Nightmares
& PREMONITIONS

By
MARCY BIALESCHKI

© 2024 by Marcy Bialeschki. All rights reserved.

Words Matter Publishing
P.O. Box 1190
Decatur, IL 62525
www.wordsmatterpublishing.com

No part of this publication may be reproduced, stored in a retrieval system, or transmitted in any way by any means—electronic, mechanical, photocopy, recording, or otherwise—without the prior permission of the copyright holder, except as provided by USA copyright law.

ISBN 13: 978-1-962467-48-3

Library of Congress Catalog Card Number: 2024948153

Dedication

To all the people in my life,
past and present, who have made
going 'Up North' so special.

Acknowledgments

A special thank you to Deerfoot Lodge and the Moccasin Bar in Hayward, Wisconsin, for all the memories and for allowing me to stretch my imagination into their world.

Table of Contents

Dedication iii
Acknowledgments v
    Chapter 1 1
    Chapter 2 5
Part I: Nightmares Can Feel So Real 11
    Chapter 3 13
    Chapter 4 23
    Chapter 5 31
    Chapter 6 37
    Chapter 7 41
    Chapter 8 47
    Chapter 9 53
    Chapter 10 59
    Chapter 11 65
    Chapter 12 75
    Chapter 13 83
    Chapter 14 91
    Chapter 15 97
    Chapter 16 107

Chapter 17 117
Chapter 18 123
Chapter 19 131
Chapter 20 137
Chapter 21 145
Chapter 22 149
Chapter 23 153
Chapter 24 161
Chapter 25 165
Chapter 26 173
Chapter 27 177
Chapter 28 185
Chapter 29 191
Chapter 30 197
Chapter 31 203
Chapter 32 211
Part II: The Future Plays Out 217
   Chapter 33 219
   Chapter 34 227
   Chapter 35 233
   Chapter 36 241
   Chapter 37 253
   Chapter 38 261
Special Bonus 271
   Chapter 1 275
   Chapter 2 283
   Chapter 3 291
   Chapter 4 299

Chapter 5 307
Chapter 6 315
Chapter 7 321
Author Bio 333

Chapter 1

Aria was going through a long, exhausting stint of sleeplessness, which was quite uncharacteristic, and both she and Mac were starting to get concerned. So far, she had not experienced an ominous nightmare or premonition, but she feared it was only a matter of time. With her extreme agitation, and CiCi to care for along with her responsibilities at MacAdoodle. Aria was nearly at the end of her rope.

"I don't know how much more I can take, Mac. I'm just so tired. All I need is one or two really good nights' rest, and I'll be fine. But I'm so anxious, and then I get to worrying about possibly having a nightmare, and I'm even more restless."

Mac understood her completely. Christopher Paloma was now home in Peoria after spending some time in a hospital for his debilitating headaches and complications related to multiple personality disorder. Aria couldn't shake the thought of some of the disturbing encounters she had with him before he left. Ever since it became common knowledge that Christopher received Tre's kidney and Calysta shared her theory, it was difficult for everyone to ignore the possible source of Christopher's odd behavior, especially Mac and Aria. It was obvious that Christopher didn't like them, and he had no problem making it known.

Now Mac had to wonder, was this hatred coming from Tre? As unrealistic as it seemed, Mac's mind was fixated on this question.

Now that they had CiCi, Aria was emotional, paranoid, and downright scared at times, especially since Christopher had an unusual attraction to her only child. Mac always did his best to quell Aria's fears, but his hugs and soothing words were a temporary fix. When Aria's anxiety intensified, Mac felt as if she needed to see a doctor. Both Mac and Aria hoped the doctor would prescribe something for her to relax and sleep. Mac thought Aria was right—a good night's sleep could do wonders.

Therefore, Mac called an old friend from the department whose wife was a doctor and explained the situation. She was happy to make a house call to first treat Aria's pounding headache and then give her something to help her rest. Before long, Aria was sleeping peacefully, and Mac was feeling much more at ease. Mac watched her resting for a moment, relieved to finally see Aria calm for the first time in days. Satisfied that she could now get some rest, Mac kissed her forehead and left her sleeping peacefully.

It wasn't long, and Aria's agitation began to make a slow but subtle return. Still asleep, the muscles in Aria's face began to twitch and wince as if she were seeing something disturbing. This reaction was brief and served as a catalyst for bigger things to come. Fast asleep, Aria was on the brink of one of her most foreboding premonitions ever. At a time when she should have been terrified, her body relaxed rather than clinching from the most intense terror right in front of her. Tre Halprin was standing before her with the same smug, sinister smile she remembered. Even though he was one of the most evil men she ever knew, Aria was not afraid, and she waited for him to speak.

"Well, well, well, if it isn't Mrs. McDonald Brunner. Two bullets—one for you and one for me—and look at us! Aren't we resilient!"

"You're dead, Tre. Mac shot you, point blank, between the eyes. No one can survive that."

"Oh, now, listen to you! A medical expert now, are you?"

Aria was silent. She refused to give Tre's sarcastic jab the satisfaction of a reply, but now there was an awkward silence, and his smirk seemed to effortlessly mock her.

"I must say, I hate you and that asshole husband of yours with a passion, but your little baby, CiCi, why, she's a doll. A *real* doll. Interesting name, by the way—*CiCi*."

Aria's senses went on high alert the moment CiCi's name came out of Tre's mouth, but she tried to show no fear and still remained silent.

"You'll be seeing a lot of me. Gotta go for now. Take care of *my* CiCi. She's a doll!"

With his last word, Tre was gone, and Aria shot up in bed, awake but terrified.

"MAC!"

After Aria told Mac the entire disturbing experience, he was sickened, and he knew it was time to discuss Calysta's theory about Tre and Christopher further.

"We know that kidney was Tre's, and Christopher's hatred for us is actually coming from Tre. It's a plausible explanation, Aria."

"But medically, is that even possible? If we try to explain this to anyone, we'll be the ones locked up," she replied harshly. "First of all, how do I explain my *abilities*? And then how do I explain the fact that we think Christopher has been turned into a diabolical killer because of a kidney transplant. Do you hear how that sounds?"

Mac sensed her frustration and wished more than anything that he could do more to help. What had them both rattled this time was that CiCi was involved, and they had to be extra careful.

"Mac, I'm so sorry that my nightmares and premonitions keep us constantly looking into the future, but we've been through this before. We know better than to jump too far ahead and try to figure things out. There's a reason we're still standing, and she's right through that doorway asleep in her new 'big girl' bed," Aria said, smiling and lifting up on her tippy toes for a kiss.

Mac instantly felt better but knew Tre Halprin coming to Aria in her dreams couldn't be good. Mac got the dreaded feeling that their number one enemy was not defeated even though Mac himself had put a bullet right between his eyes. If Christopher Paloma was the link Tre needed into this world, Mac and Aria's lives just got complicated—again.

Chapter 2

Aria was going to get that good night's sleep one way or another, and since the prescription medication seemed to bring on a nasty premonition, Aria decided a home remedy was in order. All day at work, she could hardly concentrate thinking about a hot and sensual evening alone with her sexy husband. Glen and Cheryl were taking CiCi for the night, and Aria had big plans to drink a shit-ton of wine, seduce her husband, and fuck herself into a deep and satisfying sleep.

At exactly 5:01 pm, Aria left the closing responsibilities at MacAdoodle to Cheryl and ran up the stairs to the main hallway, got into the elevator, and made her way to their quarters in their massive property on Merchant Street. She knew she had about forty minutes to get the babysitter out of there, cuddle with CiCi, get her fed and packed up for a fun night with Aunt Cheryl and Uncle Glen, and then get some candles lit, some music on, and slip into that new black teddy she'd been dying to wear. It would be a race, for sure, but she was definitely up for the challenge.

All tasks were completed, including opening a bottle of wine and pouring herself a glass, when she heard Mac's key in the door. When the door opened, Mac was unaware that he'd fallen into a trap at first because he was looking down, reading the mail. However, when he looked up, he saw his gorgeous wife looking sexy as hell in their dimly lit family room. Mac instantly dropped the mail and his keys, slammed the door, went to his wife, and met her open mouth with a sensual kiss that made her spine tingle.

"Welcome home," she said in her sexiest voice.

"Damn! This is quite a welcome. Where's CiCi?"

"She's having a sleepover at Aunt Cheryl and Uncle Glen's."

Mac didn't respond with words. He took off his jacket, unbuckled his belt and let his pants drop to the floor while Aria unbuttoned his shirt and pulled it over his head.

"You look amazing," he said, sliding his hands down her sides, keeping his thumbs to the front so they intentionally passed over her hardening nipples. When his hands got to her hips, he slipped them around to her backside, squeezed, and pulled her even closer to him. She could feel his hardness pressed up against her, and she moved ever so slightly to feel the surge of pleasure rubbing her just right. Mac sensed her motive and moved his hands up and down on her backside, slightly lifting her, making the rubbing more intense. Aria's eyes closed, and her head tilted back.

"You like that, don't you?"

"You know I do."

Mac kept the same rhythmic pace a little longer and then moved his hand between her legs, rubbing his fingers up and down over the top of the lace. Aria was wiggling and moaning now, and Mac knew her cues, but he quite liked driving her wild. He had learned that she was capable of climaxing from even the slightest touches if done correctly. He thought he'd have some fun with this despite the fact that she was damn near begging him for more than she was getting.

He moved both hands to her breasts now and first slipped the straps of her teddy down and then slowly pulled the rest of the fabric away, exposing her perfect little pebbles that he lightly brushed up and down with his thumbs.

"Gorgeous," he said, still only lightly touching them, just a tickle that made Aria's back arch.

Mac was squeezing now and rolling her rock-hard nipples between his thumb and forefinger.

"Mac, please!"

Mac's only response was to remove one hand and slip it between her legs. When he pulled the lace of her teddy to the side, Aria gasped, and Mac finally ran his fingers up her slit to her pulsing spot, aching for his touch. Mac's touch was light at first—still a tease, and Aria looked at him with desperation in her eyes. Mac couldn't continue his charade. Not so much because her pleading eyes were irresistible but because he wanted her so badly.

He took her hand, led her to the bed, slipped her out of the teddy, and positioned her on her hands and knees and spread them wide, shoulders and head down. She felt so vulnerable, so sexy, so hot. She was sure Mac was going to slip inside her, but when she felt his tongue run the full length of her, going all the way up, she was breathless. And when he started to do it again, she was exploding, and he was up and in her, thrusting, making her orgasm over and over again. Aria had never experienced such a wild and strong sensation, and when it was all over, she was just about to ask where in the hell he got *that* move when Mac offered up the humbling truth.

"Wow! I guess it pays to change your mind at the last minute."

"What?" At first, Aria was confused.

"I was all ready to just hit it, and it just looked too good to pass up."

Aria threw the covers over her head. She thought she was over being embarrassed with Mac, but that was *too much*. "Oh, Mac!"

"What?" he asked, laughing and digging under the covers to tickle her. "And the response was so good on the first pass, I had to do it again."

"Mac!!" Aria was now trying to get out of bed but started laughing when Mac was finally successful in tickling her.

"I knew that second lick would do you in, Aria. You're so easy."

These words stopped Aria in her tracks, and she threw the covers off of her head and looked at Mac with a half grin-half glare. "What did you say?"

Mac knew he wasn't really in trouble, so he repeated his words slowly and deliberately.

"I said, you're so easy." And his grin was both sexy and devilishly onery. Mac knew he was playing with fire but also hoped he was about to get burned.

"Hum," Aria replied, lifting an eyebrow. "You're pretty easy as well," she said, getting out of bed.

Mac watched her and wondered what she was up to. He was getting a little worried when he saw her going to the dresser and getting some panties and pajamas out. Surely, their night of play wasn't over. She wasn't really mad, was she?

"Umm…what are you doing?"

"I'm getting ready for bed. Why?"

"Well?" Mac said, confused.

Aria could hardly keep up her act when she saw Mac's disappointed look. She knew what he expected since they finally had an entire night to themselves. But Aria had a point to make, and she was ready for the kill shot.

"See how easy you are?" Aria said, turning to him with a sly grin. And then, he watched as she pulled the pajama top off over her head. There they were again— her perfect little nipples, still perky and waiting to be sucked. She straddled Mac on the bed while pinning his arms above his head, and Mac was ready for whatever she had in mind, and he was even okay with being duped.

"Alright, you win! Thank goodness!"

After *round two*, Aria opened some more wine, and she told Mac her plan to get a good night's sleep. He said he was sorry she was so sleep-deprived, but anytime she needed to use him as a sleep aid, he was willing. After getting something to eat and some more conversation unrelated to Christopher Paloma or Tre Halprin, Mac said he had some work to do and that he would just sleep in the spare room so he would not disturb her coming to bed. Finally, he gave her a goodnight kiss and left her to get some rest.

Aria decided to finish her wine and read for a bit, and when her eyes got heavy, she shut off the light, settled into her pillow, and drifted into a long, deep sleep.

Part I: Nightmares Can Feel So Real

Chapter 3

CiCi Brunner dreaded her upcoming snowmobiling trip to Wisconsin over her winter break, and she wished she was going home to Peoria to see her parents instead. CiCi also wished she was going without Dex, her now 'on again, off again' boyfriend. Currently, they had a difference of opinion whether or not they were a couple.

In CiCi's eyes, they had downgraded their relationship to 'friends,' and CiCi wished she had the strength to make a clean break and tell Dex they were through. But every time she started that conversation, Dex put on the charm, and she lost her nerve. Deep down, CiCi longed for the old Dex she once fell in love with. So, every time she broke up with him, she changed her mind, took him back, and then regretted it when he fucked up again. So, here she was, about to head out on a six-day vacation with their relationship status *unconfirmed*. Everything about that situation gave CiCi anxiety.

They met at freshman orientation and felt an instant connection, each needing something stable in a place and time that seemed so different from their usual lives. Right from the start, they had a sexual attraction that was fiery and insatiable. Before finding each other, neither Dex nor CiCi had ever had sex; therefore, they had no idea if their sexual relationship was typical. Nonetheless, they fell in love, and for the first three years of their lives at Millikin University, they were incredibly happy.

CiCi was positive the exact moment of Dex's transformation was the summer before their senior year when he discovered she was rich—mind-blowingly rich. They had gone together for three years, and CiCi never had any reason to mention or flaunt the fact that she would someday be the sole heir to a massive fortune. Dex found out she was an heiress quite unexpectedly while doing some unrelated searching online, and he was more than a little pissed that CiCi hadn't disclosed this information in the past three years.

"Seriously? We've been together our entire college experience, and you've never mentioned the fact that your parents are Mac and Aria Brunner? *THE* Mac and Aria Brunner!"

"You've met my parents. I didn't hide their identity."

"But you didn't disclose it either!" Dex fired back.

CiCi had grown up rather normally despite the fact that her parents were some of the richest people in the world. To her, that fact made no difference. Besides, her dad always told her to keep her identity somewhat under wraps for fear that kidnappers might try to take advantage. And when she went away to college, he wanted her to be extra careful who knew about her wealth. At first, when she tried to explain all of her reasons for keeping her family fortune a secret, Dex just grew more distant.

After Dex recovered from the initial shock, he and CiCi seemed to move on, and CiCi had high hopes that the man she loved would return. But Dex still had a hard time processing how his life might change if he stayed with CiCi. He also became resentful of her budding successes and feared that a life with such a wealthy and talented woman might always put him in the shadows. These insecurities seemed to make Dex lash out in uncharacteristic ways, and CiCi was growing impatient.

Their communication and interaction were now different, and CiCi began to think she would never see the return of her old Dex. She got the feeling that Dex didn't really want to be with her, but he also didn't want to let her go. Therefore, every time she took him back, he proved that he never really changed, and she scolded herself for being so gullible.

Dex was a talented graphic designer and wicked smart, but he was enjoying his final year of college with more parties than classes. CiCi, however, was determined to finish strong. A few months into their senior year, Dex noticed that in the time he was fucking around, CiCi had become more focused on school and her future career. CiCi's new goals and dreams were just another irritation for Dex, who was already insecure about his talents compared to hers.

"I get that you want a *good* job, but why does it have to be the *best* job? You don't always have to be the best, CiCi," Dex scowled.

"Why wouldn't I want the best job?" CiCi argued.

CiCi knew her aspirations threatened Dex, and lately, whenever he felt threatened, he ridiculed her family money, saying that it must be nice to have your mom and dad fund even the stupidest of dreams. Deep down, he didn't believe that at all, so every time it came out of his mouth, he swore he'd never stoop that low again. But here he was, repeating past mistakes, just like always. And just like always, CiCi defended herself and began feeling more and more disconnected from Dex. CiCi just couldn't understand why Dex would say such hurtful comments if he loved her.

"For once, don't you want to earn something on your own and not rely on your parents' money to buy it for you?"

Those comments always had a spiteful sting and put CiCi on the defensive, and CiCi's witty comebacks absolutely enraged Dex.

"For once, can you not bring my family's money into an argument because you feel threatened?" CiCi fired back.

"I'm not threatened by you!" Dex snapped.

"Bullshit!" CiCi countered.

Dex's face got beet red, and he was at a loss for words. CiCi's calm, unwavering stance pissed him off, and he walked away, like always. It was petty but hurtful arguments like this one that kept eroding the foundation of CiCi and Dex's once rock-solid relationship.

CiCi was studying Marketing and Business Management, along with Graphic Design, and her design talent was cutting edge. Graphic Design was her passion, and it was her father's idea to include the business degrees. Now that she was getting closer to graduation and applying for jobs, she was quite pleased she had put up with all the aggravation.

It was apparent that Dex and CiCi were growing apart, and at some point, Dex knew CiCi would be out of his reach and moving on, which is probably why he did the stupidest thing ever at the Halloween party.

First of all, his alcohol consumption was out of control, and trying to get him to slow down or stop made him furious. His behavior worried CiCi, but she decided to distance herself from Dex because, frankly, she was tired of dealing with his bullshit.

After some time, the guilt set in, and CiCi got worried. She had not seen or heard anything from Dex for quite some time and thought that he might be passed out somewhere and something awful might happen. She was mad at him for his abysmal behavior, but she would never forgive herself if something happened to him. So CiCi started looking, hoping everything was okay.

At first, she went to the obvious places: his room, the basement party room, and the bathroom. But there was no sign of Dex.

He has to be here. There was no reason for him to leave. The party is at his house.

So CiCi widened her search to the bonfire in the backyard and the deck off the kitchen. Still, no sign of Dex.

Perplexed, CiCi stood on the deck and then an awful feeling came over her.

What if he took his car somewhere?

He was definitely in no condition to drive. Walking toward the driveway, CiCi saw that Dex's car was still there, and a sigh of relief swept over her. But upon closer look, she saw movement inside. Walking closer, CiCi was heartbroken to see Dex inside with another girl making out. She had never been so humiliated and hurt in her entire life. Dex was her *person* and her best friend. How could he do this to her? Sure, they were having some problems, but they were still together.

When Dex realized CiCi was outside, looking in, he abruptly stopped his business in the car, collected himself, and hurried out to stop CiCi's abrupt retreat to the house. By the time Dex caught up with her, CiCi had made her way to Dex's room to grab her things and leave. She was crying but not sad. Rather, she was furious.

Entering the room, an obviously drunk Dex was spewing excuses and lies, and CiCi was in no mood. In her attempt to gather her things and get out, Dex grabbed her hard, which resulted in bruised arms for days after. Desperately trying to explain his disloyalty, Dex shook her, scaring her. He had never laid a hand on her, but CiCi was fearful this episode would escalate. They were alone, and the music was loud. No one would hear her even if she screamed.

CiCi grew up with a father who worked in law enforcement, and her Godfather was a martial arts expert and self-defense instructor. She learned to handle herself very early on in life. But never in a million years did she think she would be defending herself against her own boyfriend. But it was time to act before this scenario got out of hand. Swiftly and with all her might, CiCi thrust her right knee up hard, connecting with Dex's groin. He instantly let go of her and doubled over in pain, giving CiCi the opportunity to run out.

Looking back, CiCi identified this incident as the beginning of the end. And although Dex said he didn't remember any of the acts CiCi told him the next day, the proof was all around him. She had bruised grip marks on her arms, and he had an aching crotch. With further inquiries, it came to light that the girl Dex was with was Maggie Graham, one of his friend's girlfriends, causing even more trouble for Dex. Even though all of the evidence was staring him in the eyes, Dex continued to say CiCi was making up the whole incident as an excuse to break up with him.

From that moment on, CiCi knew she couldn't trust him, and they fought more and more. This was a glaring reason to make a clean break, but she didn't. Even though she took him back with conditions, their relationship did not improve, and Dex clearly did not learn his lesson. As usual, their fighting would frustrate Dex, and he once again began taking cheap shots at her parents and their money.

Shortly after the Halloween incident, CiCi began to identify the pattern with Dex and also with herself. At first, she was critical of his behavior, but then she took a hard look at herself. He would do something stupid, and she would be so adamant about calling it quits. Then, he would be so sweet and remorseful that she gave in. However, CiCi had come to realize that Dex never made an effort to fix his ways. He had gotten used to fucking up and then asking forgiveness afterward.

"Well, why wouldn't he?" CiCi asked herself. "I've allowed it."

And just like that, CiCi decided that she wanted more than Dex was capable of providing. Therefore, this trip up North for winter break was a source of stress for her. She didn't want to lose all the ground she had gained by succumbing to a weak moment and be right back in the palm of Dex Robertson's hand.

The Wisconsin trip with two other couples started as a grand plan after a full day and night of drinking during fall break. Bored and disappointed that they didn't have exciting fall break plans, the group of six decided their current condition wasn't going to be a problem during their winter break. To ensure this promise, they booked a snowmobiling adventure for winter break at a resort near Hayward, Wisconsin.

CiCi made these arrangements before the relationship-altering incident at the Halloween party. After that defining moment, she was ready to call off her participation in the winter break trip. But CiCi's friends begged her to go, and she didn't want to disappoint them. Besides, their time together was growing slim, and she really did want one last trip full of memories with her best friends. Therefore, CiCi agreed to go to the lodge with Dex as long as they had separate rooms.

Dex, on the other hand, was sick and tired of being the laughingstock of his friends. He never should have told anyone that CiCi was withholding sex because of his behavior on Halloween, and there was no way he was looking any more foolish by having separate rooms. The ribbing he constantly endured from his buddies about his sexless relationship with CiCi was getting old, and Dex saw this trip as a way to revive their relations. Even though Dex kept that secret from CiCi, his ego let his intentions slip when talking with his friends.

"I don't know why you're even going on this trip, Dex," his buddy Vic said, snickering. "It's cold up North, and you aren't *gettin' any* to stay warm."

When the room erupted in laughter, Dex was livid.

"Don't worry about my dick, Man. Worry about your own," Dex fired back.

"I have zero worries. I get pussy whenever I want it," Vic said, still laughing.

"Well, I'm done with her bullshit. I'm getting laid on this trip. I don't give two fucks what CiCi wants."

Dex hadn't told anyone, but he canceled CiCi's room, and he believed that under those conditions, she would have no choice but to stay with him. He knew she would be furious at first but figured she would soften up and maybe see the gesture as romantic. Therefore, he would be back in her good graces and back in her pants.

"Isn't that exactly why her legs closed in the first place? Better watch it. CiCi's about had it with your shit, Dex," Greg Wilson, another friend going on the trip, added.

"Like I said, don't worry about me. I'll get more pussy than all of you on this trip," Dex boasted, even though no one in the room believed it, including him.

Now, it was time for the winter break trip, and CiCi had not spoken with Dex for a couple of weeks. As far as she was concerned, they were *not* a couple, and CiCi planned to look and act single on this trip. As awkward as it would be, she wanted a guilt-free vacation fling or maybe even to meet someone who was relationship-worthy. The fact that Dex would be there to witness it would be awkward, for sure. But Dex's sad presence was certainly not enough to deter CiCi. She was a woman on a mission.

Chapter 4

It was about a nine-hour drive from Millikin in Decatur, Illinois, to the lodge in Hayward, Wisconsin. CiCi dreaded the isolated, *alone time* in the car with Dex, so without him knowing, she asked her friend Dessie and her boyfriend Greg to ride with them. When their friends arrived, bags in hand, Dex was more than a little put off. He was looking forward to some alone time with CiCi to prime her mood with some talk about the 'good ole' days.' Dex had discovered that revisiting fond memories always made CiCi a little sentimental, and he was hoping it would make her more inclined to get back together and, of course, put out.

Now, they had extra riders, and his *alone time* wasn't going to happen. When they stopped for the first time, Dex had words.

"Really, CiCi, you can't stand to be alone with me for a few hours?" Dex said, with obvious anger and disappointment.

"I thought it would be more fun this way," CiCi responded.

"Whatever," Dex said, not wanting to start a big fight.

In reality, CiCi didn't want an all-out fight she couldn't escape, and she definitely didn't want to be alone with Dex and hear all of his sentimental chit-chat. Or worse yet, she feared she was still vulnerable, and she could fall for Dex's charming ways, take him back, and start the dysfunctional cycle of their relationship all over again. Deep down, CiCi admitted that she still loved Dex, but she loved the old Dex, and she was tired of waiting for him to reappear. At least with Dessie and Greg, the conversation would not be about them reconciling and about all their fun sexual encounters over the past few years. As it turned out, Dex drove silently most of the way, even when addressed.

"It's nice that the roads are clear," Greg said. "But I've been keeping a close eye on the snowfall up there, and it looks like the trails up North have plenty of snow."

Greg was probably expecting his comment to be a conversion starter, but Dex was moping. Greg thought he'd try again.

"How much farther, Dex?"

But when Dex remained silent and brooding, CiCi was at her limit, and she decided to call him out.

"What the hell is wrong with you, Dex? You're just being rude," CiCi said scoldingly.

"Rude? Ha! That's funny," Dex responded.

"What's that supposed to mean?" CiCi asked, obviously irritated.

"Well, since you asked. I'm paying for this whole damn trip, and you don't even want to be with me. Why didn't you just cancel?" Dex bellowed.

Greg and Dessie suddenly wished they had taken their own car but sat in the back, silent, hoping this argument would blow over.

"Really, you're worried about money? Fine, I'll give you the money," CiCi replied, hoping that would end his tirade, but it just seemed to make things worse.

"Of course, you have *all* the money. You have no problem paying for *everything*," Dex blasted, sarcastically mocking CiCi's wealth again.

"Do you even hear yourself? First, you want me to give you money, and then you feel threatened when I offer it," CiCi shouted.

"How many times do I have to tell you I am not threatened by you, CiCi!"

"Until I actually believe it, I guess," CiCi replied. And then she couldn't help herself and mumbled "asshole" under her breath.

"That's right, I'm always the asshole," Dex replied.

"Yes, you are, right now," Greg added, coming to CiCi's defense.

"Fine, you wanted me to talk, and I did. Are you fucking happy now?" Dex said, hoping he was getting the last word.

CiCi let it go and looked out the window. With Dex's outburst, she didn't have to worry about giving in to his advances. She had absolutely no attraction to him whatsoever. This was the fight they needed. This was the end. It was more than a little unfortunate that she now had to spend six days of her winter break with him.

They pulled into the lodge a little after 4 pm, and there were so many snowmobilers coming and going, loud music playing, and alcohol everywhere. It was like a cold and snowy nightclub, and CiCi's mood instantly improved. The girls all went inside to check in, and the lobby was filled with even more people seeking shelter from the cold outside. CiCi looked around and saw the lobby bar was also packed. Good! She would have plenty of chances to meet someone to make her trip fun. Dex was on his own. She was definitely finished with his petty nonsense.

"Good afternoon," CiCi said as she approached the check-in desk. I have a reservation for Celeste Brunner."

The woman behind the desk searched for the reservation, and a pensive look came over her face.

"No, Ma'am. I'm sorry. I don't see that name."

CiCi was alarmed. What did this mean? Were all of their reservations missing? She suddenly became anxious. She had booked the rooms. If something was wrong, everyone would hate her.

"Try Dexter Robertson," CiCi asked, trying not to panic.

"Yes, Ma'am. That room is in a block of three. It looks like a fourth room was canceled recently."

Canceled? CiCi was confused, and then she figured it out. Dex canceled her room, so she would have to stay with him. Well, she would show him.

"Well, can I get a room then?"

"No, I'm so sorry. We are completely full all week," the woman replied regretfully.

CiCi was livid, but she calmed her demeanor when Dex strolled up beside her. She didn't want to give him any reason to think he had gotten one up on her. In fact, she was about to give him a taste of his own medicine.

"What's wrong, CiCi?" Dex said with a smile.

"I don't have a room for some reason," CiCi stated. And then the mocking smile on Dex's face confirmed what she suspected. "You canceled my room, didn't you?"

"Yes," Dex admitted, still smiling.

"Well, I'm taking yours, and you're the one who's going to need to find a place to sleep.

"Ma'am?" CiCi said, addressing the woman behind the check-in desk again. "Ma'am, this gentleman has offered to give me his room. He says he has some friends he can stay with. The name is Dexter Robertson."

The smug grin on Dex's face was instantly gone, and before he could protest, CiCi had taken what she wanted, and now she was the one with the mocking smile.

"You're pathetic!" she said as she grabbed the key and headed upstairs.

Once in the room, CiCi was shaking. How could he do such a thing? She knew he was manipulative, but this was the last straw. She didn't want to have anything to do with him, and she felt bad that he would become someone else's problem on this trip, but she was not letting him think he could get by pulling shit like that.

Once CiCi was all unpacked, she texted Dessie.

CiCi: Is he with you?

Dessie: Yes, and I'm fine with it. He was being a dick to you in the car. He just left with Greg and Vic to take a look around.

CiCi: I'm done with him. Text Izzy and meet me at the lobby bar.

❖ ❖ ❖

CiCi was a striking young woman who didn't need much effort to turn heads. Therefore, she quickly freshened up and changed into something a little sexier before heading down to meet her friends at the bar.

Taking in all the sights and sounds on her way down the grand staircase, CiCi didn't realize it, but she was causing a great deal of interest among the unattached young men there for a week of snowy fun. Finding her place at the bar with Dessie and Izzy, CiCi ordered a Goose Island draft and let her mood absorb the cheery atmosphere.

"This place is crazy!" Izzy said, looking around. "I've never seen so many men in my life!"

"We are definitely the minority," CiCi added.

"I kinda feel like some of these guys are looking at me like a snack," Dessie offered, causing CiCi to nearly spit out her beer.

"I hate to say it, but I kinda wish this was a girls' trip," Izzy said, wide-eyed.

"Well, we'll have to live vicariously through CiCi. She's the only single one," Dessie stated.

"Don't tell me. Dex was a douchebag on the way up, and you broke up?" Izzy asked.

"As far as I'm concerned, we've been broken up for a while," CiCi clarified.

"Don't cave this time, CiCi. You can do way better. I'm still pissed that you took him back after the shit he pulled at the Halloween party," Izzy added.

CiCi still got chills when she thought about everything she had been through with Dex. She never in a million years thought Dex would ever hurt her. She wondered how someone she had been with for so long could be so different. Now Izzy was telling her she thought what happened that night was horrible, and no one but CiCi herself knew the entire truth. Even Dex didn't remember, which is why he sometimes chose to believe CiCi was making it all up and being dramatic.

All of these old memories were killing her mood. But her trip down memory lane did two things for her: it reminded her that she never wanted to be with Dex Robertson again and that she was horny as hell.

The girls didn't even finish their first drink before three guys approached them, wanting to strike up a conversation. CiCi, of course, was all for it. Her friends, however, were guarded, not being single like CiCi. When Izzy and Dessie excused themselves after a quick 'hi,' CiCi knew her friends would be no help getting her laid this week. And she was well aware that sitting there alone just looked desperate. Therefore, CiCi also excused herself and headed up to her room to get a warmer jacket. She thought it was time to take in the sights around the beautiful lodge, so she grabbed her ski jacket and headed outside.

Chapter 5

CiCi was pretty sure Vic and Izzy were in their room fucking, and Greg and Dessie were probably entertaining Dex but wishing they were fucking. And here she was, freezing her ass off, staring at a frozen lake, wondering if there was even a remote possibility that she would meet someone and have a week's worth of naughty, no-regrets sex before heading home to Peoria for Christmas. She knew damn good, and well, once she got home, her opportunity for a good fuck was over. For one thing, she never could find a decent date in her hometown, and for another, her parents would monopolize her time.

It was getting dark, but CiCi was enjoying the crisp North Woods air and was reluctant to go back to the lodge. She realized, however, that her short walk had actually taken her quite a way down the shoreline. In the distance, CiCi saw several snowmobile lights coming her way, and after a little more time, she heard the roar and hum getting louder. It was a group of snowmobilers who had been out all day but were now headed into the warm shelter of the lodge.

CiCi waited for the approaching group of six that slowed their pace when they saw her. Stopping, the man in the lead addressed her.

"You need a ride back?"

CiCi thought about it for a minute and then threw caution into the wind.

"Sure, thanks!"

The man handed her his spare helmet, CiCi hopped on, and the group roared on toward the lights of the lodge.

Once back with the party atmosphere, CiCi was ready for another drink, but first, she was dying to get a look at the man behind the snowmobile gear who gave her a ride. CiCi liked that he was tall. When he removed his helmet and goggles, she was unprepared for his intense green eyes and long dark lashes. It looked like he was sporting a two-day beard, probably too busy having fun to shave. He looked older but was certainly sexy. She felt a little surge of hormones when he ran his hand through his wavy caramel-colored hair, attempting to fix a severe case of helmet head. But CiCi didn't mind that he wasn't freshly shaven and that his gorgeous head of hair was currently a bit disheveled. She thought he was about the sexiest thing she had ever seen.

"Let me formally introduce myself," the man began. "I'm Christopher."

"Thanks for the ride, Christopher," CiCi managed. "Oh, and I'm CiCi," she said with a coy smile.

"CiCi– that's a pretty name," he confirmed, nodding his head and smiling ever so slightly. His words, paired with his smile, were just enough to make the pit of CiCi's stomach drop slightly.

"Let's get a drink," he suggested.

CiCi was on cloud nine and temporarily unable to respond. She'd been there an hour and met quite possibly the sexiest man in the whole fucking place, and he wanted to have a drink.

"Sure, that would be great."

But when she spotted Dex at the bar alone and brooding, she got nervous and worried he would make a scene. CiCi intentionally bypassed Dex's area and hoped he would be too self-absorbed with his pity party to notice her and her snowmobiling Prince Charming.

"What would you like?" Christopher asked.

"I'm not sure. What are you drinking?"

"An Old Fashioned, of course. When you're in Wisconsin, you have to drink an Old Fashioned," Christopher said quite definitively with that sexy grin, which was much more prominent now.

"Sure! Sounds good," CiCi confirmed.

While her handsome new friend was at the bar, CiCi took a moment to check him out from all angles. She had already established that he was tall and jaw-droppingly sexy, but after shedding some of his bulky gear, she could also tell he was muscular and strong. But right in the middle of her not-so-covert appraisal, Christopher glanced back and caught her checking him out, so he flashed her a grin and winked. CiCi knew she was blushing, so she smiled and looked down. Christopher smiled to himself, picked up their drinks, and walked back to the table to an embarrassed CiCi.

❖ ❖ ❖

From the moment Christopher stopped to pick CiCi up, he was hooked. Her long, light brown tresses lay perfectly over her shoulders and down her back. Even with the last of the sun's rays sinking, he was hypnotized by her bright blue eyes. And mostly, the way that ski jacked hugged her told him she had some killer tits.

Nightmares & Premonitions

All the way back to the lodge, with her arms wrapped around his torso, he hoped she couldn't feel his growing excitement. When they pulled up to the bustling lodge, Christopher knew he needed to extend his time with this gorgeous woman and didn't hesitate to ask her for a drink at the bar.

In the bright lights of the lodge lobby, Christopher could tell his passenger was young, really young, and his heart sank a little. Still, he was going to give it a shot. When CiCi accepted his offer for a drink, he was relieved, but he still needed to know how old she was. When he saw her giving him the once over while getting their drinks, Christopher worried a little less about her age; now, he was looking at her as if he knew her somehow. But he quickly dismissed that thought when he saw her sitting there, blushing, smiling, and looking at him. She was young and couldn't be anyone he knew, but most of all, she certainly looked and acted old enough to fuck.

"One Wisconsin Old Fashioned for the lady," Christopher said, starting to place the drink on the table but then pulling it back. "You are old enough to drink, right?" he said with a cunning smile.

"Yes, I promise. I'm twenty-two," CiCi clarified.

Fuck! I knew she was young, but damn, twenty-two!

"In college, huh? Let me guess. You're on holiday break," Christopher predicted.

"You're pretty good! Yes, I go to Millikin in Illinois. I have one more semester."

"Millikin is a great school. I'm from Illinois, too," Christopher offered.

"Really, where?" CiCi asked.

"Peoria, I live here now, but I grew up there, and my folks still live there," Christopher explained.

"No way! I live in Peoria," CiCi said, completely surprised.

The conversation was going nicely, and Christopher was off to the bar to grab a couple more drinks when CiCi locked eyes with Dex, who looked far beyond pissed off. To make matters worse, he downed the rest of his drink, slid off his barstool, and began his drunken stumble toward her.

When Dex reached CiCi's table, he had to grab the edge to steady himself. He had been drowning his sorrows since they got there, and he had just enough courage to confront her.

"We've only been here a few hours, and you've picked up someone. Nice!" Dex said with a drunken slur.

CiCi was caught off guard and didn't know what to say.

Spying CiCi's awkward demeanor and her obviously uninvited guest, Christopher bypassed waiting on the drinks and moved back to his table.

"Excuse me, it looks like the lady is not enjoying your company."

"Lady? Ha! Okay. You just met her, right?" Dex said in the most hurtful way.

CiCi had no idea why Dex would be saying such untrue, hurtful things.

"Okay, that's enough," Christopher said as he grabbed a hold of Dex's shoulder and pulled him away from the table. Christopher had no trouble forcing the drunk and unstable Dex out the door and then hollered for his backup.

"Mitch! This guy needs to sober up before he comes back in."

"Yes, Boss."

CiCi was confused. *Boss??*

"I'm sorry about that. You know him, right?" Christopher asked.

"Yes, unfortunately, he's my ex. Thank you," CiCi said, still confused. "Boss? What…"

"I own this lodge," Christopher confessed, walking back to the bar to pick up their drinks.

"Cheers!"

Chapter 6

Christopher escorted a tipsy CiCi to her room, thinking all the thoughts a red-blooded man would think, but was resolved to leave her alone in her room, maybe get a kiss good night. When they arrived at her door, CiCi had a sudden burst of fear. She wondered if Dex was in their room.

"What's wrong?" Christopher asked.

"I don't know if Dex is in there or not," she confessed. "He could have gotten a key. The room is in his name,"

"Let's get you another room," Christopher suggested.

"I already tried. The lodge is full." CiCi was almost in a full panic.

"Come on. You're not staying here," Christopher declared. "Put your coat on. We have to take a ride."

Common sense told CiCi not to take off with a man she barely knew, but common sense also told her she was probably a lot safer with this stranger than Dex. So, CiCi put on her coat and Christopher's extra helmet, and they roared off into the night. But they didn't go far. Dex's personal cabin was only about a mile and a half up a remote snowmobile trail. It wasn't excessively large or lavish, but definitely a very nice place hidden by the tall pines of the Northern woods.

The cold night air had sobered CiCi up considerably, and once inside, she found her thoughts violently swaying between fear and lust and everything in between.

"Do you want a drink or soda?" he asked.

"No, I'm fine, thanks. I really appreciate this."

"No offense, but that guy's an ass."

"I know. I finally made a clean break, though," CiCi replied.

"Are you sure about that?" Christopher probed.

Feeling a bit interrogated, CiCi responded again. This time more forcefully.

"Yes, I'm very sure."

Christopher sat looking at her, partially as if he didn't believe her and partially because she was so fucking sexy. He'd be lying if he didn't admit that her tight sweater had been a source of his uncomfortable erection all night long.

"What?" CiCi asked, feeling as if she was being seduced by his intense green eyes.

"I was just wondering what a drop-dead stunner like you would ever be doing with a prick like that."

"He wasn't always this way, but enough about Dex, okay?"

But Christopher's icy green eyes were still on her, and CiCi desperately wanted to kiss him. As if he knew what she was thinking, Christopher said, "Do it." And in the next moment, he was pulling her to him, granting her wish by meeting her open mouth with his eager tongue.

His kiss was electric, with just the right amount of force paired with sensual gentleness. When the kiss was over, CiCi opened her eyes to that irresistible smile that made her blush earlier when he caught her staring at him. CiCi knew she was a goner. She was about to do something she had never done before—have reckless sex with a man she just met, an older man, at that.

Christopher stood up, took her hand, and led her into the bedroom. At the edge of the bed, he stopped and gently cupped her face in his hands and kissed her slow and deep. Those sexy eyes seemed to seduce her as he brushed random strands of hair from her face. Then, moving all of her long locks to one side, he kissed her neck, giving CiCi goose bumps and making her want him more than she had ever wanted anything in her life.

When Christopher pulled away, he slowly pulled CiCi's sweater over her head, revealing her large, perfect breasts. He was momentarily in awe. He had been fantasizing about what was under that sweater all night long, and it was even more remarkable than he imagined. He watched as CiCi unhooked her bra, further freeing his goal. She stood before him, half-naked and breathless, anticipating his next move.

"You're gorgeous," he said, leaning into her neck and gently teasing her with his tongue. He hated to ruin the moment, but he had to ask, "Are you on the pill?"

"Yes."

Christopher unbuckled his pants and freed himself, and for one brief moment, CiCi wondered if she would be good enough for a real man. She had only ever been with Dex. But CiCi could not dwell on those fears. She had not known the touch of a man or the full pleasure of sex for weeks. Somehow, she understood that her excessive wait brought this remarkable reward. She slipped out of her jeans and panties, and Christopher laid her gently onto the bed. She wanted to beg him to be inside her, but she also wanted to see exactly what this sexy man was going to do.

Sex with Dex was never like this. Christopher lasted so long and was so attentive. And when it was all over, he didn't jump up, get her a towel, and then get on his phone. Rather, he held her, and they talked until they fell asleep.

Chapter 7

Christopher wondered if CiCi had any idea how old he was. Part of him thought it shouldn't matter and that thirteen years difference was no big deal for an adult relationship. But in a lot of ways, Christopher felt much older than thirteen years CiCi's superior, and not telling her felt like deception. Christopher knew he would not stop second-guessing himself until he told her the truth.

She was still sleeping, naked in his bed, and she looked so sexy. But he knew he couldn't continue to pursue her until he was honest with her. It may be the end of things, but he had to come clean. When he heard her stirring in the bedroom getting dressed, he poured her a cup of coffee and waited for her to emerge. Finally, a somewhat sheepish and shy CiCi appeared, and his gorgeous smile assured her that he had no regrets.

"Coffee?"

"Please."

"Do your friends know where you are? I mean, do they know you're safe?"

"Yes, I texted them last night and just now. I told them I'd meet them for breakfast at the lodge."

"Does that include Dex?"

"Probably, but he'll be okay. He's usually very apologetic after acting like an ass when he's drunk."

"Your friends have your back, right? I mean regarding him."

"They are all very protective," CiCi said, smiling. "I'll be fine."

"Sorry, I just don't want to put you in a precarious situation."

"Don't be sorry," CiCi said, moving closer. "I appreciate your concern." And then CiCi leaned down and kissed her protector with the kind of kiss that can start a fire.

"I have to tell you something," Christopher confessed.

And then, just like that, CiCi's good mood went south, and she felt a little insecure, wondering what he was about to say.

"I'm thirty-five years old."

And when these words came out of his mouth, Christopher questioned his decision to be forthright when there was an awkward silence before CiCi's puzzled answer.

"So?"

Christopher was never so relieved in his life. Not only did he want to pursue things with CiCi, but he also didn't want her to feel like she was tricked into having sex with him, and he didn't want her to have any regrets. When Christopher let loose with one of those drop-dead gorgeous smiles, CiCi melted.

"Come on. I'll take you back to the lodge, but you're riding with me today on the trails. I'll take you and your friends to some of the best places. Even Dex, I guess," he said reluctantly and then cracked a grin. CiCi was on cloud nine. She couldn't wait for Dessie and Izzy to see this gorgeous man. She was even ready to face Dex.

But when they arrived at the lodge, Greg and Vic were in the lobby, pissed off and pacing.

CiCi and Christopher walked in, and CiCi immediately knew something bad had happened.

"What's wrong?" she asked.

"Your fucking boyfriend just stormed out, took his car, and left us all here. There's no way all six of us with luggage and gear will fit in my car going home," Vic snapped.

"First of all, he's not my boyfriend," CiCi clarified.

"Well, maybe if he was, we wouldn't be in this mess," Vic responded with obvious sarcasm.

"Look, we have five days to figure this out. Let's not ruin our entire week on the second day," CiCi proposed, trying to bring some peace and civility to the situation. "Christopher has offered to be our trail guide today, and he knows some of the best places. Let's have some fun, and I'll call my dad tonight and work out a ride home."

"She's right," Greg said. "I don't want to ruin my vacation. I came up here to get out on the trails."

Vic knew they were right.

"Fine, let's get the girls, have some breakfast, and take off."

Christopher winked at CiCi as a quick 'goodbye' and told her to enjoy her breakfast and that he would be back very soon to take them out. But as an hour passed, and then another, everyone, including CiCi, was getting a bit perturbed. All the other riders were already out, and there they sat, waiting for their guide to come back for them.

When Christopher returned, he apologized and said he got caught up in some work stuff and was detained a bit longer than he planned. His excuse was accepted fully once they were all out on the trails. As promised, Christopher took them on quite a wild ride that was worth the wait.

The guys especially loved it because Christopher was able to take them on trails that no one else had been on yet. And to further make up for being late, Christopher treated them to happy hour drinks at a cool pub across the lake that was hoppin.'

"Thank you," CiCi said sweetly in a private moment at the bar.

"Do they know?"

"Oh, yeah!" she said with wide eyes.

"And do they think I'm some old pervert?"

CiCi thought that Christopher's obsession with their age difference was okay at first, but now his worries and comments were getting a little annoying.

"Look, I don't give two shits about how old you are, and it's none of their business. You need to stop overthinking this," CiCi said, placing her hand on his thigh and leaning in to place a kiss on his cheek.

Christopher knew she was right, and he was going to blow it if he didn't cool it with his unwarranted fears. He just couldn't figure out what it was about this girl that had him so worked up. Sure, she was gorgeous, but he knew and dated a lot of gorgeous women. CiCi, however, was different; he just didn't know how to explain it.

Their age difference also seemed to preoccupy his mind. And then for just a brief moment, Christopher forgot exactly how old he was because foggy thoughts and memories clouded his mind. When the haze finally receded, he realized he was only thirty-five, but sometimes he believed he was much older. Thirteen years was no big deal, but something inside him seemed to keep bringing their age gap to his attention, and now he wondered why.

Feeling a lot more confident after his newfound clarity, Christopher vowed to stop with all of his comments about their ages and just enjoy her infectious smile, her piercing blue eyes, and her fucking hot body. But deep down, he didn't understand why this woman had captured his heart and, even more puzzling, why she seemed so familiar when he was quite certain he had never met a CiCi Brunner before. But this was no time to dwell on his peculiar thoughts. His gorgeous CiCi was sitting dangerously close to him, and he could feel the heat rising between them.

"Even though *what's his name* is gone, you're staying with me again tonight," he said quite authoritatively.

CiCi kissed him, stared into his eyes, and looked incredibly sexy as she bit her bottom lip.

"Can't wait."

❖ ❖ ❖

The trails were exhilarating, and everyone was exhausted and starving when they rode back into the lodge at about 6 o'clock.

CiCi's friends appreciated Christopher's hospitality while out on the trails, but for some reason, back at the lodge, Izzy got a bad vibe.

"There's just something creepy about him," Izzy said softly to Vic as they watched some sweet exchanges between Christopher and CiCi.

"How old is he, anyway?" Vic asked.

"CiCi says she doesn't know. I think it's more like she just won't say. I mean, he's nice, and he's certainly sexy," Izzy added, receiving an eye roll from Vic.

"Well, he owns the place, and we got a personal trail tour that I'm pretty sure no one else gets. So, I'm fine with it," Vic concluded.

"I just hope she doesn't get too carried away trying to prove something," Izzy added.

"Who cares? It's her life."

"I know, but I feel like we need to keep an eye on her. She's vulnerable with Dex finally out of the picture for good. Please, just keep an eye on her," Izzy asked.

"Yeah, okay," Vic agreed.

❖ ❖ ❖

Christopher had some work things to take care of, so he kissed CiCi goodbye and left her with her friends to enjoy the evening. The group all had a terrific time enjoying drinks, talking about good times, and relaxing before the start of their final semester.

CiCi was not even a little concerned about Dex. In fact, she was pissed that he left them stranded there and that their relationship problems were affecting their friends. She dreaded going back to school and resuming real life, which most certainly meant running into Dex. They had classes together, and they each had so many personal items at each other's places. They would definitely have to see each other again, and it would be awkward. But that was over a week away. CiCi had the rest of her vacation to enjoy, and she planned to do so.

Chapter 8

Christopher Paloma was incredibly confused. He spent every extra moment wondering why he was falling so hard for a twenty-two-year-old he just met. He couldn't explain it, but it was like he was being drawn to her without a will of his own. Not only that, he was starting to feel incredibly possessive, and he knew this controlling factor could be the end of his chances with a woman like CiCi. She had just broken free from a long-term relationship that definitely had control issues written all over it. There was no way she would stand for another man dictating her every move.

You have to play it cool, Man. You can't push too hard or come on too strong.

This approach made perfect sense to Christopher, but there were parts of his mind that refused to comply. Once again, he had no idea why his thoughts were being manipulated by something— he didn't know what— that was beyond his control.

All this confusion and contemplation gave Christopher a headache. He thought these intense pains were gone, but recently, they had resurfaced, and Christopher was distressed by their return. Although he never took naps, he felt as if he needed one to relax and reset his thoughts. CiCi was having dinner with her friends, and he wasn't meeting her until later at the bar, so he had time to try and ease his aching head by laying on his couch and resting.

Christopher fell right to sleep, but his peaceful rest was soon interrupted by a vivid dream. Christopher saw himself leading a woman to a remote area by gunpoint. He was consumed by thoughts of hatred and revenge as they moved closer to his final destination. In his dream, he knew the woman, and when he looked back at himself, he appeared to be someone totally different.

But the dream did not stop, and he was still walking with the woman, feeling that very soon he would kill her. When he looked closer at the woman's face, she was familiar. He was still convinced that he didn't know her, but her face and stature and the way she carried herself were so common.

Without warning, Christopher felt the scorching, piercing pain of a gunshot right between his eyes, and he felt himself falling to the ground when he suddenly woke up in a drenching sweat. Sitting straight up, panting, Christoper was surprised that he was alive. His dream was so clear and so real. He was sure that he was dead.

Heading to the kitchen for some water, Christopher struggled to understand his dream. The headache he had before he laid down was gone, but he made a troublesome connection. His headaches were eerily similar to the pain he felt from the gunshot in his dream.

Christopher had not had any of these confusing, disturbing episodes for several months, and he was distraught that they had returned. But for now, he was pain-free, so he hopped in the shower and tried to push his inner turmoil aside. After a few minutes in his hot, steamy shower, Christopher's mind cleared, and just like that, his focus returned to the stunning, amazing college co-ed waiting for him at the lodge.

Christopher had to slow his pace after seeing his gorgeous date sitting at the bar. It was a fishing and hunting lodge, but CiCi had the foresight to pack a sexy black jumpsuit and heels that accentuated all her most alluring assets. Christopher should have been flattered, but he began overthinking and arrived at the conclusion that CiCi's sexy attire was once intended for Dex, and this realization took some of the excitement out of her appearance. Still, part of him wondered why he was so worried about her ex. She was there with him now, and she dressed sexy for him. He was stumped as to why he couldn't accept this effort as good enough.

As he approached, he received a beautiful, welcoming smile, and out of nowhere, a faint but noticeable pain persisted in the back of his eye. However, when he leaned down to meet CiCi's hello kiss, all of his pain and reservations subsided.

"You look amazing," he affirmed.

"Not bad yourself," CiCi replied. "Did you get all of your work done?"

"Yes, thank you. I figured you could use some time with your friends anyway," Christopher answered.

"Yes, our dinner was delicious," CiCi confirmed.

"I'm glad," Christopher answered, gently putting his hand on her thigh. CiCi could instantly feel all her senses heighten, and she secretly begged for him to move his hands to her most sensitive parts and get her off right there at the bar. They had only been there for half an hour, and CiCi couldn't concentrate. She had still not recovered from Christopher's sensual touch and attentive lovemaking the night before. Now, her mind was drifting to the possibilities yet to come that evening.

Sensing CiCi's restlessness, Christopher ceased his conversation and hailed the bartender for their check. He had shed all his doubts, weird feelings, and fears for the time being. Now, he was ready to explore CiCi Brunner further, so he proceeded to pay the bill.

Downing the last drops of her wine, CiCi mentioned that she was not dressed for a snowmobile ride to his cabin, but she had a perfectly good room right upstairs. With the tab covered, Christopher assisted his date off her stool, and the two of them headed up the stairs with overwhelming anticipation.

Just inside the door, Christopher pulled CiCi to him, and she released an uninhibited sigh of pleasure when he met her open mouth with his sensual tongue. CiCi had been waiting on this moment all day, and she was finally in his arms again. He was holding her so close she could feel he was ready to make love to her. CiCi boldly stroked him through his pants until she could tell he was about to lose his mind. Not letting him off the hook, she undid his belt and fly and went down on him, eliciting the reaction she hoped for because it wasn't long, and Christopher was begging.

"I need to fuck you right now!"

In the next few seconds, CiCi was out of her jumpsuit and on the bed, awaiting what she knew would be one of the best fucks of her life. Christopher pulled her to the edge of the bed, placed her legs up on his shoulders, and pushed in, causing her to gasp much louder than she planned as he gripped her hips and pulled them hard into his body again and again, hitting that spot every fucking time.

She was almost out of her mind from this wonderful misery when Christopher pulled out and stood there looking down at her. After a few seconds, he carefully bent her knees and placed her feet on the bed. Out of modesty, CiCi naturally kept her knees together, but Christopher smiled that smile, and her stomach did that flip.

"Now, it's no time to be shy," he said, placing his hands on her knees. When his fingers touched her, CiCi felt herself melting into the sheets. As he ever so slowly pulled her knees apart, CiCi was both terrified and exhilarated by her complete exposure.

Christopher took several seconds just looking at the beauty before him. He took his fingers and lightly brushed them down over her, and CiCi let out a breathy gasp.

"You're mine now, CiCi."

Christopher got to his knees and officially staked his claim while CiCi arched her back in satisfied appreciation. And just like that, he was back inside her, absorbing all the pleasure of her lingering spasms, and he was hitting that spot again, extending her pleasure. When it was all over, CiCi was rendered motionless and finally opened her eyes to Christopher smiling his perfect white smile, looking so sexy, knowing he was good— very, very good.

"I…I…" CiCi began but was interrupted by a deep, sultry kiss.

"Yes? You were saying," Christopher teased.

"I could never get tired of that," she finally managed.

"Good," Christopher replied, pulling on his pants. "I'm going down to get a bottle of wine and an ice bucket. When I get back, I'll let you decide what you want first…a drink or another mind-bending fuck," Christopher said, looking back at her still naked on the bed. Then he flashed that irresistible smile and winked. CiCi made her mind up right then and there that another glass of wine could wait.

Chapter 9

CiCi was late meeting her friends for breakfast after her eventful night with Christopher and felt more than a little embarrassed walking down the stairs into the lobby. Dessie and Izzy knew that look all too well and shared a concealed snicker.

"It's about time!" Vic said with more displeasure than he intended.

"I'm sorry! I'm sorry! I overslept," CiCi explained.

Dessie and Izzy shared another *knowing* moment, and Vic expressed his apology for being so brazen.

"No worries. But let's get in there and eat!"

CiCi was quiet at breakfast, and after Vic got his fill of 'all he could eat' bacon and eggs, he was curious.

"So, what's the deal with this Christopher guy? He's a little old for you, isn't he?"

Caught off guard, CiCi wasn't quick with a reply, but she finally responded.

"There's no *deal*," CiCi began on the defensive. "He's thirty-five, and it doesn't really matter, does it?"

Sensing CiCi's annoyed tone, Vic thought better of pressing her for more answers, but CiCi, still feeling the need to defend her actions, concluded their conversation.

"Besides, it's just a vacation fling, right? It's not going anywhere."

CiCi wasn't sure she believed the words that came out of her mouth, but at least her comment might get her friends off her back. What she didn't know was that Christopher had walked up behind her to greet the group and heard every word.

After feeling his heart drop to the floor, Christopher felt he should at least say something to the group so he wouldn't look as stupid as he felt.

"Good morning. I hope your trip is going well. I'm unavailable for trailing today, but I'm sure you'll have a nice time." And rather than addressing CiCi personally as he would have normally done, he turned and walked out the door.

CiCi felt a hot rush come over her face.

"Was he…"

"Yep," Dessie confirmed.

CiCi put her face in her hands. She couldn't believe he heard that. Why did she feel the need to minimize her feelings for him? Why didn't she just keep her mouth shut? She felt horrible. She wanted to run after Christopher and explain, but even her explanation was degrading. She excused herself and headed up to her room—the same room where she spent the most amazing night of her life with Christopher. CiCi was disappointed in herself and felt physically sick, knowing she hurt a man she really cared for.

When Izzy and Dessie knocked on her door, she didn't even want to get up and let them in, but she did, trying to act normal.

"Hey, I'm not feeling so good. I think it was something I ate. I'm gonna hang back here this morning. If you come back sometime this afternoon, maybe I'll feel more like going out on the trails."

Izzy and Dessie weren't buying it. They knew her too well.

"You have feelings for him, don't you?" Izzy asked.

Unable to lie, CiCi felt a tear forming and then broke down.

"That was so stupid of me. I didn't mean that. I was just caught off guard, and it does seem a little weird that I like him so much. I didn't want you to know, especially the guys, since Dex and I just broke up. It makes me look like a slut."

"First of all, we all know that look you get on your face when you're around him, even the guys. And no one thinks you're a slut. We just want you to be careful. That's all," Izzy said, putting her arm around CiCi's shoulder.

"Well, it doesn't matter now. He thinks I was just looking for someone to fuck on vacation. I feel so bad."

"But don't ruin your fun over it. Come out with us," Dessie said.

"No, I'll hang back here and hopefully see him and try to smooth things over and catch up with you guys this afternoon. Come back and check on me, okay?"

"Alright. Good luck," Izzy replied as Dessie gave CiCi a little hug.

❖ ❖ ❖

Christopher was completely distraught. He just had the most magical night with the most wonderful woman, only to find out that she was using him as a vacation hook-up. Christopher walked briskly to his snowmobile, checked all his gauges, and roared off into the Wisconsin woods.

I should have fucking known! Immature college women! She's too young for me anyway.

As he tried to convince himself, Christopher suddenly felt a pain in the back of his head that he knew all too well.

Damn it! Why can't I shake this fucking pain? I thought it was gone, but now, all of a sudden, it's back. Too much stress, I guess. That CiCi Brunner is more fucking trouble than I signed up for.

Christopher quickly turned around and headed back toward the lodge. He didn't want to be out too far if his head got too debilitating. Pulling into camp, he decided he would go to his office and take a nap. That seemed to do the trick the last time his headache flared. The return of these headaches baffled him, and he wished he knew both the cause and a certain cure. For now, he felt a nap might help.

As he walked into the lodge lobby, CiCi spied him. She had been waiting, hoping he would return so she could explain herself. As she locked eyes with her target, his malice and disdain were evident, and she was crushed. But she knew she owed him an explanation, so she got up and headed his way. CiCi knew that she deserved to be ignored and dismissed, but she hoped he would listen to the truth.

When she approached him, CiCi began her plea.

"Look, I feel a little weird being here with Dex's friends and all of a sudden being with someone new. I said those things this morning because I know what they were thinking. I know they think I'm moving too fast. I didn't mean any of it. I said those things so I wouldn't have to justify sleeping with someone right after Dex and I broke up."

Christopher was just staring at her, not saying a word.

"I'm sorry," she said, finally.

Since Christopher had not spoken or given her any indication that he understood and forgave her, CiCi turned to walk off.

"I don't want you to be embarrassed to be with me," he said, finally.

CiCi turned around and looked him directly in the eyes.

"I'm not. Please believe me. But I have to go home to the real world with these people, and I have no idea where you and I stand when this week is over," CiCi confessed.

Christopher didn't even honor her comment with a reply. Instead, he took her hand and kissed it.

"I thought I made my feelings perfectly clear last night," Christopher stated.

CiCi was on thin ice here but felt as if there was no better time to be honest and lay it all out.

"I'm sorry. But where I'm from, spending the night with someone doesn't mean you have feelings for them," CiCi stated.

Christopher was a little hurt and confused.

"I didn't just spend the night with you. I made love to you. Couldn't you feel that?"

CiCi felt worse than ever. Maybe she had found that one special guy who was a romantic and not just out to fuck and leave.

"You have to admit, me having expectations after a couple of nights together would be a little clingy and weird. I just didn't want to try and make this something that it's not," CiCi explained.

Christopher thought for a second and then took her hand and led her back upstairs to the room where they had made love all night long.

"I guess I have some convincing to do then," Christopher said right before he laid her down on the bed. And just to make himself clear, he whispered some words that made CiCi's heart race.

"When this week is over, *we* are not over."

Chapter 10

CiCi was more confused than ever. How could she let her feelings get so far gone so fast? She just ended a three-year relationship and thought she would be single for a while, doing all the things single girls do. And now, here she was, involved in another relationship.

There were lots of red flags about the whole situation, but CiCi chose to ignore them initially. For one, even though she had strong feelings for Christopher, she felt as if he fell too hard, too fast, and CiCi didn't like that he was more invested in the relationship than she was. Sure, he made her heart flutter with his romantic words and gestures, but his comments about their future were way too advanced for no longer than they had known each other. And the way he said, "You're mine, CiCi," seemed sexy at the moment, but who really says that after only a couple of days?

Still, CiCi chose to overlook Christopher's possessive nature so she could be with him over her break. He was handsome and sexy, and CiCi could not deny that he had a way of making her hot and then putting out that fire. Just the thought of being with him gave her shivers.

"You don't want to fuck that up, CiCi," she said to herself.

So, CiCi ignored her intuition, pushed the warning signals to the back of her mind, and resolved to have a fucking great time on her vacation with this gorgeous man who just couldn't get enough of her.

There are worse things than having a sexy man who knows how to fuck infatuated with you.

❖ ❖ ❖

That night at dinner, Vic was stressing again about the ride home. None of them wanted to call their parents and ask to be picked up; there was no train service close to that route, and a ride service would cost a fortune.

"Has anyone thought of a solution to our ride problem?"

"Well, as a matter of fact, Christopher's parents live in Peoria. He said he could give us a ride. He was going home to see them for Christmas anyway," CiCi offered.

"Hallelujah!" Vic shouted. "He has a big SUV, so our stuff will fit just fine."

"That solves that problem. Now maybe Vic can get the stick out of his ass and have some fun, " Izzy said, rolling her eyes.

"Hey, it was a big deal!" Vic said, defending his position.

"My parents would have come up to get us if it came to that, so I wasn't really worried," CiCi explained. "I mean, because it is kinda my fault."

"Nonsense!" Dessie offered quickly. "Dex should have known you were coming up here single instead of thinking he could get in your pants."

"I don't think he was going to try to 'get in my pants,'" CiCi answered sarcastically.

"Oh, he was bragging that 'he was going to get some no matter what'…blah, blah, blah…" Izzy added.

"He said that?" CiCi questioned in disbelief.

"Yeah," Greg confirmed.

"I can't believe I wasted so much time on that prick," CiCi responded.

"But he wasn't always like that," Dessie shared.

"Yeah, but it's the way he ended up that matters. I don't want anything else to do with him ever," CiCi confirmed.

"Let's talk about something a little more pleasant, like tomorrow and what we're going to do," Izzy said, changing the subject.

"Christopher is taking us ice fishing," Greg said with obvious excitement.

"That sounds absolutely horrible!" Dessie confirmed.

"Yeah, I'm going to pass on sitting out on a frozen lake," Izzy added.

"You could take the car and go into town and do something," Vic suggested, looking at Izzy. "How's that? Is the stick out of my ass now?" Vic said jokingly.

Everyone laughed. The group of friends were having a wonderful time on their vacation, and now that they had a way home, even Vic could relax. They spent the rest of the evening hanging out at the bar, laughing and talking about old times. It had been a long day, and everyone except CiCi was tired pretty early and decided to go up to their rooms. She was more than a little upset that Christopher hadn't met up with her that evening as they planned. She was annoyed that he could get upset at her for being casual about their relationship and then turn around and be so distant and inconsiderate. She was wondering if maybe she had it all wrong. Was *she* the one being used in this situation? Was all his smooth talk just a way to get what he wanted?

CiCi grabbed her coat to take a walk around the grounds. Her thoughts were scattered. On the one hand, Christopher seemed incredibly interested in her, even beyond her week vacation. And then, on the other, he would disappear for hours, and there was no word from him. She wondered if he was seeing someone else and had to admit that another woman would explain his behavior and secrecy.

CiCi was getting cold, and she was tired of worrying about where Christopher was and what he was doing. When she went back to the lodge and headed up to her room, there was still no text or sign of Christopher.

❖ ❖ ❖

Christopher's head was pounding. He was so sure his sick headaches were gone, and he couldn't figure out why, all of a sudden, his torture returned. He was going to go mad if he didn't get some relief. He could hardly get his head off his pillow, let alone go to the doctor. Remembering he had some pain pills left over from breaking his ankle the past summer, he mustered all his strength, made his way to the cabinet to get the pills, and then went back to bed.

After about twenty minutes, Christopher got a little relief. He still had pain in the back of his head, but it was not that skull-pounding pressure that kept him helpless. Christopher was also able to relax enough to fall asleep, but his newfound relief would not last long as he began to drift off into a horrible nightmare.

In his visions, Christopher saw two people, a man and a woman. The man seemed familiar, and he was pretty sure the woman was the same one from his previous dream. The couple were living comfortably and seemed exceptionally content. Then he saw the woman with a baby, and he immediately felt a connection to the child. He couldn't understand why, but he wanted to take the child from the woman, and he began to resent her for having the baby he wanted.

As Christopher walked toward the couple, the man looked up at him, but his face was blurred. Christopher could tell, however, that the man was glaring at him with a menacing scowl. This whole situation seemed familiar like he had seen it all before somewhere, and even though the man's presence made him hesitate, Christopher wanted that child. He was even willing to risk his life to take it from the woman. But as he reached for the baby, the woman resisted and had words.

"I know who you are, and there's no way in hell you're even touching my baby, let alone taking her." The woman's voice was strong and determined. His mind was clouded, but his desire to take the child had not lessened, and he was resolved to take her forcibly if necessary because he hated this woman even more than before.

In the next seconds, Christopher saw a gun in his face. The man was standing over him. His face still blurred and unrecognizable, but with a look of hatred that was undeniable. And then the gun fired. Christopher was dead one second, and he woke up in a sweat the next.

Now, with only the faint remnants of his headache, Christopher had a new worry. Why was he having these nightmares, and who were these people? Christopher lay his head back down on the pillow and closed his eyes. Until now, he believed he was safe from his past. He was exhausted and defeated and, most of all, terrified by these visions and this pain. In the past, these episodes led to nothing but trouble. Christopher covered his face with his hands and prayed that somehow, someway, he would not revert back to the troubled soul he had once been.

"I don't know how much more I can take," he said, lying there weary but wide awake, afraid of sleep and the mayhem in his head. Finally, Christopher's mind relaxed, and he fell into a deep sleep, absent of nightmares.

Chapter 11

Christopher woke up headache-free the next morning. He felt horrible about not texting CiCi the night before, but he could barely open his eyes, let alone text. Surely, he didn't owe her too much of an explanation. They weren't a proper couple or anything. Still, had he not been incapacitated by the excruciating pain in his head, he would have been with her or at least texted her. But he was about to see her soon. He planned an ice fishing excursion for CiCi and her friends, and he was looking forward to the day ahead. He was sure that she would understand when he told her he was sick.

> CHRISTOPHER: Good morning! Sorry I didn't get a hold of you last night.
> I was sick and just stayed in bed.

When CiCi's phone pinged a notification, she was filled with tense nervousness. She hoped it was Christopher, even though she was mad at him. When she read the text, a frown came over her face.

Really, Christopher? Not too many people are so sick they can't send a simple text. And here you are this morning, fine and shit.

CiCi was baffled. When she was with him, he was attentive and certainly acted like he was interested in her, maybe even interested in a real relationship.

Maybe it's the age difference. Maybe people his age don't feel obligated to text regularly.

But CiCi couldn't quite make herself believe that explanation.

Well, he better not have something shady going on like another girl or even a wife.

Although she doubted he was married, it wasn't impossible.

How much do I really know about him?

When she asked herself that question, she shuddered slightly. She was being reckless, and she knew it.

That's it! I have to cool it. This is ridiculous anyway.

She tossed her phone back on the bed and finished getting ready to go into town to do some shopping with the girls. She decided she'd put a little space between them. And better yet, she was quite proud of herself to be giving Christopher a taste of his own medicine by not replying. After all, she needed to start treating this like the vacation fling it was and not be clingy.

Christopher was getting a little steamed, wondering why CiCi hadn't texted him back. Surely, she could understand that he was sick and not mad about the night before. As he got ready for his day on the lake, he tried to let his worries go and decided he would just see CiCi when she showed up to go fishing, and everything would be alright.

When Christopher met Greg and Vic down in the lobby, he was not concerned at first that the girls were not with them. Even though they would be on a lake in the middle of nowhere, these girls would put on makeup and do their hair. When he greeted the guys, he was pleasant. But when Vic asked if they were ready to go, Christopher had to ask.

"Where are the girls?"

"They headed into town to do some shopping. None of them thought ice fishing sounded very fun," Greg offered.

Christopher's face instantly changed. Now he was not only worried that CiCi was upset with him, he was also pissed that she went off into town without telling him where she was going. He knew his face was speaking volumes, but he couldn't control the intense anger that was filling his core.

Greg and Vic instantly noticed the change in Christopher's mood. His sudden anger concerned them, and the questions they had about his character multiplied. They couldn't quite figure him out. One minute, he was the nicest guy on earth, and the other, he didn't appear to be human. Not knowing what to say or do, Greg and Vic stood there watching their guide gain control of his emotions. Just as quickly as Christopher's anger consumed him, it seemed to subside.

Vic and Greg noticed that his face and body language completely changed, and he seemed to be back to normal. They wondered what could make him so mad. Surely, the source of his rage wasn't that CiCi went into town. The guy barely knew her.

"Oh, okay. Well, let's get packed up and head out," Christopher said casually.

As Vic and Greg continued to prepare for their trip, they were guarded, thinking that they didn't want to see that look on Christopher's face again, especially if they were all the way out on the lake. Luckily, Christopher seemed just fine for the remainder of their time that morning, and Vic and Greg had almost completely forgotten their fears after a short while out on the lake.

❖ ❖ ❖

Christopher never understood why he would have sudden emotional outbursts of feelings that didn't seem like his own. He thought he had outgrown these bizarre experiences, but now, for some reason, they were back, and Christopher dreaded the outcome. He was worried that he would have blackouts like before, with periods of time where he knew nothing about his whereabouts and actions. And he now specifically worried that his strange behavior would cause problems with CiCi, maybe even put her in danger. He was already consumed with worry that she hadn't texted him back, so he stole a moment to shoot her a quick text before heading out to the lake.

> CHRISTOPHER: Have a good time in town. Make sure to go to the Moccasin Bar. See you later on today.

In the backseat of Vic's car, CiCi opened her text from Christoper and couldn't help but smile.
Maybe he was really sick.
She knew one thing; she was getting some answers to some of her nagging questions as soon as possible before continuing to fall any harder.

The guys were semi-successful on their ice fishing expedition. Christopher was an excellent guide. He not only knew the area of the North Woods like the back of his hand, he was also a skilled hunter, trapper, and fisherman.

Once back at the lodge, all the guys noticed they had texts from their girls. It sounded like they had a great time shopping and were heading to the Moccasin Bar, as Christopher suggested, and wanted the guys to join them when they got off the lake.

"You'll have to drive, Christopher," Vic said.

"No problem, but my Bronco is up at my cabin. We'll have to take the snowmobiles up and get it."

"Cool! I've been wanting to see your place since CiCi first mentioned it," Greg added.

The guys were blown away by Christopher's property and cabin. Although the ground was covered in heavy snow, they could tell he had a huge yard cut out in the middle of the woods. And just as CiCi described, the inside looked like a taxidermy museum, which freaked both guys out more than they had planned.

"I know. It's a lot," Christopher laughed. "I've got my keys. Let's go."

Christopher wasn't sure why at first, but he had a strange urge to take an alternate route into town. Driving out to the main road made the guys remember how remote their lodge was. It was nothing but trails and woods for miles. When none of this scenery seemed familiar, Vic noticed that they weren't on the usual road that headed out to the main highway.

"Where are we, Man? This isn't the road we came in on?" Vic said, curious and just a little concerned.

"That road needed more clearing," Christopher answered, hoping his explanation was sufficient. "I probably could have gotten through it, but there was already a car in the ditch. This way is a little longer, but we'll get there."

The new route was extra eerie. The trees seemed taller, and the road was narrow. Then Greg spotted a small shed out in the middle of nowhere and thought it was odd.

"Why in the world would there be a shed way out here with nothing else around?" Greg asked.

"It does seem odd," Vic added.

At first, Christopher was silent and pensive but then offered a suitable reason.

"With all the trails, people sometimes need a place to stop and drop off or change gear."

And then, Christopher felt a weird surging in his veins and felt compelled to fuck with their minds a bit. "Who knows, maybe it's where the North Woods stalker hides his victims."

Christopher laughed and even he did not recognize his voice.

No, no! This can't be happening!

The rest of the car was silent and completely creeped out by Christopher's inappropriate comment and eerie laugh. They didn't know why, but his words hit them the wrong way. They knew it was meant as a joke, but they didn't think it was remotely funny coming from Christopher. Needless to say, the rest of the ride in town was uncomfortable and far too long.

The Moccasin Bar was an odd novelty for the two city boys, and the whole vibe was so unique Vic and Greg forgot about Christopher's *joke* and took in the sights. There was cold beer, and their women were a couple drinks in and a little flirty when they arrived. How could life be any better?

Christopher locked eyes with CiCi the minute he walked in as if he knew right where she would be. For a brief moment, he felt anger surging through him, and then just like that, it was gone. CiCi thought he had a look of disapproval on his face, but quite quickly, he cracked that gorgeous white smile that made her insides flip.

"Hey, I told you the Moccasin Bar was cool," Christopher said as he approached and gave her a 'hello' kiss.

"Very cool," CiCi agreed. "Are you feeling better?" She asked to start the conversation. She thought that a general, unthreatening question would eventually give her an avenue into a deeper query about his absence the night before.

"Much. I get these sick headaches, and I can't even open my eyes or lift my head. It's an awful, debilitating pain. I thought I had kicked them, but after several months, they're back," Christopher explained.

Well, now CiCi just felt silly. His explanation sounded one hundred percent legitimate, and she was feeling as if she should have checked on him or tried to help instead of thinking the worst.

"I'm so sorry. I probably should have checked on you," CiCi said, lightly rubbing back and forth between his shoulders as part of her sincere apology.

"Don't be silly. You were having fun with your friends, I'm sure."

"Yes, I was. But I have to admit. I was getting a little upset that I hadn't heard from you," CiCi confessed.

Christopher felt a sharp pain in his forehead and had a brief moment of fear that he would succumb to a full-blown headache right there at the bar. As the pain and his fear slowly waned, Christopher felt an uncontrollable rage growing in his chest.

No! Please, God! No! I can't go back there.

He was suddenly furious that she expected him to text or call to constantly check in. Plus, he had a similar episode when she exercised some independence and went shopping without letting him know. Part of Christopher was extremely confused. This part could not explain why he would be so possessive. He knew he was being irrational, but his anger was too strong. Christopher dreaded what was coming next, but he had lost all control, and his face seemed to morph into someone CiCi didn't even recognize.

CiCi noticed the change in his demeanor right away and knew she had hit a nerve even though she felt it was a legitimate question. At first, she was not particularly worried, but when he spoke, his tone was menacing, and it scared her.

"It was one night I didn't text," he said with malice in his words.

CiCi was scared but also put off. Christopher seemed to have his own set of rules and totally different expectations for her. She suddenly felt the familiar double standard rule rearing its head. The last thing she needed was to go from one moody, possessive boyfriend to another.

"I understand your reason now, but I thought it was inconsiderate at the time."

Christopher laughed loudly, making CiCi extremely uncomfortable and catching the attention of everyone in the bar, especially CiCi's friends, who were now a little worried for her. Greg and Vic put their drinks on the bar and moved a little closer to CiCi, but this only infuriated Christopher more.

"Inconsiderate? That's funny. I've been nothing but hospitable," Christopher said while laughing again. "And your friends there," he said, pointing to Vic and Greg, "can back off. You all have no problem getting free trail excursions and ice fishing, but you're quick to turn on a guy."

CiCi was more than a little uncomfortable and began her slow trek anywhere but where she was, pinned into the bar by Christopher. Trying to move away from Christopher and get closer to Vic and Greg seemed like an excellent plan until Christopher put his hands on her shoulders to stop her progress. Greg was livid.

"Hey! That's enough, Man. Leave her alone."

Christopher backed off but maintained intense and unnerving eye contact with Greg, who was intent on standing his ground.

"I think I've been very accommodating to you all, especially the twenty-two-year-old who's trying to fuck away the memories of an old boyfriend," Christopher said, looking accusingly at CiCi. "You know he's a prick, right?"

CiCi was stunned. She had to take a second to process what he just said. When her mind was straight, she pulled away from Christopher and let him have it.

"Don't you *ever* come near me again. You hear me? You have a problem, and I'm removing myself from your bullshit."

And with those words, CiCi began to walk toward her friends when Christopher grabbed her wrist forcefully, preventing her from going any farther.

"You're staying right here," Christopher commanded.

"Let go of me!" CiCi said quite forcefully.

With Greg and Vic right in front of him and the whole bar watching, Christopher decided to let go. Humiliated and furious, he stormed out the door.

"We had your back," Vic said, giving her a hug.

"Why do I attract the crazies?" CiCi said, with fear still in her voice.

"I knew there was something not quite right with that guy," Izzy said.

A man at the bar who had been watching the entire scene spoke up.

"That's Christopher Paloma from Deerfoot, right?" he questioned.

"Yes," CiCi answered, rolling her eyes.

"Yeah, he's an odd one. I've seen him do some weird shit, but I've never seen him treat a woman like that."

"Weird? Like what?" Greg asked.

"Sometimes he's just a normal guy, but he's known for talking to himself a lot. And anger is an issue, too. No one will go hunting with him anymore because they don't trust to be around him with a gun."

CiCi suddenly felt sick to her stomach.

Wow! And I was at this guy's cabin alone. I had sex with him!

"I say we just get out of here and go home to have a few extra days with our families," Vic suggested.

"I don't want to go back to the lodge and possibly run into him," CiCi said. "But all of my things are there."

"We can go back and get everyone's stuff," Vic offered. "We'll do that and check out and meet you back here."

"Okay, I'll call my parents. My dad will come up and get me and whoever else needs a ride. I'm so sorry, guys," CiCi said, almost crying. "This whole vacation has been a disaster from the start, and it's all my fault."

Even though her friends were inclined to agree, they knew CiCi felt horrible, and none of them really cared about the two days they were missing. Izzy and Dessie stayed with CiCi while the guys headed back to the lodge. CiCi guessed there were worse places to wait than a bar, but it would be at least nine hours before her dad would be there. Under different circumstances, she would have enjoyed herself and had a few more drinks. But that afternoon, she was so confused by her emotions that she wanted nothing to do with drinking. Under the circumstances, she felt she needed to keep a clear head. She couldn't wait to crawl in her dad's car and sleep while he drove her home, far away from this nightmare. She dreaded the call home to explain their situation, but she knew her dad would drop everything and come to her rescue, so she made the call.

Chapter 12

Mac was up at the lodge in record time to pick up CiCi and her friends. CiCi omitted the part of her distress that included Christoper when she called her dad, knowing he would not approve of her reckless behavior. Even though the most damaging part of her story was unknown as far as her dad was concerned, she was still nervous about seeing him. She was certain that her dad would not be very happy having to drop everything and come get her all the way up in the North woods. But Mac wasn't mad at her. He was pissed at Dex. He hoped he would get the chance to give him an earful someday and let him know that his actions put a lot of people he cared about in a very precarious situation.

CiCi was thankful she didn't have to go back to the lodge and risk running into Christopher; however, she totally forgot to tell her dad to pick them up at the Moccasin Bar instead. She was more worried about her dad finding out about Christopher than where she needed to be picked up.

"No one is allowed to mention the ordeal with Christopher," CiCi ordered. "As far as my dad knows, Dex and I had a fight, and he left, which is actually true."

Nightmares & Premonitions

Mac pulled into the lodge at about 10 pm, and the party atmosphere was in full force. Mac was somewhat perplexed as to why CiCi and her friends would want to leave early. It seemed like the perfect winter break getaway, and instantly, Mac was sorry he wasn't staying.

Mac walked up to the desk and inquired about CiCi and her friends, only to hear that they had checked out. Confused and a little worried, Mac texted his daughter.

> MAC: I'm here to get you. Where are you?
>
> *Ugh! I forgot to tell him we were waiting in town, not at the resort. Now, he's going to be even more upset.*
>
> CiCi: SO SORRY! We had to check out, so we are at the Moccasin Bar in town.

Mac wondered why they had to check out but didn't give it much thought. Now, he had to figure out how to get in town.

"Excuse me again. My navigation wasn't working very well on the way up here. I need some directions to the Moccasin Bar," Mac asked.

Thinking it was more than a coincidence, Christopher, who was coming down the stairs, heard 'Moccasin Bar' and turned his attention in that direction. The very moment he laid eyes on Mac, Christopher got that shooting pain going right through his skull, and he had to close his eyes for some relief. Once the pain subsided and the throbbing began, Christopher was at least able to open his eyes. There was something familiar about that man, and while he was sure it was CiCi's dad, Christopher wondered why he would think he was familiar.

Mac got his directions, turned to leave, and nearly ran into Christopher, who had come up right behind him.

"Excuse me," Mac said. "I guess I shouldn't be in such a hurry."

"No worries," Christopher replied. "I'm Christopher, and I'm the owner here. I couldn't help but hear that you are looking for the Moccasin Bar.

"Yes," Mac confirmed.

"It can be pretty tricky to find places up here if you aren't familiar, especially in the dark. I wouldn't mind riding with you, so you get there safely without getting lost," Christopher offered. "I could get a ride back, no problem."

"That would be great! I'm in a bit of a rush. My daughter and her friends got stranded up here. Apparently, they've been waiting at the bar all day for me to arrive," Mac stated. "Oh, I'm Mac, by the way. I don't know if you got to meet my daughter CiCi while she was here, but she was here with her boyfriend and other friends for a few days."

Christopher was trying to act naturally, but he almost laughed out loud when Mac asked if he had a chance to meet CiCi. Christopher wondered if he should mention that 'yes, he got to meet his precious daughter, and she's one hell of a lay.' But he thought that could wait.

"There have been so many people up here with the tremendous amount of snow we've had this year. I can't be sure," Christopher answered.

The two got in Mac's Tahoe, and Christopher pointed Mac in the right direction to head out onto the road that hooked up with the main highway to Hayward. About a mile into the ride,

Christopher began to feel some familiar and disturbing sensations, and a sinister cloud shrouded his mind, giving him a negative physical reaction to Mac.

Mac caught his passenger staring at him with an intense gaze that immediately told him something was wrong. This was not the same cordial man who introduced himself at the lodge and generously offered to be his guide into town. Mac was suddenly aware of his .45 resting in his shoulder holster and began to think of the best way to access it if necessary.

After trying to engage in more conversation to no avail, Mac noticed Christopher had something shiny in his hand that he kept manipulating. It wasn't a weapon or anything that could be a makeshift weapon, but Mac still couldn't make it out until the man brought it to his lips and seemed to kiss it. Mac was horrified when he recognized the item as CiCi's bracelet, the one they bought her for her twenty-first birthday. Mac would know it anywhere. He and Aria had designed it themselves and wondered why the man would have it. Mac was more nervous than ever and was now almost sure this man not only knew CiCi but might be the reason she called him to come get her.

"What do you have there?" Mac asked, hoping he made the right choice, calling Christopher out.

"Nothing!" Christopher said with an irritated tone, and he shoved the bracelet into his pocket.

"I recognize that bracelet. It belongs to my daughter," Mac said calmly.

"I found it. I was going to give it back to her when we got to the bar," Christopher snapped back.

Christopher was flustered. He could kick himself for allowing Mac to see the bracelet in his hand. He was so thrilled to find it left in her room after Vic and Greg hastily packed. Missing

CiCi, he went up to her room when he returned to the lodge after his embarrassing departure from the Moccasin Bar. Finding CiCi's bracelet was such a welcome surprise, but now Mac was going to want it back. Christopher just didn't know if he would be able to part with it.

Mac decided to change the subject because he could see Christopher's distress. Frankly, Mac was a little worried that they might not even be heading in the right direction, so he thought he'd ask.

"Are we getting close to a main road?"

Christopher was silent and looked to be deep in thought. Mac knew he was walking a fine line with this man. He could go off any minute. Then Mac got a text from CiCi that popped up on his information screen.

Are you about here?

Seeing the message, Christopher's mood began to lift, and his brooding scowl softened.

Mac was bewildered. This man now seemed perfectly normal, but Mac knew better than to relax. He had witnessed how quickly Christopher melded into his first dark episode. Thinking he better answer CiCi, Mac started to push the 'talk' button on his screen, and Christopher bristled.

"No! We're almost there. You don't need to answer her," Christopher demanded.

Mac was starting to put some pieces of the puzzle together. This man definitely had something to do with CiCi and her friends' shortened vacation. That would explain why he had to pick them up somewhere other than the lodge.

Pulling into town, Mac saw the lighted sign right outside the Moccasin Bar and headed that way without asking for or getting any additional directions. Christopher seemed anxious and irritated again and fidgeted in his seat as Mac got closer and closer to the bar. Mac got the feeling that by having Christopher in his car, he was delivering danger to his daughter and her friends, so he stopped before reaching their destination.

"Thanks for the directions. I can make it from here," Mac began. "I'll give CiCi her bracelet," Mac said, extending his hand, letting Christopher know he expected to receive it.

Christopher's demeanor changed again for the worse. He looked Mac in the eyes, and it was like an awakening of his mind. Suddenly, he knew who Mac was. He was the enemy, and Christopher hated him.

"I'll give it to her myself," Christopher said with a dark authority that made Mac even more worried.

In the next instant, Mac pulled his .45 from his holster so fast Christopher couldn't process what happened. But then he realized he was staring down the barrel of a .45 that was inches from his face. Christopher had never had a gun pulled on him, yet this was a memory he seemed to be reliving. Even though Mac had not pulled the trigger, Christopher saw it all quite vividly—the flash and the spinning bullet exiting the barrel. At the end of it all, Christopher slumped down in his seat. He had passed out. Mac breathed a sigh of relief, holstered his gun, cuffed Christopher, and grabbed CiCi's bracelet that Christopher had dropped on the floor. Mac then dialed the emergency number for the police and texted CiCi.

❖ ❖ ❖

MAC: Stay inside the bar and don't come out until you see police lights.

CICI: WHY! What's wrong?

MAC: I'm fine. We have the entire ride home for me to explain. Stay inside!

❖ ❖ ❖

When Christopher came to, he felt the familiar tightness of handcuffs around his wrists and let out a sinister laugh. He was still in the passenger seat of Mac's Tahoe and saw the flashing red lights and heard the familiar piercing squeal of sirens. Christopher was reliving it all, but he was aware that it wasn't *his* memory, and he struggled to sort out his thoughts. It wasn't until they put him in the back of the police car that he understood what was happening.

He watched as CiCi came running out of the bar and into her dad's arms for a long hug. When the hug ended, Mac gave his daughter a kiss on the forehead and then hugged Izzy and Dessie, who had also come outside with the guys to see what was going on. Christopher watched as Greg and Vic shook Mac's hand and even leaned in for a shoulder hug and a couple pats on the back. Christopher had never been so sad. He knew this whole fiasco ruined any chances of having a normal relationship with CiCi. He would never get a handshake from her father, and he would never be accepted by her friends.

These thoughts initiated that hot sensation in Christopher's chest that always turned him into someone he didn't recognize. As this sensation spread, Christopher was consumed with hatred. He saw CiCi's dad talking to the officer, probably telling him lies about what happened. And when he laid eyes on CiCi, his feelings were mixed. He knew she was also saying damaging things about him, but he wasn't worried. He would make bail and be out before he knew it. Although he was completely in love with CiCi, her betrayal and the way she dismissed him so quickly pissed him off, and he could not control the look of disgust that consumed his face.

And then Christopher made a connection that he had not made before. His life was going great until he met CiCi a few nights ago. After picking her up on the snowmobile, his headaches started again. He thought he had outgrown them, but CiCi was his trigger this time, and they were back.

But Christopher's malice for CiCi was fleeting, and as he looked out the window, he caught her looking at him. He remembered the first night she came to the lodge, and he went to the bar to get their drinks. When he looked back at her, she was staring at him. But now, her stare was one of disgust and fear rather than hopeful curiosity and lust.

Many times after that night, CiCi wished she had never looked Christopher's way. Once she locked eyes with him, she could not break his chilling gaze. And when the police car began pulling away from the parking lot, CiCi saw something she would never forget. Christopher cracked his sexy white smile and mouthed, "See you soon," sending chills up her spine.

Chapter 13

By the time the police questioned everyone, it was late. CiCi and her friends didn't talk much on the way home. They gave Mac a simplistic version of what happened with Christopher, and then they fell asleep from exhaustion, leaving Mac with a lot of questions that would now have to wait.

When they got home at about 10 am, Aria was waiting with some disturbing news. Dex's mother called and said she talked to Dex before he left for home four days ago, and he never made it. After hearing the news, CiCi was consumed with fear and guilt, wondering where Dex was and if he was alright.

"What do you mean? He didn't come home? Or he's missing, like there's been an accident?" CiCi questioned, fearful of the answer.

"He's missing," Aria confirmed.

CiCi looked back on their arguments at the lodge, and she knew she would have reacted the same way if the tables were turned. It was very soon for her to be moving on, and to blatantly pursue someone else right in front of Dex was cold. Now, for many reasons, CiCi wished it had never happened.

"What's happening? Are they looking? Does anyone know anything?" CiCi asked in a growing panic.

"Yes, the police are looking, but no word yet," Aria answered.

"CiCi, I think it's time you and your friends told us everything that happened on that trip," Mac said with a concerned but authoritative tone.

CiCi knew he was right, but she dreaded reliving all the details and worried what her parents would think of her. When the entire story was revealed, Mac told CiCi she had to tell the police everything about Christopher's controlling behavior and menacing threats. But when he dialed the Hayward Police Department, Mac was furious when Chief Jackson told him Christopher Paloma made bail and was released an hour ago.

"What the hell? This guy is a stalker. He is definitely unstable and has some kind of obsession with my daughter. He's made threats to her!" Mac pleaded.

"Mr. Brunner, no one is more upset about Christopher Paloma being released than I am. We've been trying to get that guy for years now. We have too many unexplained accidents and missing persons around that area for it to be a coincidence. We believe when Paloma has a beef with someone, he takes care of it—his way. But we can't prove any of it. This incident with your daughter is the first time he's been a little too reckless and sloppy."

Mac had a chilling feeling Christopher now had something to do with Dex's disappearance, but he hesitated to mention it, not wanting to worry CiCi.

"I'm getting some rest, and then I'm heading back up there," Mac said. "I'm 'all in' on the Dexter Robertson case. I'll see you soon."

When Mac hung up, CiCi wrapped her arms around his neck and gave him a tight hug.

"Dad, I'm so sorry for all of this," CiCi said, starting to cry.

"None of this is your fault. Don't worry. I'll find Dex, and I'm going to make sure that creep Christopher stays far away from you."

❖ ❖ ❖

Dex Robertson wondered if he would die before anyone found him. He had spent four long days and nights chained to a metal pole and locked up in a cold shed with nothing to eat but some snow that had blown in under the door.

Looking back, Dex knew he never should have left his friends at Deerfoot. He was just pissed and didn't want to stay there and extend the misery of seeing CiCi with another guy. But now, none of that mattered because he had bigger problems.

The day he left, Dex wasn't even on the main highway yet, and a snowmobile came out of nowhere and ran him off the road and into a deep snowbank. He couldn't be sure at the time because of all the man's gear, but he thought it was that snake Christopher who was making the moves on CiCi. When the man approached, Dex saw that he had a gun and then pointed it at him.

"Start walking," the man ordered, and Dex had no option but to comply.

Dex had no idea where they could be going. They were out in the middle of the North woods without a soul around, so he was almost certain the man was going to kill him. Then Dex saw a small shed in the distance, right in the middle of nowhere, and he figured they were headed there. When they arrived at the shed, Dex knew the man was Christopher because he told him that he would never be able to hurt CiCi again.

Even before this unfortunate incident, Dex regretted his hateful words about CiCi and knew they were not true. He also knew CiCi had every right to hate him. He tried to convince himself that he didn't know why he had gotten so spiteful towards her lately, but the truth was that CiCi was right. He was threatened by her.

"This is all fucked up," he thought. "I was just supposed to go home and then smooth things over after a few days." But Dex knew that plan was flawed from the beginning. He had really blown it this time. He didn't understand why he continued to take advantage of CiCi's love and kindness even though he regretted it every time. For too long, he would really fuck up and simply say he was sorry a few days later. That pattern had become a little too easy. Dex knew CiCi didn't deserve such treatment, but he continued to be a jerk, and she continued to believe he would change, and he never did.

Now, with nothing but time to think, Dex's mind went back to all of the hurtful comments, despicable actions, and petty arguments, and his heart hurt. As graduation approached, he knew that when they entered the real world, she would be the shining star, and he would always take a backseat to her accomplishments. His stupid pride told him to distance himself to prevent getting hurt. Now, facing a slow, painful death, he wished he could apologize. He wanted to tell her she was right, and his abysmal behavior lately was driven by his jealousy and fear.

But now he was almost certain he would never see her again, and she would never know how he really felt. He began to cry when he thought about dying, and CiCi's last memory of him was being a drunk asshole. He knew she deserved so much better. They had once meant so much to each other. In the lonely, cold days and nights he spent at the shed, he often wept uncontrollably, knowing that his fragile ego made him hurt the person he cared for the most.

After the Halloween party, Dex was so ashamed that he hurt his best friend, and the only person left who still believed in their relationship. Even though CiCi's friends told her to dump him and move on, CiCi continued to hope he would get back to the kind and selfless person he had once been, but he disappointed her, and not only that, he really hurt her.

Now humbled and desperate, Dex had lost all hope. He wished he had been a better man for CiCi, and now he would die out in the middle of the North Woods, and CiCi would never know how sorry he was. He had to find a way out of there. He couldn't die without apologizing, really apologizing, to the only woman he ever loved. She may never feel the same way about him again, but she deserved an apology, and now he feared he would never have the chance to give her one.

❖ ❖ ❖

When Christopher and CiCi returned from his cabin that first morning after making love, Christopher was livid that Dex Robertson would be so petty and selfish to leave CiCi and her friends stranded.

Fucking prick.

After hearing Dex's selfish decision, Christopher hastily excused himself, geared up, hopped on his snowmobile, and went flying off down the road. It wasn't long until he caught up with Dex who had to drive slowly on the fresh snow.

Christopher didn't have a plan at first. His main goal was to make sure Dex Robertson was never CiCi's problem ever again. Part of Christopher's thoughts told him to kill Dex, but the other half was unable to agree with such a gruesome solution. Therefore, Christopher decided to leave Dex in the shed, and he'd come back in a week or so to bury him. The end result was the same awful fate for Dex, but this way kept Christopher's hands a little cleaner.

As Christopher led Dex to the shed by gunpoint, he worried about what he would do with Dex's car. If he pulled it out of the snowbank, where would it be stored? He certainly didn't want to have it anywhere on his property. Christopher decided to just leave it in the ditch. Anyone who found it would assume the driver took off walking or got picked up.

Christopher was confident the shed was a relatively unknown place to the general public. It was barely visible from the remote trail that led from Christopher's cabin to the main road. Honestly, no one but Christopher was ever out that way, mainly because everyone knew Christopher's reaction to trespassers.

It wasn't the first time Christopher used the shed to hide someone. And it wasn't the first time someone died chained to that pole. He hoped it would be several days before anyone made the connection between the car and Dex Robertson's disappearance. And he hoped Dex was long gone and buried by then as well. Christopher coldly walked out of the shed that morning, leaving Dex alone without food or water, knowing his horrifying fate.

After getting released from jail, Christopher felt more vulnerable than ever, and a little paranoid about the secret he had stashed in the shed. Logic told him that Dex was secluded enough that no one would find him. However, annoying pangs of worry and guilt assaulted Christopher's mind, and he stressed over the idea of someone finding Dex in the shed before he got back there. If that were to happen, fingers would certainly point in his direction.

Therefore, Christopher's first stop after getting released was the remote shed. He figured it had not been enough time for

Dex to die, but he knew Dex would be weak and unable to sustain the elements without the protection of the shed. If Christopher released him, Dex would most certainly collapse and die in the woods. After discovering Dex's car, everyone would think he died trying to get to the main road for help.

Dex was asleep when Christopher came in. The past few hours had been especially painful and difficult as he grew weaker and weaker from the lack of food and water. When Christopher unchained him and left without a word, Dex was confused and unsure of what his next move should be. He watched as Christopher calmly made his way out the door and back to his snowmobile and then roared off in the direction of the main road.

If Dex had been stronger and able to think clearly, he would have jumped him or done something. Now free to go, Dex really didn't feel any better and didn't know how being unchained was going to help his situation. He was so weak, and he knew he was deep inside the woods. He'd never make it out to find help. But he had to do something. He had to try.

Dex mustered every bit of strength he had, went outside, and attempted to get his bearings. He could see Christopher's tracks in the snow, so he figured he would follow them. Christopher had to be going somewhere, a main road maybe. Dex decided that following Christopher might keep him from getting more lost and even save his life.

❖ ❖ ❖

Chuck Dempsey had one more lake road to plow before heading back to Hayward. He'd spent the past ten hours digging people out from the latest snowfall. As he slowed his plow to make the turn, Chuck saw a weak, struggling man emerging from the tree line, attempting to wave him down. Chuck put his plow in neutral, set the break, and hopped down to help the desperate man.

Before seeing the plow, Dex had made peace with death. He was certain he was in his final hours if someone didn't find him soon. Spotting the plow was a true miracle. Chuck could tell Dex was in bad shape and immediately called for an ambulance. There was no way this man was strong enough to climb up into his plow, and frankly, Chuck was afraid if he did, he would die there.

Chapter 14

Mac was almost packed to head back up North when he got a call from the Wisconsin State Police.

"Mr. Brunner, this is Trooper Nathan Curry from the Wisconsin State Police. Chief Jackson over in Hayward gave me your number. I wanted to let you know we found Dexter Robertson in the woods. A snowplow spotted him and called for help. He's in Memorial Hospital in Hayward. They think he's gonna be okay, but he'll be there for several days."

"Have you contacted his parents?" Mac asked.

"Yes, Sir."

Mac was relieved to tell CiCi they found Dex and that he was alright. She was so overcome with emotion that she couldn't talk, but she cried happy tears. Mac was also relieved that he didn't need to make another nine-hour trip up North. Dex's parents were going, and Mac was sure the Wisconsin State Police and the Hayward Police Department had everything under control.

CiCi thought she would give Dex some time to get well, and then she wanted to have a heart-to-heart. This whole experience left her feeling extremely grateful and very, very lucky. She didn't want much time to pass before giving Dex the explanation he deserved. She also planned to let him know how she felt, even if he could never forgive her.

Aria was relieved Mac was staying home because Christmas was only two days away, and they were invited to a big Christmas Day celebration at CiCi's Way. Although she had gotten up there in years, Calysta pulled out all the stops for the party with her biggest tree ever. There was no way Aria wanted Mac to miss the holiday with family and friends.

Being home and safe with her family was just what CiCi needed. She had to admit that her vacation was stressful rather than relaxing. Needless to say, CiCi spent Christmas Eve reading, relaxing, and catching up with her parents. In a little more than a week, she would begin her final semester of college. She had a lot of work to do before it was all over, and she knew she needed to get her head straight, especially about Dex, who would remain a big part of her life, being so entwined with the same classes and friends.

She thought she would probably never see Christopher again, and she was perfectly fine with that. Even though he made that eerie threat that he would 'see her soon,' she doubted that he could ever pull that off, and that thought had CiCi breathing a bit easier. But when her dad gave back her bracelet that she thought was gone forever, it gave her chills knowing Christopher once had it. The bracelet was so special to CiCi, and she was cussing Vic and Greg in her head for forgetting it from the bathroom vanity. But then again, she appreciated the fact that they went back and got all her stuff, so she wouldn't have to be anywhere near Christopher. From that perspective, she couldn't be too upset. Besides, she had it back now, and that was all that mattered.

On Christmas Day, CiCi and Aria did some baking and last-minute wrapping for the party. CiCi was excited to wear her new sweater dress and tall boots she didn't get to wear on vacation, and she decided to do something special with her hair, hoping that would help her get into the Christmas spirit.

CiCi was sad that Dex had to spend Christmas in the hospital and even more depressed that this was the first Christmas since she had known him that they were not together. CiCi wrestled with the thought of calling him. She had been wondering if it was appropriate and also wondering if he'd even talk to her. Honestly, she kind of thought he would have texted by now, but maybe he was thinking the same thing.

Taking a deep breath and pushing #1 on her contacts, CiCi took the leap. When a bewildered 'hello' came through, CiCi was at least glad he answered.

"Hey, I've been wondering how you were doing up there and wanted to wish you Merry Christmas," CiCi offered, sounding a bit nervous.

"I'm getting better. They say I'll be able to make the trip home in a few days," Dex answered.

After an awkward silence, CiCi felt as if she had made a foolish decision.

"Well, I'm glad you're okay. Merry Christmas," and she didn't wait for a reply because she was terrified, she either wouldn't get one, or she would get one, she would just as well not hear.

That was a disaster.

CiCi wondered what she even expected and what she wanted from that call. Was her guilt rekindling old feelings, or was it loneliness? CiCi just knew that the unsatisfying conversation did nothing to improve her mood.

Dex was so surprised by CiCi's call that he was literally speechless. He wondered how in the world she could even stand the thought of him, let alone reach out. Dex had spent a lot of time lying in his hospital bed, planning what he wanted to tell her once he got home. Her calling him was definitely not expected but a welcome gesture. And then he thought about how dumb he probably sounded, and he knew he blew it. That was evident by her rushing to hang up before he could even muster up a word or two to keep the conversation going.

Dex thought about calling her back or at least texting, but now he was more confused than ever, and when he did have a conversation with CiCi, he wanted it to be thoughtful and planned. So, instead of calling or texting, Dex lay in his bed overthinking and miserable on Christmas.

❖ ❖ ❖

Once out into the fresh air, infused with holiday music and energized with jolly guests, CiCi's mood lifted. She was filled with fond memories of past Christmases. They had always gathered there at the infield of CiCi's Way for Christmas, and she loved the warm, familiar atmosphere of Calysta's parties.

Everyone was supposed to be there: Grandma Connie and Grandpa Rob, Aunt Cheryl and Uncle Glen, Calysta, Pauly, the Johnsons, Mallory, Jason, and their two boys and their wives. Mallory and Calysta were always a little blue for a while on Christmas because they hoped and prayed Mallory's oldest son would come home. As far as CiCi knew, he never did because she had never met him. He had some troubles, and she heard he spent some time in a hospital and then moved away. He kept in contact with his parents, but he rarely saw them, as far as she knew. But usually, after the initial disappointment that he didn't show again, Calysta and Mallory reconciled with the fact that he wasn't coming and settled in to enjoy themselves.

By the time CiCi got outside, there was quite a buzz of activity. Calysta had rented a couple of specialty drink trucks: a hot chocolate one for the kids and a martini bar for the adults. CiCi thought she could go for a grasshopper martini, so she began walking that way and ran into Mallory who was quite excited that her oldest son had, in fact, finally made it home for Christmas this year. About that time a hauntingly familiar figure rounded the side of the martini truck.

"Hello, CiCi. Merry Christmas!"

CiCi bristled and could feel her palms getting sweaty and a giant lump growing in her throat.

"Oh, Christopher, I didn't know you knew CiCi," Mallory interjected with a puzzled look. "I know you moved away when she was very little."

"Yes, I definitely know Ms. Brunner," Christopher said with that killer smile that had once seduced her. Now, just thinking about it nearly made CiCi sick. For Mallory's sake, she would be cordial. CiCi managed a simple 'hello' and immediately excused herself.

Shaking with fear, CiCi was frantically looking for her dad. How could this be? How could the menacing Christopher from Hayward, Wisconsin, be Mallory and Jason's estranged son? Suddenly, all of the things that she knew about Mallory and Jason's oldest fit Christopher perfectly. He had some problems with what Jason called a "multiple personality" and moved away to "spare his family the effects of his condition."

Calysta also bragged about how her oldest grandson was an outdoors expert and that he was a successful business owner now somewhere in the far North. After putting all the pieces together, CiCi wondered how she hadn't figured it out sooner. Christopher had even told her his parents lived in Peoria.

Nightmares & Premonitions

With her mind racing, CiCi was still unable to find her dad, and now she was nervous about what he would do if he saw Christopher. When CiCi stopped to take a deep breath and think clearly, Christopher slipped up behind her without warning and firmly grabbed her, locking his arm around her neck. He quickly muffled her screams by cupping his other hand over her mouth, nearly dragging her behind the hot chocolate truck. CiCi always thought that if she was grabbed from behind, she would know exactly what to do, but she was completely caught off guard, and Christopher had such a grip on her that she could barely move, let alone get away.

"I told you I'd see you soon, CiCi," Christopher whispered in her ear.

CiCi was terrified, and the feel of his hot breath on her neck was making her sick to her stomach. She wondered what he planned to do and hoped he was not deranged and reckless enough to try and get her even more out of sight and away from the party.

"Don't you look delicious," he said, intentionally rubbing his arm and then hand across her breasts. "Don't worry. I'm going to let you go this time because I'm not going to ruin our family Christmas, but I *will* have you all to myself someday. Merry Christmas, CiCi."

And just like that, Christopher let go, turned, and walked away.

Chapter 15

CiCi was frightened out of her mind and began desperately searching for her dad. In her distressed state, several people tried to stop and talk with her, yet she maintained her pursuit of Mac. When CiCi found him, she also saw her worst fear coming true. Christopher was standing not too far behind her parents, glaring intently at them with sheer hatred in his eyes. When he spied CiCi, that glare transferred to her, and she struggled to maintain her composure as a deadly cold chill went down her spine.

CiCi instantly locked eyes with her former lover, and she saw his face briefly relax. The slight snarl of his lip turned to a sexy but terrifying smile. His sinister gaze was hypnotizing, and CiCi was paralyzed to react. She was absolutely terrified of this man, and he knew she wouldn't ruin Calysta's joyous party by making a scene.

Christopher got a lot of satisfaction from seeing the terror on CiCi's face when he casually greeted her and wanted to repeat the rush by catching Mac off guard the same way. Christopher was fairly certain Mac would also be uncomfortably surprised but not make a scene.

Christopher still had a cocky grin, and his eyes were locked on CiCi as he began walking toward Mac and Aria. CiCi was alarmed when his grin turned into a sinister scowl that made CiCi despise him even more than before.

A few feet into his pursuit, Christopher stopped and put his hand to his head. A debilitating pain shot through his temple that stopped him in his tracks. Once recovered, Christopher stood looking at Aria, wondering where he had seen this woman before. She was not with Mac at the Moccasin Bar, but it seemed he knew her.

Mac and Aria were busy chatting and oblivious to the potential peril behind them. CiCi, however, had a front-row seat, and her priority was preventing Christopher's sneak attack on her parents. She knew her dad wouldn't give a single fuck about spoiling Calysta's party if it meant teaching Christopher Paloma a lesson.

Christopher had resumed his pursuit and transferred his disturbing stare back CiCi's way. When she noticed his grin melted back to a snarl as he approached her parents, there was only one thing she could do to throw off Christopher's plans.

"Dad, Mom! Hey, come here, please."

When her parents headed CiCi's way, Christopher's devious plan was derailed. CiCi knew her dad would go ballistic seeing Christopher, especially if he was confronted unexpectedly, so she had temporarily solved the problem. She just needed the time and opportunity to tell her dad Christopher was there and prevent the all-out brawl she envisioned.

When Mac and Aria instantly turned and walked in CiCi's direction, Christopher's rage was evident. He wanted to boldly confront Mac and make him pay for his embarrassing arrest that night at the Moccasin Bar. But somehow, being in such close proximity, Christopher felt like he had more of a history with Mac than just their brief meeting up North. He just couldn't put his finger on the reason why.

He also now believed he had some connection to Aria, and when he got a better look at her entire face, the connection finally became clear. Aria was the woman who sometimes appeared to him in his horrible nightmares. Now, he struggled to understand how this strange coincidence was even possible.

Christopher couldn't explain any of the odd feelings Mac and Aria Brunner elicited in him, but he knew he harbored a powerful hatred for them that ran deep in his veins. CiCi distracting them was unfortunate but not enough to stop his malicious pursuit. The more he stared at them, the more his anger and malice grew, and he was more determined than ever to not only confront Mac but attack him.

When CiCi saw Christopher's entire facade change from a brooding scowl to a murderous glare, she knew it was time to react. She could no longer just watch this deadly pursuit for fear of spoiling the party.

"Dad! Watch out behind you!"

Mac instinctively turned around to see Christopher approaching. Without hesitation, Mac drew his .45 and instantly had Christopher in his sights.

Christopher stopped in his tracks when he saw the barrel of Mac's pistol once again. He remembered it all too well from the ride to the Moccasin Bar, and staring at the black metal so close to his face made a debilitating pain shoot through his skull. That familiar sight also brought a wave of memories from deep within him. They seemed so very real, but yet he was certain they were not his own. Still focused on the gun barrel, Christopher's piercing pain shot again, this time dropping him to his knees. Holding the sides of his head tightly with his hands, Christopher was obviously in agony.

Having no sympathy, Mac brutally confronted the tortured man before him.

"What the fuck are you doing here?"

"Mac, who is this?" Aria asked with her heart racing.

"This is the asshole from Wisconsin—the reason our daughter and her friends had to leave their vacation early."

Mac walked closer to Christopher, who was on the ground, still holding his head.

"I'm going to ask you one more time. What the fuck are you doing here?"

"He's my grandson! He's family!" Calysta yelled as she hurried over to help Christopher, who was still writhing in pain on the ground.

Mac's mind was all scrambled now. He was too worked up to try and make sense of Calysta's words, but he dropped his arm, taking his gun sights off of Christopher's head.

Mallory and Jason came running when they heard the commotion. They knew it had something to do with Christopher. Everything bad in their lives always had something to do with their oldest son. When they saw him incapacitated and holding his head, Jason's heart sank, and Mallory closed her eyes and turned away.

"His headaches are back. He called me a few days ago and said he had been headache-free for nearly a year, but now they were back with a vengeance," Jason said with obvious sadness.

It was all Mac could do to refrain from blurting all the dirty details of Christopher's behavior towards CiCi while she was up North. He would do anything to keep his daughter safe, but he also realized Christopher was Jason and Mallory's son. If Christopher struggled with some issues beyond his control, Mac should try to give him a break. But then he thought about the mysterious happenings the Hayward police chief mentioned and knew deep down that Christopher had something to do with them. And, of course, Mac still wondered if Christopher was responsible in some way for Dex's disappearance. But now was not the time, not with it being Christmas and with Calysta, Mallory, and Jason around.

Mac holstered his gun and took Aria by the hand and walked away. CiCi had already removed herself from the scene, so Mac and Aria went to her. She was anxious to tell her dad what Christopher had done behind the drink truck but was leery, thinking he might pull his gun again and have no mercy a second time.

"This is fucked up," Mac said, turning to see Jason helping Christopher up from the ground. "They better take that son-of-a-bitch home."

"Shhhh, Mac! They'll hear you," Aria pleaded.

"You don't know everything, Aria. The Hayward police chief told me they have several unsolved missing persons cases and unexplained deaths that they think link to that sick bastard, but they don't have enough proof," Mac explained.

CiCi's stomach was in knots, and she felt herself getting sick. She hurriedly stepped away from her parents and vomited, thinking about how she had been alone with him at his cabin.

Mac's phone rang, and he saw it was from the police chief up in Hayward.

"Hey, Chief, do you have news?" Mac asked.

The Chief began telling Mac the most recent developments in the case.

"We finally got the green light to question Dexter Robertson. We just took his statement, and he implicated Christopher Paloma. Robertson has quite a story."

"I knew it!" Mac replied.

"We are pushing as hard as we can to find similar cases that link to Paloma. I'm pretty sure once we find him, he'll do some hard time."

"Great! And I have some good news for you," Mac began. "I know where Paloma is right now. He's right here in Peoria, Illinois, and I'm even looking at the sick son-of-a-bitch. I'd be honored to call our local P.D. and have them come get this prick."

"Man, that's great news!"

The Chief was so relieved, but Paloma was not in custody yet. He knew all too well how slam dunk captures could go terribly wrong.

"Why don't you just cuff him and keep him contained until the police arrive?" the Chief asked, hoping Mac would comply.

"I need to stay detached. I had the fucker in my barrel sights earlier tonight, and it was all I could do to keep from pulling the trigger. I'm not ruining my life over this piece of shit," Mac explained. "But I'll keep a watchful eye and make sure he doesn't try to leave before the authorities get here."

"Fair enough. Keep me posted!"

When Mac hung up, he immediately dialed his contacts at the Peoria P.D. Aria, and CiCi were dying to know what was going on, but Mac was like a machine, doing all his tasks before stopping to explain. Finally, Mac had a moment to relay the details to an anxious Aria and CiCi.

"Hayward P.D. just took Dex's statement. He said Christopher ran him off the road, took him at gunpoint to a remote shed, chained him to a pole, and left him to die."

This had been an excruciatingly troubling day for CiCi. Finding out Christopher was Jason and Mallory's son, Christopher's surprise greeting, his assault, and his threat nearly sent her sanity over the edge. But also finding out Christopher was responsible for Dex's near-fatal experience was too much. She had so much guilt for bringing this dangerous monster into everyone's lives. Once again, she burst into tears, and it was all Aria could do to console her.

"I hope the police hurry up and get here before that asshole gets away," Mac said, watching Christopher recover. "I told them no sirens and no lights. We don't want him spooked and making a run for it. I'd do it myself, but I'd probably kill the motherfucker if he made one wrong move."

CiCi knew she had to tell her dad about Christopher's assault earlier that night, but she was terrified. Wiping her eyes and mustering all her courage, CiCi began to talk, and after she got started, the words came out much easier than she thought.

"Dad, when the police get here, I need to talk with them," CiCi said bravely. "I had an incident with Christopher tonight. He grabbed me from behind and dragged me behind the hot chocolate truck. He groped me a little and let me go. But as he walked away, he made a chilling threat. He said he'd be seeing me very soon, the same way he promised after being arrested at the Moccasin Bar."

Mac's veins were popping out of his forehead. Aria had to grab his arm and stop him from rushing over to Christopher and doing something stupid.

"I swear…that asshole…I know I have to trust the justice system. But if they don't make a charge stick for Dex's kidnapping and attempted murder, I'll kill that bastard myself."

"Just calm down and wait for the police to get here," Aria said, still holding his arm tightly.

About that time, Calysta made an announcement.

"I'm so sorry everyone, but under the circumstances, I think we need to postpone our Christmas celebration. Jason and Mallory are taking Christopher home, so he can rest and hopefully get to feeling better."

"No, no, no," Mac said under his breath. I want to see that fucker in handcuffs, going to jail."

As if on cue, Mac spotted two police officers walking across the huge infield. Mac had a sinking feeling Christopher was not going down without a struggle, so he covertly drew his .45 and told Aria to take CiCi inside. Aria put up some resistance, but Mac was adamant.

"CiCi has already been through too much. Get her inside. I have a bad feeling about this," Mac said sternly.

When Calysta saw the police officers, she was fuming mad. She wondered who had the audacity to call the police. Christopher was just having an episode. He wasn't going to hurt anyone.

Before anyone could address the police officers, Christopher spied them, broke free from his father's arms that had been assisting him and tried to run when his middle brother Jeffery stopped him.

"It'll be better if you just give yourself up," Jeffery said calmly.

Until that moment, all Christopher wanted was to escape, but seeing his brother step in out of genuine concern was too much for Christopher. Suddenly, Christopher's urge for freedom faded when he saw the compassion in his brother's eyes. That was it. Jeffery was right.

"But he hasn't done anything!" Calysta insisted.

"Grandma, there has to be something. There's always something," Jeffery said sadly. "We just don't know it yet."

As the officer placed Christopher in handcuffs, he turned and shot a sinister glare Mac's way. Unaffected, Mac returned a hateful stare. Mac knew it couldn't be true, but for one brief moment, he sensed a haunting experience from the past. It had been twenty-two years since Mac stared Tre Halprin in the eyes, but he would know that evil look anywhere. And just as fast as that dreadful Halprin glare came, it was gone, and Christopher hung his head as he was escorted out of the courtyard of CiCi's Way.

Chapter 16

Mac didn't want to be the bearer of bad news and the revealer of Christopher's unlawful deeds, but he felt as if Calysta and Christopher's parents deserved an explanation. Calysta was devastated that Christopher was arrested, and for the life of her could not figure out why. Mac knew she deserved the truth. He just hated being the one giving it. He was also interested in anything Christopher's parents or Calysta could offer regarding his mental health status. He was certain they could provide some insight that might explain Christopher's bizarre behavior and criminal acts.

Calysta seemed stunned and still unable to understand what had just happened. Jason and Mallory, on the other hand, were somewhat used to these events and were disappointed but not surprised.

"Let's go inside," Mac said. "I have some news I need to share."

Calysta sat straight-faced as Mac explained all CiCi had been through. It wasn't that she didn't believe Mac. She just didn't want to. At one time, Calysta was fearful that Christopher receiving Tre's kidney would affect him in some way. She wondered if having such an evil man's vital organ could change

Christopher's personality. All these years, she had pushed that worry aside. Even when Christopher was diagnosed with multiple personality disorder, Calysta refused to believe that darkness was the reason for her grandson's torture. But now, after all that had transpired, she was being forced to believe it, and she felt compelled to share her theory. She thought back to that stressful time when she and Pauly asked Mac to find the origin of Christopher's kidney. She remembered never getting an answer, thinking that meant Mac had never discovered the truth. Still, with all the evidence before her, Calysta's old fear was now back at the forefront of her mind.

Taking a deep breath, she began.

"When Christopher got his kidney, I am fairly sure it came from my brother Tre," Calysta began. "I once asked Mac to look into it, but I never received confirmation one way or another, which made it easy for me to eventually dismiss my fears when things were going well for Christopher." Mac and Pauly shared a knowing look, both remembering that day when Mac showed up at the house with his news regarding his findings. That day, Mac and Pauly decided that they would be the only ones who bore the burden of knowing Christopher's kidney came from St. Lucia. And although that did not necessarily mean it was Tre's, the coincidence was a bit too eerie.

"Anyway, my worry was that a vital organ like a kidney would put Halprin's blood running through Christopher's veins. And that blood would somehow turn my grandson into Tre. I know it sounds impossible, but I think we all have to consider this possibility in light of the circumstances."

At the very thought of such horror, Aria's spine tingled, climaxing with an uncontrollable shiver.

"I never wanted to believe it was true, but I now think Christopher's multiple personality condition and his headaches are a direct result of having Tre's evil blood running through his veins."

Now it was Pauly's turn to shed some light on this matter, knowing what Calysta was saying looked more and more possible.

"You said you never received information about the origin of Christopher's kidney, but I did," Pauly confessed. "Mac told me the organ came from St. Lucia."

Feeling a bit of guilt, first for never telling Calysta where Christopher's kidney came from and second for calling the cops to deal with her grandson, Mac put forth his opinion.

"Christopher seems to be caught between his own beliefs and the wishes and behaviors of Tre. I've seen it for myself. Tonight, I could swear it was Tre Halprin giving me the stare-down, but I kept that information to myself because it just sounded crazy."

Mac continued to process his thoughts aloud and share an explanation for this odd circumstance.

"It also explains how Christopher was doing fine for years, but when he met CiCi, his symptoms returned. This reaction had to be Tre sensing who CiCi was and hoping to either hurt Aria and me by getting close to her or by using her to lure us into his vengeful plans."

Everyone sat motionless, trying to wrap their logical minds around Mac's words. He decided it was time to tell what else he knew about Christopher Paloma, even though he knew this news would hit hard.

"I have other bad news," Mac said, dreading to continue. "Christopher was arrested tonight because I called the police. Hayward P.D. has been suspicious of Christopher for years and hoped to connect several missing persons and unexplained death cases to him. Today, they got what they needed to begin the process. Dex Robertson made his statement saying it was Christopher who kidnapped him and left him for dead."

The silence continued but now hung heavy in the room.

Finally, Calysta spoke.

"He needs help. He needs to be back in the hospital. Christopher, *our* Christopher, is being tortured. Even in death, my brother is calling the shots, and Christopher is paying the price."

"If Christopher's behavior is caused by Tre's presence in his body, the only relief he'll ever have is if he can get rid of the kidney," Pauly offered.

"Or die, " Jason solemnly added.

Aria was confused by the strangeness of it all, and when she found her voice, she made her stance clear.

"Do you hear yourselves?" Aria interjected. "This is crazy talk. How can Tre be manipulating Christopher just because of a kidney? Christopher may be sick, but he has a lot to atone for. Tre Halprin was a bastard, but is it fair to blame him for Christopher's behavior and crimes?"

Once again, nothing but silence filled the room until Calysta finally spoke again.

"Of all people, Aria, I thought you would never underestimate the malevolent powers of Tre Halprin."

Calysta had a point, but still, what she and Mac were proposing seemed so farfetched.

"All I care about right now is that Christopher is somewhere he can't hurt anyone or hurt himself," Mallory stated.

"They'll be extraditing him back to Wisconsin tomorrow, I'm sure," Mac said.

"I know it's Christmas Day, but it sure doesn't seem like it. I hate to interrupt our lawyer's holiday, but I'm giving him a call right now," Calysta added.

After some brief goodbyes, everyone seemed to disperse, and the *party* was over.

The ride home to Merchant Street was a numbing existence for CiCi because she was still in shock. This whole ordeal was so unbelievable. It seemed like they were all characters in someone's nightmare, but it felt very, very real. She could not let Christopher off the hook for his actions. She didn't care that he had a tortured mind. He threatened her, and she was fearful that he would somehow make his threats a reality.

Now, all she could think about was Dex and him spending Christmas in the hospital with only his parents. She thought about how much he had been through, and she was thankful he was alive. She would never forgive herself if something had happened to him. More than anything, she wanted to see him. She had an idea, and she hoped her dad would go for it.

"Dad, I want to go see Dex. Christmas in the hospital wouldn't be much fun, especially with no visitors but your parents—no offense," she said with a little grin. "Besides, I feel as if I need to give a more thorough statement to the Hayward police. The night Christopher got arrested, I just wanted to get out of there and get home. I worry that his release might be partially my fault for not taking the time to recount all of the details of my experience. Can we please go up to Hayward and see Dex?"

"CiCi, it's nearly 9 o'clock. We wouldn't get there until 7 am," Aria argued.

"I know, but I'll take my turn driving."

Mac never could resist his little girl. She hardly ever asked for much, so when she made her case to head out for Wisconsin,

Mac knew it must be extremely important to her. He shot a look Aria's way as if to say, "Let's pack." The next thing they knew, the Brunners were on their way up North.

❖ ❖ ❖

Dex was eating breakfast when CiCi and her parents walked into his room. CiCi was so glad to see Dex for herself and see that he was getting well. Her enthusiasm immediately took her to his bedside, where she gave him a big hug. Dex was so surprised and overjoyed to see them, especially CiCi, that his emotions got the best of him, and tears welled up in his eyes.

"I didn't know you were coming, but I'm sure glad you're here," Dex managed.

"I just missed you, and I hated that you were up here, stuck in this bed on Christmas," CiCi replied, holding his hand.

"You look good, Dex," Mac added.

"Yeah, really good," Aria confirmed.

"I feel good, and they're talking about letting me out of here soon—maybe tomorrow," Dex responded enthusiastically.

CiCi had so much she wanted to say, but all of that could wait for now. She wanted to tell him all about Christopher showing up in Peoria, but her dad beat her to it.

"Well, the guy who did this to you was arrested in Peoria last night. Turns out we know his parents. It seems Christopher moved away from home because he had some issues with multiple personality disorder. It seems this guy might be connected to several missing person cases in this area. You're one lucky man, Dex."

"Wow! That's unbelievable that he already had a connection to you. I'm just so glad you are safe, CiCi. I know you spent some time with him. You're pretty lucky, too," Dex said with a genuinely grateful tone.

CiCi looked into his eyes and saw the Dex she once knew. She saw the Dex who brought her chicken noodle soup across campus in the rain when she was sick. She saw the Dex who nervously kissed her for the first time at a bonfire party, and she saw the Dex who first told her he loved her out of the blue while watching Netflix one night. They had so many sweet memories that had recently been tainted by hateful comments and actions that pushed them apart. But now, looking into his eyes, CiCi saw the Dex she loved, and she wished with all her heart that he was there to stay.

"Lucky, yes, and stupid…yes," CiCi managed. "I brought this monster into everyone's lives, and you, the person I care the most for, got hurt…really hurt. I am so sorry, Dex. I'm sorry for everything," CiCi unloaded, starting to cry.

Mac and Aria felt this had turned into a private conversation, so they slipped out and went looking for Dex's parents, who he said were trying to find someone who could tell them exactly when he could go home.

"You're not stupid. I pushed you away, and I know that now. I've had a lot of time to think up here in this bed, and even… well, you know," Dex said as if he couldn't bring himself to say his awful truth about his time in the shed.

"You were right. I was threatened by you, and I know now that I should have been your biggest supporter, but instead, I was bitter and jealous. I'm the one who should be sorry," Dex replied.

CiCi's heart was exploding with joy. Dex had just given her a sincere apology, which she knew had to be difficult. Dex had spent so much time pushing her away with hurtful comments; it was so refreshing to hear something sweet and genuine. Dex admitting he was wrong was a huge milestone in their relationship. She had no reservations about it. She instantly forgave him.

Overcome with emotion, CiCi couldn't help but lean down and kiss Dex, which didn't feel awkward at all. Instead, it felt familiar and wonderful, and when she looked at Dex afterward with a huge smile, his eyes spoke volumes. CiCi somehow knew her Dex was back. Without hesitation, he slipped his hand around the back of her neck and pulled her to him for a long, slow kiss that they both had missed so much the past few months.

Mac and Aria found Dex's parents, who were also extremely thankful to have someone up there to visit. The Brunners and Robertsons had grown quite close in the three and a half years CiCi and Dex had been together. Aria and Fiona, especially, were troubled by the recent state of their children's relationship, and both thought the trip to Wisconsin would be just the thing to get them back on track. As it turned out, amid horrific trauma and tragedy, it appeared they were right.

"It looks like we'll be heading home with Dex tomorrow," Doug Robertson shared.

"So glad to hear that," Mac answered.

"Is CiCi here?" Fiona asked.

"Yes, their conversation was getting pretty personal, so we slipped out," Aria replied. "She was adamant about coming up here. If we wouldn't have come, she would have made the trip on her own."

"We just love CiCi. I'm so shocked that you all just left your Christmas celebration to drive here. Thank you," Fiona added.

"No problem at all, but I am starving. I'll see if CiCi wants to go get something to eat. Join us for breakfast, won't you?" Aria asked.

Aria knew there was no way she was getting CiCi away from Dex's bedside, but she decided to ask. Of course, her daughter didn't want to leave but asked her mother to bring her back something. As Aria left Dex's room, Dex called out to her.

"Mrs. Brunner! Thank you for making the trip. I really appreciate it."

"You are very welcome, Dex. I'm so thrilled to see you are almost well. Your mom and dad say tomorrow is the day," Aria said with a smile.

"I was hoping,' Dex replied. "Thanks again."

Dex knew he had been a real ass lately, and he worried about his relationship with CiCi's parents. They were such great people, and he wanted them to know that all of his stupid, hateful, jealous ways were behind him. He knew he would have to prove himself, especially to Mac, but Dex was up for the challenge. He had almost lost CiCi. His time chained up in that shed and now recovering in the hospital gave him a lot of clarity. The method was tragic and painful, but Dex learned a lesson, and he would never again take CiCi for granted.

Chapter 17

After Mac and Aria returned from breakfast and CiCi ate hers, Mac wanted to go to the police station and see how they were coming with the case. And he knew CiCi needed to give her full statement. Even though CiCi wanted to make things right with her information, pulling her away from Dex's side was nearly impossible. Finally, Mac just said he was leaving and walked out the door.

"Go, CiCi. You need to do this. I'm not going anywhere," Dex said with a little laugh.

"Okay, you're right. We'll be back, and I'll tell you everything we find out," CiCi said right before giving him a quick goodbye kiss.

At the station, Chief Jackson was expecting them. He somehow got the feeling Mac would not leave this case alone for long. Mac was thrilled to hear Christopher would be transported back to Wisconsin the next day. Chief Jackson also told him that they were waiting on a search warrant for Christopher's cabin and the entire grounds at Deerfoot.

After CiCi relayed her complete experience with Christopher, Chief Jackson told her she was a very lucky young woman. Although she thought that herself, hearing it from the Chief made a lump appear in her throat, making it difficult to swallow or even breathe. Thinking about how horrible things could have gone made that lump grow, and when she responded to the Chief, her voice cracked, and she hardly recognized it. It would be a long time before CiCi completely recovered from this experience, but she would recover. Christopher was not going to have the last say. Now, all they could do was wait for justice to be served.

❖ ❖ ❖

Christopher lay in his jail cell, jaded and brooding.

"This is unacceptable," he thought. "I'm not spending my life behind bars."

And with that declaration, Christopher began thinking of ways to fix his problem when his grandma came in. It broke Calysta's heart to see her grandson behind bars. She believed he needed to be back at the hospital, where they helped him get rid of his headaches and odd behavior the first time. Although she knew Christopher didn't like that place, she was certain he would prefer it over prison.

"Hello, Christopher."

Christopher was not expecting any visitors, but his grandma was his biggest fan and even though he ruined her Christmas Day celebration, he knew she would forgive him.

"I'm so sorry, Grandma. Sometimes I don't even know myself. I'm right back where I was before," Christopher said with genuine remorse. "...headaches and strange behavior I don't recognize. I'm so sorry."

"This time, we're really going to help you. I promise, but you'll have to spend some time in that hospital."

"I'm going to prison, Grandma. I've done some very horrible things. Things I can't even think about without feeling sick to my stomach," Christopher confessed.

Calysta had a hot sinking feeling go down her spine. She had never thought so before, but with these words, Calysta worried that Christopher did those horrible crimes up North Mac mentioned earlier.

"Your headaches and your malicious behavior are not your fault. You're being manipulated by a very evil man. I can't explain all the details right now, but your lawyer is arguing that you are unfit to stand trial. We're trying to get you admitted at Brownbridge Hospital rather than go to prison," Calysta explained.

"Grandma, I deserve to go to prison. I don't want to hurt anyone else."

"They'll help you get past this setback at Brownbridge. You won't get any help or relief from your headaches in a maximum-security prison," Calysta said with a rather desperate tone.

Calysta harbored a great deal of guilt for never telling anyone but Pauly about her cryptic dream many, many years ago. She had always held the knowledge of this experience and how it connected to Christopher's ailment buried deep inside her as if guarding it with her life. Until yesterday, she had never revealed all the details of her belief that Tre's kidney was responsible for Christopher's devious behavior. Knowing that medical science would scoff at her assumption, she held onto her conclusion and often wondered if revealing it sooner could have helped Christopher in some way.

Calysta remembered the chilling dream like it was yesterday. Tre was mocking her and flaunting the fact that he now controlled Christopher. He had been given new life, and he would use this new existence to continue his wrath against the people he hated the most. His particular targets, of course, were Mac and Aria. Calysta assumed by getting close to CiCi, Tre believed he could hurt his enemies more by hurting their precious daughter. What baffled her the most was Christopher understood very little of what was happening to him. It was time to tell him her thoughts on his peculiar ailment.

"I have something to tell you, Christopher. It's going to sound crazy and unbelievable, but please hear me out. When you got your kidney, I believe it came from my half-brother, who was a very malicious and spiteful man."

As Calysta talked, Christopher could feel the hot stabs in his forehead beginning lightly at first, and his whole demeanor changed. Calysta couldn't help but notice Christopher's sudden transformation, but she kept telling her story.

"I believe it's his kidney that has tainted your body and mind."

Christopher couldn't control a rising rage building from his feet to his head. He thought to himself that it was a good thing he was behind bars because he had an uncontrollable urge to snap his grandmother's neck. He couldn't keep quiet any longer.

"Shut up, Bitch!"

Calysta was rendered speechless. Out of fear, Calysta got up from her seat and moved a bit further away from the bars that separated them. Not only were her grandson's words shocking and hurtful, but his voice was also different. It had been twenty-two years since she had heard Tre's diabolical voice, but she was certain she had just heard it coming out of Christopher's mouth. Calysta's recourse was to talk to her grandson as if he were Tre.

"Why are you doing this? What pleasure do you get from harming an innocent person like Christopher?"

Christopher was silent, but his evil eyes were locked on Calysta. And then, without any other provocation, Christopher began to laugh, and again, Calysta could swear it was Tre's laugh. He was mocking her the same way he did in her horrible dream many years ago. Even from the grave, her brother had a powerful grip on her and her family. Her betrayal was his downfall, but she could not keep paying for her disloyalty. She broke ties with Tre because she could no longer accept his devious and unscrupulous ways.

"I betrayed you. I said I would never do that, but I did. But was it really betrayal when our goals and ideals changed, and I no longer wanted the same things as you? I'm sorry that destroying you was necessary, but it was. You were a dangerous man, obviously. Surely you can understand that it was a battle, and at the time, there had to be a winner and a loser," Calysta explained.

"Winner? You think you were the winner?"

"No, Tre. *Now,* there is no winner," she said dejectedly.

"Don't get soft and let your guard down, Calysta. At least one of us still plans to win."

Calysta was broken and at the end of her rope. She had hoped to help her grandson fight this inner war, but now she knew that would be impossible. Tre had too much control over Christopher. The only way to truly combat the evil presence inside him was to end Christopher's life, and Calysta would not entertain that idea even for a second.

"Okay, then, you win, Tre," Calysta said as she motioned for the guard to let her out. As she looked back at her grandson one last time, she said those words again.

"You win."

❖ ❖ ❖

Calysta sat motionless and emotionless in the back of her Town Car heading home to CiCi's Way. That would be the last time she would ever see Christopher, and she left feeling hopeless and helpless. Tre made sure of that.

Her grandson's condition and his tumultuous life had been a constant source of worry and stress for twenty-two years. Calysta was worn out. Her heart and mind were defeated. Not being able to help her grandson was a crippling roadblock that Calysta now knew she could never get over. Without the strength to sustain the ongoing conflict and with no solutions in sight, Calysta closed her eyes and let herself go. She passed away knowing the ones she left behind would have a long, rough road—one that she was too tired and weak to travel any longer.

Chapter 18

Christopher was agitated and paced the floor of his cell. He felt hot and sweaty, and his heart was racing. Every part of his body was shaking. He had never experienced such a violent assault from the inside out. His headaches were horrible, but always before they had been contained to his head. The explosive feeling he was having now encompassed his whole body. It ached, it stung, it felt heavy and scorching hot. The more he paced, the worse it got. But he could not stop pacing. All night, Christopher was vigilant until they came to get him and transport him back to the Hayward County Jail.

Even in transport, Christopher was agitated. They had given him a sedative to calm him and make his long journey north more pleasant, but Christopher got little relief. When his transport van arrived at the jail, Christopher was cursing and spitting at the guards until everyone had enough of dealing with Christopher Paloma. Chief Jackson finally called for an ambulance. They were taking Christopher to the hospital for a mental health evaluation.

During the past several hours of Christopher's unusual agitation, he had not experienced a typical headache, but when they wheeled him into the ER, a nagging, familiar jolt in his head began to present itself. When he felt his headache coming on, Christopher didn't know how much more he could take. His heart was racing, his anxiety was sky-high, and now he also had the onset of a headache that could develop into a disaster. Why now? Why was his pain so strong so suddenly? At one time, he made a connection between his pain and Mac and CiCi. But that couldn't be the problem now. He was certain the Brunners were hundreds of miles away in Peoria.

With his tortured mind running rampant and his adrenaline pumping, the guards put Christopher in a strait jacket for everyone's safety. An orderly and three guards wheeled Christopher Paloma out of the ER and across the lobby to the elevators, where they waited to go up to the 8th floor for Christopher's evaluation.

Dex was released from care just prior, and the two families were elated to be heading down to the lobby to finally go home to Illinois. When the elevator doors opened, a wave of shock and fear rippled from inside. CiCi, Dex, and their parents were witnessing their worst fear as they realized Christopher Paloma was right in front of them, waiting to enter their elevator.

CiCi was frozen and unable to move as Christopher locked eyes with her and formed just the slightest makings of a sinister smile. Before Mac could rush CiCi out the elevator doors, Christopher whispered ever so softly, "See you soon, CiCi."

With those words, Mac was uncontrollable.

"Get that crazy son-of-a-bitch out of here before I fucking knock that grin off his face!"

As the guards wheeled Christopher into the elevator, his headache was pounding, but he tried to ignore the pain. At that moment, Christopher was more interested in making an impression on CiCi. But his smug pleasure backfired as he saw Dex spring from his wheelchair to be closer to a terrified CiCi. Holding her close with his arm wrapped tightly around her waist, Dex supported her. CiCi, now feeling safe, leaned on his shoulder for comfort as they hurried through the lobby. Suddenly, Christopher was fuming, and he yelled at the top of his lungs.

"Are you fucking kidding me? She's mine, Asshole! That's *my* CiCi!"

The elevator doors closed, and they could still hear his muffled rants.

Both CiCi and Dex were shaken to the core, and their once joyous celebration of Dex's release had been tainted with unimaginable fear. Not only was their great mood ruined, but now dark anticipation and dread lurked around them. CiCi wanted to cry but held back her tears. She could not let Christopher get to her like that. Even though she was able to ward off her tears, CiCi was powerless to shake her biggest worry. So far, Christopher had always made good on his threats, which meant it was just a matter of time before she would see him again.

❖ ❖ ❖

Dex and CiCi planned to ride together to have some prime time to talk, but in light of their recent run-in with Christopher, Mac decided they needed to ride in his car. Neither Dex nor CiCi complained and actually welcomed their company. It was just as well that neither CiCi nor Dex had to drive. At first, they were consumed with worry and anxiety after seeing Christopher, and after a little while, they were mentally exhausted and slept for several hours of the trip.

"What do you think about Calysta's theory that Christopher's kidney from Tre is influencing him?" Aria asked Mac.

"It sounds so crazy, but if you look at the facts surrounding his behavior and his ailments, I think it's possible," Mac answered.

"At first, I thought this was the most ludicrous idea ever. But now…"

Mac interrupted her thought

"You really can't deny all the coincidences."

"So, we're dealing with Tre Halprin again after all these years. But this time, we can't just kill him if it comes down to that because he's actually Calysta's grandson," Aria said with a worrisome tone. "I hope he stays locked up somewhere for a very long time."

Just then, Aria got a text from Pauly.

> I'm sorry to inform you over text, but Calysta passed away yesterday afternoon. I'm just now in the right state of mind to contact everyone. I'll see you when you return.

"Mac! Calysta is dead!"

"What? What happened?" Mac asked in disbelief.

"I don't know. That was Pauly. He just said he'd see us when we got home. I'd call, but he said he was having a really hard time, so I don't want to bother him."

CiCi was just waking up and heard her mother say Calysta was dead, and she wondered if she had heard her correctly.

"Mom, Calysta is dead?" CiCi asked.

"Yes, I don't know any details, though."

When they stopped the first time, Aria decided to call Mallory and extend their condolences and get some details in the process. Mallory was doing well with the news, considering Calysta's death was quite sudden. She told Aria that Calysta had been to see Christopher at the city jail before he was transferred back to Wisconsin, and she passed away in her Town Car on the way home. Mallory didn't know anything more and added that the details of Calysta and Christopher's conversation would probably never be known.

Aria dreaded arriving home and having to accept that Calysta was gone. She knew Pauly had to be devastated. CiCi and Dex still had the week between Christmas and New Year's before having to return to school, and CiCi hoped her fear of Christopher showing up randomly could be debunked by news that he was either incarcerated or locked up in a mental hospital. She wondered why she told him so much personal information like where she went to school. All of this information now gave him ammunition to find her and harm her if he ever got free.

Once home, CiCi and Dex felt a little better, putting so many miles between them and Christopher. With their minds eased a bit, both were eager to have some alone time to talk, plan, and reconnect. Dex's parents had planned a cruise over the holiday and with Dex making such a remarkable recovery, he told them to go and have fun. Reluctant at first, the Robersons relaxed and took their son's advice when Mac and Aria invited Dex to stay with them to continue his recovery.

"Are you sure, Dex?" his mother asked. "We can go home to Bloomington with you and forget about the trip."

"Don't be silly," Dex answered. "I have the cutest little nurse in the world taking care of me right here. Honestly, I'd probably spend all of my time with her here in Peoria anyway. So go!"

When the Robertsons left, Dex settled into a huge suite connected to Mac and Aria's renovated home on Merchant. In all the years Dex had been with CiCi, he never knew the Brunners owned the entire building that was damn near a block in size. He had only been in the main living quarters. As he looked around the room, he was in awe and felt silly for fighting with CiCi last summer about her *secret* wealth.

Even though Dex had his own place at the Brunners, he spent a lot of time with the family. Dex was still feeling weak and not quite himself. He and CiCi enjoyed romantic evenings, and Dex was relieved there was no pressure to be physical. This left more time to talk and repair their relationship. In fact, all of their past issues were exposed and resolved, and after a couple of days, both Dex and CiCi were head over heels in love again, creating some steamy anticipation regarding their first sexual encounter in months.

When Dex showed up at CiCi's room with flowers and a sexy smile, CiCi didn't make the connection at first. But when Dex set the vase on the table and pulled her to him, meeting her mouth with his eager kiss, she was brimming with curiosity.

"Well, Dex Robertson, that was quite a kiss," CiCi stated, still wrapped in his arms.

"I thought I'd let you know I'm feeling quite strong and energetic," Dex said, kissing CiCi's neck.

"Hum... strong and energetic, huh?" CiCi repeated.

"Yes, and I might also add, very, very horny," Dex said, pulling CiCi's mouth to his and giving her a passionate kiss that made her knees a little weak.

When the kiss ended, Dex took CiCi by the hand and led her to his suite. Today was the day. This was what both of them had been thinking about since their reunion. Dex closed and locked the door and turned to CiCi with pure passion in his eyes.

They both knew full well they were about to unleash months of pent-up passion from being apart. In a lot of ways, this encounter seemed like their first time again, and this thought made CiCi hot and tingly all over. She led Dex to the chaise lounge in the center of the room and gently pushed him down. Even though she was very eager, CiCi proceeded to seduce Dex with a slow and sexy strip tease.

Pulling her sweater over her head, CiCi's lacey bralette exposed just enough of her breasts to make Dex's heart skip a beat. When she wiggled out of her jeans, she was left in her thong underwear that made Dex exhale loud and slow, proving CiCi's alluring effect on him. Dex was in heaven watching CiCi slowly remove her clothes. She was so beautiful and so sexy, and now she was his again, and life could not be better. He grabbed her arm, pulled her down onto his lap, and engulfed her with a sexy, open-mouth kiss that trickled down into passionate kisses on her neck and breasts. Dex took the liberty of slipping the straps of CiCi's bralette down past her shoulders, letting the fabric drop, leaving her naked breasts exposed and aching for his touch and tongue.

CiCi turned to straddle Dex, rubbing his crotch with her most sensitive parts.

"I've never seen you so sexy," Dex whispered in her ear, giving CiCi goosebumps that made her tingle all over. She wanted Dex inside her, and hesitated to ask, but decided this relationship was their reset, and CiCi was going to be honest and bold, so she spoke up.

"I want you inside me. Please," CiCi managed.

Dex was quick to comply, gently helping CiCi up off his lap, removing his jeans, and slowly removing CiCi's panties, eliciting a tiny groan as she anticipated his next move. Dex carefully laid her down on the chaise while kissing her deeply with his tongue. They had made love so many times, but this reunion was truly special. In the end, they lay in each other's arms, and no words were necessary for what they were thinking and feeling.

Chapter 19

The doctors hesitated to tell Christopher that his grandmother passed away, but thinking that he would feel deceived if they didn't, they decided to approach the task very carefully. He had calmed down, and his headaches were gone, but his personality had not returned to normal. Christopher was not Christopher anymore. He didn't feel like himself, think like himself, or act like himself. His most recent violent pains seemed to be the symptoms of a permanent transformation.

Therefore, when given the news of his grandmother's passing, he merely shrugged his shoulders and maybe even had to catch himself to keep from smiling. The doctors felt his reaction was inappropriate, but they weren't really surprised either. Although they had a very short time with Christopher so far, they had come to see him as an enigma. He was unlike anyone they had ever treated, and even the best doctors were intimidated by the magnitude of his needs.

But he stayed there at the hospital, and the doctors continued to study his behavior for several weeks while Chief Jackson hoped for and waited on the day Christopher Paloma would be released and would have to stand trial. But as time moved on, the Chief began to wonder if Christopher would ever pay for his crimes. He also continued to think there were more nefarious incidents that could be traced back to Christopher Paloma. He just needed the proof.

One day, the Chief finally got the break he'd been waiting for. His petition for a search warrant for the shed where Dex was kept, Christopher Paloma's property, and the entire grounds at Deerfoot Lodge were granted based on Dex Robertson's statement implicating Paloma. That was all the Chief needed to orchestrate a full-blown investigation at all three sites. Even if Paloma was never deemed fit to stand trial, Chief Jackson hoped to provide closure for some families who needed answers.

When Luke Younker, one of Jackson's patrol officers, radioed in that they found something while searching out at Deerfoot Lodge, the Chief was in his cruiser and out there in record time. When he arrived, the Chief found Younker and two other officers down by the boathouse with a cadaver dog that made a hit. They were waiting for the Chief to arrive before they began to dig. In the third spade of dirt, a bone emerged, and Chief Jackson was brimming with excitement.

"I think we got him! I think we finally got this son-of-a bitch!"

As the dig continued, more and more bones and other human personal items were uncovered, and it became clear that what they found belonged to more than one person. Chief Jackson halted the dig and, against his will, decided he needed to call the Feds. Waiting for them to arrive, the chief and his officers carefully sorted through what they had found when Officer Greene made a chilling discovery.

Five years had passed since his brother disappeared. Kelley Greene left to go hunting one morning and never returned. Officer Greene searched the woods himself several times over the years and found nothing. Unfortunately, everyone, including Officer Greene, thought his brother might have been a victim of foul play, and their prime suspect was Christopher Paloma.

Christopher was an avid hunter and spent a lot of time in the woods. As more and more accidents happened and more people went missing, the rumor was that Christopher was responsible. Officer Greene had a lump in his throat when he saw a silver cross necklace caked with dirt lying on the ground. When he picked it up and knocked the dirt off, it was exactly like the one his brother used to wear. At first, a tear ran down his cheek, and then he yelled a victorious cheer.

"We found him! We finally found Kelley. This is his necklace!"

After that discovery, it was difficult to refrain from digging any further before the Feds got there, but Chief Jackson knew they had to play by the book. Apparently, Officer Greene's brother was shot and buried in this shallow grave in Christopher Paloma's boathouse. Although forensics had not confirmed this claim, Officer Greene was satisfied seeing the cross necklace and pins that once held a right knee together. His brother Kelley had the exact repairs made to his knee after a car accident a few years before he went missing.

All in all, the Feds uncovered four bodies in the boathouse. These discoveries certainly helped clear some of Hayward's unsolved crimes, but the Feds were hesitant to leak the information. Everyone thought Christopher was responsible, but with his current condition, they didn't want his lawyers to have extra time to find ways to impede the case and ultimately get Christopher off the hook for these heinous crimes. Therefore, their discovery was temporarily hush-hush. Even Officer Greene couldn't leak information about his brother to other family members. They knew their secret would eventually get out, but the Feds wanted the first crack at interrogating Christoper, and they didn't want him tipped off.

❖ ❖ ❖

The doctors thought Christopher had made some big strides of late and began to have some hope. He continued to be headache-free, which made a big difference in his overall health and was a huge step in his recovery. Additionally, his fits of rage had disappeared, and he didn't constantly threaten and curse the hospital staff. In fact, Christopher had become quite complacent.

Quite satisfied with Christopher's calm behavior, no one realized that he had made a full-blown transformation. His improved behavior and mental health concerns were the result of undergoing this process. Once Christopher was not really Christopher anymore, his actions were not typical, but they were also not violent. Christopher Paloma had lost all of his own thoughts and feelings, and the force inside him that had tortured him for years was in complete control. This personality was definitely sinister, but it was also very good at disguising its true purpose.

Therefore, Christopher appeared to be getting better, and it was just a matter of time before he would be released and be held accountable for his crimes, which now included at least four counts of murder.

When the Feds arrived to interrogate Christopher, his doctors insisted he was entitled to legal representation and urged Christopher to seek it. Christopher, however, felt he had nothing to hide, so he dismissed the doctors' suggestions and settled in to have a conversation with Federal Agent Lucy Rice and her partner Agent Dale Mankle.

Christopher's shifty mind was reeling, thinking about how he wanted this conversation to go. He had to manipulate the situation just right to achieve his purpose. He wanted to be released from the hospital and transported to prison. Therefore, he wondered if he should confess to whatever they had on him or simply talk and then ask for a lawyer. His plan, however, also hinged on being deemed sane and fit to stand trial. Christopher decided to just have a conversation at first, hoping the Feds could find a way to get him out of there.

When Agent Rice and Agent Mankle entered the room, they were surprised at Christopher's amicable presence. In fact, he looked like a regular guy and acted rather *normal*, for the lack of a better word.

"Mr. Paloma, I'm Agent Rice, and this is Agent Mankle. Do you know why we are here today?"

Christopher was initially silent and appeared pensive but eventually spoke.

"Are you trying to trick me into saying something that might damage my character, Agent Rice?" Christopher said, looking very serious and then slowly forming a faint smile.

"No, we don't trick people, Mr. Paloma. We try to arrive at the truth. That's all we want—the truth," Agent Rice countered.

"I see. What other questions do you have?"

"We've been doing some digging at your lodge, and we've found some disturbing things. Do you know what I'm talking about?" Agent Mankle asked.

Again, Christopher was pensive and honestly wondered how he should respond to arrive at his goal.

"I'm afraid that my steady improvement here is going to bring my release, and when that happens, I'm certain to be sentenced for the crimes against that kid from Illinois. I'm not sure

I want to answer and allow you to bring Federal charges as well," Christopher said honestly.

Christopher decided that he didn't have to incriminate himself to get out of there. He just had to be considered sane enough.

"Well, you do seem rather aware of what's at stake. And we certainly don't see any reason to think that you could not understand court proceedings and the charges against you. So, yes, Mr. Paloma, I would say you will eventually stand trial," Agent Mankle confirmed.

"Then I want my lawyer so I can prepare," Christopher stated.

There— he thought he played that pretty well. But the Feds were giddy that he asked for his lawyer, which meant he was cognizant of the magnitude of his crimes and the charges against him. Additionally, they didn't have to play their hand and come right out and say they were charging him with four counts of murder right away. Therefore, each side left the meeting getting what they wanted.

Agent Rice and Agent Mankle immediately began the process of preparing their evidence for the prosecutor and also beginning their push to get Christopher Paloma considered fit to stand trial. Christopher continued to maintain a healthy outward mental state, so his doctors would have to order his release when the Feds pushed for it. He wanted to transfer back to the Hayward County jail, and he was about to get what he wanted.

Chapter 20

Chief Jackson hated that he had to relinquish the Paloma case to the Feds, but honestly, he didn't want the responsibility either. This was some big-time shit, and he definitely didn't want to be the one to blow it. Besides, he still had a solid case regarding Dexter Robertson's kidnapping and attempted murder, so Paloma was going away no matter what when he was released.

Still, Chief Jackson spent a considerable amount of time looking for commonalities among the victims and other missing persons in the area. And he had a team of officers scouring cold cases in their down time that went all the way back to Paloma's arrival in Hayward. He wanted nothing more than to find justice for those families, and if that also meant piling on charges for the Feds to deliver, well, that was the cherry on top.

After considerable time and much stress, Chief Jackson finally got the news he was waiting for—Christopher Paloma would be released from the hospital and transported back to the jail in Hayward since the charges against him were under Chief Jackson's jurisdiction. This was great news. Chief Jackson began the process of preparing for Paloma's transport and arrival. From what he had heard, Christopher was in a much better state mentally than he was the last time he was in jail. But Chief Jackson knew not to let that fact trick him into letting his guard down. He knew all too well Christopher Paloma's ruthless and dangerous nature.

The hospital also began preparing for Christopher's discharge. Once Christopher learned of his release and transport, he tried not to show too much emotion, but inside, his elation was bursting. He went through his plan in his head again and again. He was lucky to have Mitch, his right-hand man at the lodge, on the outside, helping make his plan possible. Mitch visited him many times, and he and Christopher had the escape down to the very last detail. There was no way Christopher was going to stay behind bars.

The transport back to the Hayward jail was uneventful, and Chief Jackson was quite relieved. Now that Paloma was secure in his jail, Chief Jackson breathed a sigh of relief. But Christopher demanded to make a phone call to his lawyer. The last time he was there, he didn't get his call because he was too agitated and unmanageable. Therefore, he believed he was entitled to it now.

"Fine," the Chief agreed, not wanting to make waves and give Christopher any fuel for his inevitable trial.

Christopher's call, however, was not to his lawyer. Instead, he called Mitch, who was waiting for the chance to put their plan in motion. Since the plan was entirely set, when Christopher called, his words didn't have to be too specific.

"Hey," Christopher began. "I'm back at the jail. It's time to come see me."

And that was it. Certainly nothing to send up any red flags for anyone listening.

In the next few hours, Christopher rethought his course of action, making sure he was ready and that he hadn't forgotten anything. When he got word his lawyer was there, his stomach did a flip, and he took a deep breath.

This is it!

Christopher had spent night after night planning his escape. It's fair to say that his body was now completely controlled by Tre Halprin, and Tre Halprin always had an escape plan.

The deputy led his handcuffed prisoner out of his cell and down a long hallway to the room where Mitch was waiting. Every step he took was filled with ripples of anticipation that consumed his body. Breaking free from his most recent confines was right at the tip of his fingers. He knew what he needed to do, and he had to execute his plan with absolute precision.

When the officer led him into the room where Mitch was waiting, Christopher barely got in the door, and he shoved his elbow up, connecting hard with the officer's face. Caught off guard, the officer raised his hands to protect himself, letting go of Christopher and giving Mitch access to his weapon and pepper spray. Mitch quickly grabbed both items plus the officer's keys and then sprayed him in the eyes, further incapacitating the guard. So far, everything had happened so quickly that no other officers responded.

Like expert escape artists, Christopher and Mitch ran down the hall and out a back door, where Mitch had done exactly as Christopher had planned. A snowmobile and a duffle of supplies and gear were ready and waiting. Mitch unlocked Christopher's handcuffs and handed him the officer's pistol. There was no time for words. Christopher roared off down the street, and Mitch climbed into his truck and sped off in the opposite direction. Very soon after that, both men disappeared into the vast Wisconsin woods.

Once protected by the dense pines, Christopher stopped just long enough to put on the snowsuit Mitch brought him and revisited his plan in his head. He knew better than to meet up with Mitch right away and anywhere near his property, which would be crawling with cops. Therefore, the two were taking separate paths to the same destination, where they would meet in several days.

When Christopher and Mitch parted, Mitch drove south to a small town just outside of Eau Claire, put on a change of clothes, abandoned his truck, and hit the road hitchhiking. Knowing the surrounding wooded area like the back of his hand, Christopher roared west through the woods as far as he could go on his tank of gas. Although secluded by the woods, Christopher was well aware of the main roads and tried to stay close. When his fuel ran out, Christopher dumped the snowsuit Mitch brought him and put on a change of clothes. He was relatively close to Highway 89 heading southwest, so he began walking toward the road, hoping to catch a ride as far west as possible.

Christopher and Mitch were long gone before the bloodied officer recovered enough from their assault to get help. When Chief Jackson realized Christopher Paloma had escaped, he was in absolute disbelief. He knew his ass was on the line, and it was critical that he assemble a crack team to go after the escapees. Once again, Chief Jackson hated to admit it, but he needed to call the Feds.

Agent Rice and Agent Mankle were there in record time, pissed and confused about how this escape was even possible. By the time the Feds organized their search, both fleeing men were out of the state, heading west, planning to meet up later in the week. It was two days before they found Christopher's snowmobile and just as long before they figured out the identity of his accomplice. Needless to say, their trail quickly went cold, and now Chief Jackson felt compelled to notify Mac and give him the dismal news.

"WHAT?!" Mac yelled into the phone.

"I'm sorry, Mac," I wish I didn't have to tell you that. And there's more bad news."

Mac was silent. He didn't know how it could get any worse.

"Their trail is cold. The Feds have nothing. I'm so sorry."

Again, Mac was at a loss for words. After he got over his initial anger, he kind of felt sorry for the Chief. He was a good law enforcement officer, and this one incident could ruin his whole career. But Mac didn't have time to worry about that. He had his own problems now. How was he going to tell CiCi and Aria? How was he going to keep his daughter safe when she was at school? He knew he couldn't ask her to come home. She was almost finished. Leaving would most likely keep her from graduating, and then her job in Osage Beach would fall through. Mac was consumed with worry. He knew she might be in class, but he had to text his daughter and know she was okay.

> MAC: Hey! Just checking in. How are things?

CiCi was immediately worried. Her dad never randomly texted her like that.

> CICI: Fine, what's up?
> MAC: Call me when you get a chance.

CiCi was walking to class, but she had a few minutes, so she felt they would be well-spent talking to her dad, who obviously had something important to tell her. So she dialed.

When Mac picked up, he tried to sound calm and not alarm her.

"Hey, I have some bad news," Mac said gingerly.

Immediately, CiCi's instincts told her this had something to do with Christopher.

"Chief Jackson up in Hayward just called and told me Christopher escaped from the jail with an accomplice."

"When? Today?" CiCi asked.

Mac's heart dropped when he had to tell her it had been three days since they last saw him.

"THREE DAYS!" CiCi yelled. "Are you fucking kidding me?"

CiCi had never cursed in front of her dad, but he let it go because he felt it was an appropriate reaction to the circumstances.

"Dad, he could be anywhere," CiCi said with growing fear in her voice.

"I know. That's why I texted."

CiCi stood in silent disbelief. When her head had sufficiently wrapped itself around the gravity of the issue, she finally spoke again.

"I have to tell Dex. I have to go, Dad. I'll check in soon," she said rather hastily and then hung up.

CiCi was frantic with fear. She needed to warn Dex, and she needed to be with him to feel safe, so she put in a call even though he might already be in class.

When Dex saw CiCi's name pop up on his screen, he was instantly worried. She would never call this time of day. Something had to be wrong, so he stepped outside the classroom and answered.

CiCi didn't even give him time to say 'hello' before laying out the ugly truth.

"Should we go home?" he asked.

"I don't think so. What if he tries to go to Peoria to see his parents? No, I think we have to just stay here, but be cautious—very, very cautious," CiCi said with more fear than her voice actually showed.

"Where are you? Are you coming to class?" Dex asked.

"I'm almost there," CiCi confirmed.

When CiCi walked in the door, they both breathed a huge sigh of relief. At least they were together, and this was their last class of the day, so they could walk back to Dex's place and stay put. CiCi was so depressed that this mess was stirred up again, and she wished she could go back before she ever met Christopher Paloma and do something different to change her fate. She wished that with all her heart.

Chapter 21

Once the word got out that Christopher Paloma escaped, the news of bodies found at Deerfoot leaked. This information caused a chain reaction of people coming forward and revealing their harrowing encounters with Christopher Paloma. Several made formal statements fattening the Fed's case if they ever found Christopher.

There were men who were assaulted on snowmobile trails and while out ice fishing and hunting. Many of the victims didn't report their incidents out of embarrassment or fear. But after all of Christopher's crimes came to light, these people understood there was no pattern with Christopher, and no one really knew why some people were killed, some were harmed, and others were completely spared. One thing was certain: everyone who left their experience with Christopher alive felt damn lucky after those bodies were found buried in the boathouse.

Christopher and Mitch had to lay low for a while, and Christopher knew just the place. He decided right away that the old arms compound in the desert would be perfect. As far as he knew, no one had made a connection between Christopher Paloma and Tre Halprin. Even though he thought the Brunners were suspicious, no one would initially be looking for Christopher at an abandoned illegal gun compound once controlled by the Halprins. He figured he would be long gone before anyone made a definitive connection.

Christopher, who was now Tre, realized that the old compound had been raided and deserted many years prior, but he was certain it was still there. It had been good enough one other time when he and Levi made a stop there on their way to Vegas. It would be good enough now as well. With a little TLC, he and Mitch could regroup there before moving on to his ultimate destination. Therefore, on his trip West, Tre picked up as many necessities as he could to sustain their very isolated stay at the compound. Everyday items like single paper towels from public restrooms, soap, and small packaged food items were no longer taken for granted. They were now priceless items collected for survival.

Tre asked every person who picked him up and took him a little further on his journey for some spare change or a few bucks, and they all complied, exceeding the amount of his requests. Some even gave him shoes and other clothing items, as well as personal hygiene products. Tre took it all, stuffing them in the backpack Mitch gave him the day they escaped from the jail.

Tre hoped Mitch was doing the same, collecting what they would need for a sustained time at the compound. They had planned it that way, but having no contact with Mitch since they parted ways after the escape, Tre honestly didn't even know if Mitch would even meet him. All he could do was keep heading West and worry about himself. Having companionship would be nice, but Tre was prepared to go it alone if necessary.

On his journey West, Tre ran everything through his mind, hoping he would not experience any setbacks. The compound had water when he and Levi stayed there briefly, and even if it had been shut off, Tre knew how to access the source. He knew from his earlier stay there that all of the emergency provisions were gone, so when one of his rides dropped him off at a truck stop, Tre took a chance shoplifting a few food items. He had to laugh to keep from crying, thinking that at one time, he ran multiple hotels, casinos, and other businesses. He once had a jet and a chauffeur. But now, he was stealing beef jerky and Gatorade from a truck stop.

I've started from the bottom before. I have to do this to survive and then eventually crawl my way back.

So he stuffed a few more packages of cheese and crackers in his bag, made his way to the shower area, cleaned up, and then began looking for his next ride, which hopefully took him all the way to his destination.

Tre's next ride was indeed a driver headed precisely in the direction of the compound. The journey was uneventful since he faded in and out of a fitful sleep for a few hours. When he awoke, Tre knew exactly where they were, and he began preparing to be let out. When they were about a mile from the old compound, Tre asked the guy to stop, which seemed exceptionally odd to the driver.

"Are you sure? We're in the middle of the desert, Man."

"Very sure. I appreciate the ride."

"Well, hey, take this bottle of water and my hat. I feel bad leaving you here."

"Don't worry. And thanks."

With those words, the truck driver stopped and let Tre out, and took off again, looking several times in his rear-view mirror until Tre was no longer visible.

Tre didn't walk very long, and he spied the massive compound in the distance, bringing a smile to his face. Upon arrival, he once again accessed the perimeter gate with his code and entered the same way he did with Levi twenty-two years prior. The place had definitely seen its better days, but this was a temporary stop, and it would do. Tre was hot and sweaty from his walk and headed to the very depths of the building to clean up, cool off, eat a little something, and take a nap. Before laying down, Tre activated the perimeter alarm, and to his amazement, it turned on with the generator power. This way, he would know when Mitch arrived without having to wait outside in the heat. For the first time since his escape, Tre felt truly safe. He smiled at his accomplishment and was able to sleep soundly for the first time in days.

Tre awoke several hours later to the alarm sounding, hopefully signaling Mitch's arrival and not something else. Sure enough, when Tre peeked out the main floor windows, he saw Mitch looking a little haggard. Tre pushed the button to open the gate, and Mitch seemed relieved when he walked inside, and the gate closed behind him.

Chapter 22

CiCi was very cautious in the days directly after Christopher's escape, but now it had been several weeks, and he was nowhere to be found. Every day that passed gave CiCi new hope that her ordeal with Christopher Paloma was over.

"He probably never had any plans to hurt me," CiCi said to herself. "He probably just wanted to scare me."

CiCi knew she couldn't dismiss Christopher altogether, so she was not letting her guard down. However, she also decided that she was not living her life scared and looking around every corner either. That's why, after a few weeks and no sign of Christopher, she thought a change of scenery would do both her and Dex some good.

"Let's go to Vegas and stay at my parent's penthouse for spring break," CiCi proposed.

"Seriously?" Dex asked, a little confused. "I thought you were hyper-focused on school?"

"We've worked hard, and we're in good shape going into the final weeks. We need a break and some relaxation before things get all crazy at the end," CiCi argued.

"Don't get me wrong. You don't have to sell me on it," he said, kissing her in appreciation.

"Have you cleared this with your parents?"

"No, but I don't see why it would be a problem, " CiCi responded.

"Uh…the problem is still out there, CiCi," Dex reminded her. "And I don't see your dad allowing us to go across the country just for some spring break fun."

"But no one has seen or heard from Christopher in a couple of weeks. Besides, he's not going to be in Vegas," CiCi added confidently. "Let me bring it up with my parents, and if they're okay with it, we'll make our plans, okay?" CiCi said, kissing Dex sweetly at first and then a little more passionately to seal the deal.

"You really do know how to be quite convincing, Ms. Brunner," Dex answered.

That night, CiCi called home and caught up on the news with her parents, and then posed the possibility of a Las Vegas trip for spring break.

"So, I was wondering. Would it be okay if Dex and I went to the penthouse in Vegas for spring break?"

There was an awkward silence on the other end of the phone. CiCi knew this idea might be a hard sell but was hopeful she could make her case. She began to prepare herself for a 'no' and then her barrage of reasons why she and Dex should be able to go.

Mac and Aria had a hard enough time being away from CiCi while she was at school. Allowing her to go to Las Vegas with Christopher Paloma on the loose would be torture. Mac, especially, feared any moment Christopher would appear and wreck their lives. He had no idea what he would do if something ever happened to CiCi. But he understood that they could not live their lives afraid and guarded, so he would allow it under one specific condition.

"I'll allow it," Mac began with a tone that told CiCi there was a big 'IF' coming.

"Yes?"

"Your mom and I get to come, too."

CiCi's excitement about the trip suddenly deflated. How could she and Dex be together—*really* together, under the watchful eye of her parents.

"Uh… that's not really what I had in mind, Dad," CiCi explained.

"Probably not, but it's the only way you're going to Vegas," Mac stated authoritatively.

Aria, who had been silent during this father-daughter exchange, chimed in with a compromise she thought both her daughter and Mac could live with.

"Don't forget, we own the top *two* floors at The Palace Hotel. Your dad and I can stay in a suite below the penthouse."

CiCi figured that was an acceptable compromise, and she did like the idea of having her dad around for protection.

"We don't have to do everything together, right?" she asked.

"I suppose not, but before we leave, we'll discuss some ground rules for everyone's safety," Mac added.

"Fair enough!" CiCi agreed excitedly. "Our break begins in two weeks. I have some projects to finalize, and then I'm all about Vegas!"

❖ ❖ ❖

After a couple of weeks in the compound, Tre and Mitch had exhausted their provisions, but Tre feared they had not been in hiding long enough. He knew a trail went cold after a certain point in time, and the longer fleeing fugitives stayed undetected, the better their overall chances of staying free. But with very little food and water left, it was time to move on. Just like his journey with Levi, Tre and Mitch were heading out of the underground tunnel that took them a significant distance toward the bright lights of Sin City. Once again, Tre planned on getting lost in the chaos of the Las Vegas Strip.

The trip through the tunnel took a full day, then a few miles of desert, and a long walk across town before they reached their destination. They were exhausted, hot, and sweaty, but the intense excitement immediately rejuvenated the two travelers. As they made their way down the Strip to The Palace Hotel, Tre was in awe at how much the landscape had changed over the years. In fact, they almost walked right past The Palace Hotel because it looked so different.

Once there, he and Mitch took a sharp turn off the sidewalk and walked adjacent to the building until they were far from the hotel itself but right on top of the manhole that once led down to his secret bunker. For a brief moment, Tre worried that the bunker had been destroyed or filled, but when he opened the manhole, the space seemed very familiar. Descending into the dark, condensed space, Tre smelled those familiar smells and became anxious to see their new home.

After finding the auxiliary light, Tre switched it on. The tunnel leading to the main part of the bunker had not changed a bit. In fact, the actual bunker was also quite similar. Tre smiled and began tidying the space and making room for two.

"You have all the secret spaces and shit, don't you?" Mitch said, joking.

"I guess you could say that. I'd much rather go in the front door the way I used to when I owned this place, but this will do for now."

Chapter 23

Going to Vegas always brought back both wonderful and terrifying memories for Mac and Aria. It was the place they got married and began their lives as husband and wife. Yet it was also the place where they were tricked by Tre Halprin and nearly lost each other forever.

The Palace Hotel was completely remodeled a few years prior, and while the aesthetics were different, the feelings it aroused in Mac and Aria were always the same. They didn't quite understand how one place could be the source of such dread and also such joy. They tried not to dwell on the negative aspects of their time at The Palace, but their complicated history there could not easily be dismissed.

After completing a couple of hectic weeks at school before spring break, both Dex and CiCi were thrilled to be getting away for a week. Pulling up to the grand entrance in their Town Car, both CiCi and Dex were giddy with excitement. They couldn't quite decide what they would do first until Mac suggested lunch in the new hotel gardens where Aria's newest design was placed. She had recently designed and donated a new water feature for the pool, and both Mac and Aria were anxious to see it. CiCi figured lunch on Dad wasn't a horrible way to begin their vacation, so she and Dex agreed to meet her parents there after unpacking.

CiCi always loved spending time in the penthouse, but this trip was special. This time, Dex was with her, and she could share all the luxuries and opulence with him. She always wondered what it would be like to make love on the giant terrace, looking out at the bright Vegas night sky. CiCi giggled a little to herself, knowing that at some point on this trip, she would not have to wonder any longer as she planned to make that fantasy a reality. As she stood out on the terrace overlooking the magnificent city, she mentioned her plans to Dex.

"So, before we leave here, I want to make love right here in this lounge chair with the backdrop of the luminous Vegas sky," CiCi said, spreading her arms wide and twirling around.

Dex walked up behind her, wrapped his arms around her waist, and whispered in her ear.

"Request noted."

Both Dex and CiCi enjoyed a sweet moment on the balcony and then went back inside. Dex was blown away by the space and lavish accommodations. Even though he and CiCi had been together for a few years, she had never taken him to their place there. He had to admit. It was worth the wait. And then Dex caught sight of what would be the focus of *his* fantasy on their trip.

"Look at the size of this shower!" Dex shouted, forgetting that CiCi was well aware of how big it was.

CiCi was amused at his amazement.

"Yes, I know," she answered. "There's room for two."

Dex glanced over and caught her flashing that shameless little grin that he loved so much.

"You're lucky we have to meet your parents in a few minutes, or I'd wipe that sexy little grin right off your cute face, Ms. Brunner."

This was what CiCi dreaded with her parents there. Already, their presence was cramping her style.

"I say we eat lunch, do a little exploring, and then I'm going to feel a little dirty, so I'll need a shower," CiCi said matter-of-factly as she grabbed her purse and headed out the door to meet her parents. Needless to say, Dex was left with an image in his head and growing anticipation in his pants. He couldn't wait to get CiCi back there and naked in that damn shower.

Lunch was wonderful, and CiCi was in awe of her mom's fountain. CiCi was so proud to have such a talented mom, and she could only aspire to be as dedicated and passionate about her work someday. Aria's talent for designing outdoor spaces and the features that go in them was first realized when Calysta put her in charge of designing the memorial park in St. Lucia. Ever since that first venture, Aria became the premiere designer in that venue. Even though she would never have to work a day in her life, Aria still needed to be productive and useful, and CiCi had always admired her for it.

After lunch, Aria and Mac set out to find some of the old places that would bring back memories. One stop was the jewelry store where Mac purchased Aria's diamond hoops, her engagement ring, and both their wedding rings. When they walked inside, the owner was thrilled to see them, and hugs followed. Mac and Aria always made it into the store to see her whenever they were in Vegas. Of course, Mac always wanted to buy Aria something, and she never objected.

On this trip, however, Aria had already made up her mind that she was buying Mac a new watch, so she headed him in that direction.

"I'm buying you a watch," she said with determination in her voice.

After a little resisting, Mac admitted that he needed one and began looking while Aria addressed her attention to some gold bracelets nearby. After Mac chose the perfect watch, Aria asked how long it would take to have it engraved, and the owner told her that for *them* the jeweler could do it instantly. Aria had been planning this purchase for a while and told the lady the simple but meaningful words she wanted on the back of the watch face.

My love always, Aria

Not finding anything she absolutely had to have, Aria and Mac left with the single purchase that elicited a lengthy 'thank you' kiss once out on the street.

"This place makes me feel romantic," Aria said, sneaking another little kiss.

Mac, who was feeling something a little different than romantic, couldn't help but express his opinion.

"This place makes me horny," he added, grabbing Aria and giving her the kind of kiss that made some very definite promises.

"Let's go to Nordstrom. You can help me pick out something," Aria said, raising her eyebrows and then giving a little wink.

Mac knew damn good and well what Aria's *something* was, and the thought of it only intensified his condition.

"I tell you what. We'll go to Nordstrom, and you can pick out *something*. Over the years, you've proven to be quite good at it without my help. While you do that, I'll wait for you in the bar."

Aria agreed to this plan which she liked even better. Then, her reveal would be a surprise. On the edge of the massive lingerie section, Mac gave her a kiss and headed off to the bar while Aria embarked on one of her favorite journeys—meandering around the plentiful racks of Nordstrom lingerie.

Thinking back many years, Aria remembered the light blue teddy she wore the night Calysta arranged their tryst. Mac loved that piece, and they were both disappointed when it got left in the room during their hurried departure. If she could find something like that, this trip would bring back some fond memories of their earlier times making love in Las Vegas.

Aria began her search, and it wasn't long until she saw a light blue bra, panty, and garter set. It was similar to the one from their past, and Mac would surely make the connection, but it was also just different enough to be new and exciting. Aria grabbed her sizes, made her purchase, and headed to the bar. Mac would either be disappointed that she found her items so quickly, or he could put two and two together and know that whatever she found in record time had to be perfect.

After finishing their first drink, Aria opened the top of her shopping bag and gave Mac a little sneak peek. His reaction was classic. There was no discussion about a second drink. Instead, he paid their tab, helped her off the barstool, and hastily found the quickest choice of transportation back to The Palace Hotel.

All the way back, Aria toyed with ideas for showing off her new lingerie. Even though she was now in her early fifties, Aria still had a smokin' hot body, and she knew it. But when they got back to the suite, Mac had his own ideas. Once inside the room, Mac took her hand and led her back to the bedroom.

"Put those on, and then come out and show me," he said in an all-business tone.

Aria was turned on by his take-charge approach and wasted no time doing as she was told. Waiting on Aria, Mac grabbed a beer from the mini fridge and sat on the spacious armchair, eagerly awaiting Aria's entrance. When she appeared, she looked so fucking sexy. Mac tried to prepare himself, but she exceeded even his high expectations.

As Aria lingered in the doorway, Mac took in all the details. Her supple breasts were bulging out of the bra that was shockingly low cut. Mac loved a great teddy, but he actually preferred the combination Aria chose: a bra and panty set with a garter. Her long legs looked amazing in that garter, and he couldn't ignore the fact that her low-cut panties were barely doing their job, and he liked it that way.

"Come here," he said, motioning with his finger and wearing a naughty smile.

Aria made a slow saunter towards Mac and then told Alexa to play a sensual tune. When the music began to play, Aria slowly began to dance, swaying her hips and raising her arms above her head. She knew she was throwing gasoline on a fire, but she didn't care. The soothing music and her rhythmic movement to it was turning her on, and when she locked eyes with Mac, she saw that tortured, *come fuck me now*, look on his face.

Getting anxious, Mac stripped down, causing Aria to miss a couple beats in her performance. She never could resist those abs, and he still had them, and she still loved them. With Mac waiting naked on the chair, Aria decided her movements to the music would be better with a partner, so she made her way over to Mac. She stopped right in front of him, leaned down, put her hands on the arms of the chair, and stared right into Mac's eyes. He wanted to maintain their sensual gaze, but he also wanted to look down at her beautiful breasts that were falling out of her bra right in his face. The urge got the best of him, and when he looked down, Aria smiled, knowing it was just a matter of time. She climbed into the chair, positioned herself, and began a slow rhythmic sway to the music.

Mac unhooked her bra and let it fall. His kisses were eager and steamy as Aria's pace increased. They always did think there was nothing quite like making love in Las Vegas.

Chapter 24

Dex and CiCi were almost back to The Palace, and Dex had one thing on his mind.

"So, are you feeling dirty yet?" Dex whispered in CiCi's ear, eliciting a sexy glance.

"So, very…very dirty."

Dex had never moved so fast getting CiCi back to the hotel. All he could think about was that giant shower and a lazy afternoon with CiCi upstairs in the penthouse, but his afternoon plans were about to be delayed.

As they hastily approached the hotel, Dex saw a man who looked exactly like Christopher walk up and approach another man who was sitting on a bench across from the hotel lobby doors. Dex felt as if he knew the other man, too, but couldn't quite place him. Suddenly, their hurried pace halted to an abrupt stop as CiCi also caught sight of Christopher. Both of them were temporarily frozen with fear. The men were engaged in conversation, so Dex and CiCi were sure that they slipped into the lobby door unnoticed.

"What the hell?" CiCi said in disbelief.

"It looked just like him!" Dex confirmed.

"I'm calling my dad."

Nightmares & Premonitions

Mac and Aria were alarmed by the tone of CiCi's voice when she called with her disturbing news, so they dressed quickly and made their way down to the lobby. Mac positioned himself at a curtain-covered window with a view across the street.

"Look on that bench across the road," CiCi said with mounting anxiety.

Mac delicately moved the curtain with his fingers and laid eyes on the bench, but there was no man.

"There's nobody over there," Mac revealed.

"What?" CiCi said in disbelief.

"That means he's out there somewhere," Dex added.

"That is *if* it was Christopher," Mac challenged.

"It was!" CiCi said definitively.

"Well then, we all need to be extra careful," Aria added.

"Do you think he followed us here?" Dex asked.

Mac thought for a minute. He doubted Christopher knew their plans. But then again, Christopher being there with them was one hell of a coincidence.

"It's hard to say, but I find it difficult to believe he had time to figure out our plans," Mac replied.

"This might sound farfetched, but coming to Vegas would be natural if there is some of Tre's willful influence inside him," Aria offered.

"Very true," Mac agreed. "Now I'm torn."

"Why?" Aria asked.

"Part of me thinks I need to call the Feds and report that he's out here, but the other part doesn't know for sure that it's Christopher and doesn't want to look stupid calling with so little evidence and information."

"Let's get up to our rooms and out of the public eye until we figure something out," Aria suggested.

As they all headed upstairs Mac's mind was racing. If Christopher was there, and he was most likely being influenced by Tre, he would undoubtedly go to the bunker for safety and seclusion. Now Mac wondered if he should stake out the outdoor manhole or the inside entrance to the bunker. Either way, he wanted to see if he could catch Christopher coming and going.

Once safe in their rooms, Dex and CiCi were out of the mood but stuck in the penthouse for a while until Mac and Aria came up with a safe solution to the 'Christopher problem.'

"Let's just take a nap," CiCi suggested.

After slipping into the silky sheets, the two had no problem going to sleep despite their recent stressful discovery. But CiCi's restful nap was soon interrupted by a terrible dream. It started out dark, but slowly, bits of light infiltrated the room, and when enough light appeared, CiCi saw the silhouette of a man in the distance. She knew right away that it was Christopher.

In her dream, she felt all the fear and disgust she would feel in reality. Her body was shaking, and she was terrified that Christopher would come after her. When he slowly started walking her way, CiCi began to move away but found herself on the penthouse terrace with very little room to back up. She was cornered, and her fear had never reached such a peak.

Christopher maintained his slow pace toward her, knowing she had nowhere to go. A cruel smile formed on his face when CiCi began to cry at first and then beg him for mercy. When Christopher was right in front of her, she could finally see him, but it wasn't Christopher's face. He had the same sinister look in his eyes and the same menacing scowl-like smile, but it was someone else's face on Christopher's body.

When he reached for her, CiCi instinctively climbed onto the rail, futilely trying to get away, as his hands grabbed her around the throat. His hands were hot and strong, and she felt his grip tightening. She was going to die, but if that was her fate, she wanted him to die, too. With that thought, CiCi felt her location of the rail with her foot and could tell she was barely holding on—a few more inches, and she would fall twenty-four stories down, and she was taking this man with her.

CiCi said a prayer and took the leap, but just as she did, the man let go. She was falling and would certainly die, but the man was safely standing on the balcony, looking down and laughing. And then he delivered the most sinister gesture. The last thing CiCi saw was the man waving goodbye— and then she woke up sweating and panting and riddled with fear.

Chapter 25

When CiCi told her parents about her dream, Aria had to sit down, which CiCi found very alarming. Her mother was the strongest person she knew, and CiCi recounting the details of her dream rocked her to the core. After she recovered some, Aria felt compelled to relay her own disturbing dream.

"This is a mother's nightmare!" Aria said, putting her hands to her face in agony. Mac knew what she was about to say.

"I had my own nightmare, which was very similar, except I was falling off a cliff. The person looking down on me was a young boy, a teenager, maybe. It was so confusing at the time because your dad and I didn't even know any boys that age. But now that we think Christopher is being influenced by Tre Halprin, it's all coming together."

"I'm not understanding, Mom," CiCi said, looking confused.

"You saw an older man's face on Christopher. I think you saw Tre. But at the time I had my dream, Christopher would have been a young teenager. The person we each saw as we fell was the same—Christopher Paloma being influenced by Tre Halprin," Aria explained.

"This is so unbelievably twisted," CiCi replied.

"And there's something else," Aria said guardedly.

CiCi could see that the worst of what her mother would say was yet to come.

"Do you have vivid dreams like this one often?"

"No, not really. This was the first 'real feeling' dream I think I've ever had," CiCi replied.

Mac and Aria shared a glance that didn't go unnoticed.

"What? Tell me!" CiCi demanded, almost panicked.

"What I'm about to tell you will seem overwhelmingly unreal, but I am pure proof of its validity."

Aria proceeded to share her ability that she now thought CiCi also possessed. CiCi was skeptical at first, but as her mother explained certain events from their lives and how they fit her dreams, CiCi began to listen with more intensity.

"So, if what you're telling me is true, this horrible dream predicts my future?" CiCi concluded with fear, lacing her words.

"Well, we've come to realize that your mother's visions never play out exactly as they did in her dreams," Mac offered.

"Still!" CiCi fired back.

"I'll tell you what my grandmother told me. It's best to live in the present and not let the dreams of the future rob you of any time," Aria said quite powerfully, holding CiCi's hands.

Mac decided that was enough of the dreams. It was time to live in the here and now, and he decided to continue explaining how Christopher Paloma and Tre Halprin could possibly be one and the same.

"You told the police chief in Hayward that Christopher got possessive of you, and I saw it when he had your bracelet. That's Tre's doing. He wanted to be close to you, maybe hurt you to hurt your mother and me. Who knows. Tre Halprin is a sick man who's motivated by revenge. After all these years, he's still after us. Shit! The fucking man is DEAD, and he's still after us!" Mac said rather hopelessly.

"Poor Christopher," Aria said softly. "The boy was dying and received a kidney to stay alive. He was just a normal kid. Who knows what he would have been like without Tre Halprin's kidney."

Aria's comment seemed to put things into perspective for everyone. Christopher was a victim, not a perpetrator.

"Before we get too carried away buying into this weird idea that a kidney transplant could lead to a full-on possession, I need to give you some cold hard facts about Christopher Paloma. Chief Jackson told me they uncovered remains of four bodies buried under Paloma's boathouse at Deerfoot. He's looking at being charged with four counts of murder when the Feds catch him," Mac explained.

Dex's face went white, and CiCi was stunned.

"Not only that," Mac continued. "The chief has had several people come forward and give statements about being assaulted, shot at, pushed out of a boat, and more. I would say you two and any of your friends who had anything to do with Christopher up at that lodge are very lucky."

"Dad, what are we going to do?" CiCi asked.

"If the person you saw was Christopher, and if he's being influenced by Tre, I think I know where he'll be."

"THE BUNKER!" Aria shouted. "Yes, he'd go to the bunker."

"The thing we have going for us is we know he's here, but I don't think he knows we're here. I'm going to stakeout the outdoor manhole that leads down into the bunker and see if I can catch him coming or going. Until I get back here with some answers, everyone stays put," Mac insisted. "Got it?"

CiCi and Dex were disappointed because they hadn't really done much yet, but they certainly understood Mac's order, and they slipped out of Mac and Aria's suite and back up to the Penthouse. Mac checked his .45 and started for the door as Aria placed her 9mm in her Sticky holster.

"Oh, no! You're staying here," Mac said, knowing Aria thought she was going on this stakeout.

"No, I'm not," Aria insisted. "You act like I've never dealt with Tre Halprin before."

Mac exhaled a deep breath and decided this was an argument he couldn't win.

"Come on. At least you know the terrain," he said, a little annoyed.

"Yes, I'm sorry to say that I definitely know the terrain," Aria added as they headed out their door and toward the stairs.

Both were probably thinking of the many times in their past when they hid or ran from danger in that very stairwell. But they had no time for bad memories. They very well could be once again facing off with Tre Halprin. It was time to get their minds right, so there was nothing but silence all the way to their stakeout spot, where they settled in, not knowing what they hoped for most—to see Christopher at the manhole or not.

❖ ❖ ❖

Tre thought he was seeing things when he spotted CiCi Brunner and that asshole Dex. They were rushing into The Palace Hotel and didn't see him talking to Mitch across the drive.

"It can't be!" he thought. But thinking back at exactly what he saw, Tre was now certain he saw CiCi and the asshole.

"She's definitely fucking that prick again," Tre thought.

Seeing them completely wrecked his mood. He was supposed to be going with Mitch to get something to eat after Mitch got back from buying some supplies. After witnessing *his* girl with another man, Tre was agitated and could feel the onset of a headache. He had been headache-free for several months, and now that annoying little thud deep in his skull was rhythmically pounding, and he knew it was just a matter of time before that little thud became a raging, stabbing pain.

"NO! NO!" he cried out loud, capturing more attention than he wanted.

He gave Mitch some money to go get something to eat, but Tre had to get some relief. There was nothing he could do but go back to the bunker and rest. His head was pounding, and his heart was breaking, so he climbed down into the dark bunker, lay on his makeshift bed, and closed his eyes. But instead of resting, Tre could not get the image of his CiCi with Dex out of his head.

"I should have killed him," Tre said with a flat, cold tone. "I had the chance. I should have killed him!"

Despite his overactive mind and overwhelming hatred, Tre slept.

❖ ❖ ❖

Once back to their penthouse safely, CiCi and Dex were trying to process all that had happened and all the information her parents had divulged.

"This whole thing with the kidney is freaky as shit," Dex admitted.

"It sounds so unbelievable, but all the evidence points to that conclusion—Christopher really isn't Christopher," CiCi added.

CiCi was hesitant to mention the other information they received from her mother, but she was dying to know what Dex thought.

"So, what about the other stuff? You know…about the 'ability' my mom revealed?"

Dex shook his head back and forth as if stumped.

"I guess there are stranger things. I mean, your mom wouldn't lie about something like that."

"And what if I now have the same powers?"

"I guess it's something we'll deal with," Dex answered, kissing her sweetly.

CiCi loved that he said 'we,' feeling as if no matter what, he was there for her.

Changing the subject, Dex thought about CiCi's folks.

"Do you think your mom is down in the suite alone?" Dex asked, a little worried.

"No way! She went with my dad," CiCi answered.

"He'd let her go? I mean, with it being dangerous and all?"

"*Let* her go? No, it's more like she *told* him she was going, and he knew better than to argue."

Dex had never heard the stories about Mac and Aria in their prime, fighting the Halprins. CiCi had to remember that Dex really had no idea the danger her parents faced in their lives. And he would be shocked to know that her mother shot a man point blank. But she decided those were stories for another time because now it was time to wash all of her worries and stress away. Now, she was focused on taking a shower with her sexy boyfriend.

"I was thinking that since they are both out on a stakeout for a while and there would be no interruptions, maybe you would like to join me in the shower."

Dex's eyes flashed a little sparkle. He thought that was an excellent idea, but he was going to play a little hard to get.

"Hum…I thought I'd read a little, but you go ahead," Dex answered, knowing he was a horrible actor.

"Oh, okay…" CiCi said, playing along, unbuttoning her jeans, slipping them down over her hips, and stepping out of them.

Dex was well aware that he was outmatched here, but he was intrigued by CiCi's performance, so he stayed silent and watched.

"But you do know the little sparkle in your eye gives you away, right?" CiCi stated, pulling her t-shirt over her head, teasing Dex with one of her best assets.

CiCi was a little surprised Dex had not caved yet, but she was *all in*, playing the game.

"But I guess I can shower alone if you really would rather read," she said while unhooking her bra, pulling it off her shoulders, and letting it drop to the floor. Now she was standing there in only her tiny panties, biting her bottom lip, and Dex had to confess that he wanted a shower. He really, really wanted a shower.

Dex grabbed her around the waist with one arm, slid his other hand behind her neck, and pulled her to him, stopping when their mouths were just inches apart. Her eyes were locked on his, and Dex glanced down at her perfect lips as if being so close and not kissing them was an unforgivable sin.

"I'm so fucking lucky," Dex said, still resisting her tempting lips.

"You…you know how to get me so hot," CiCi replied, also resisting but desperately wanting a deep, passionate kiss.

Dex slowly moved closer until their lips were barely touching and whispered, "I'm about to give you the best kiss of your life."

CiCi was so turned on, but she waited for his move.

"And then, I'm going to take you in that shower and make love to you."

CiCi knew her breathing was heavy, and she could feel her chest heave with every breath, but still, she waited for Dex's move. When she felt his lips on hers, it was gentle at first and then the passion that had been building took control. It was the kind of kiss you never want to end, but when it did, Dex took her hand, and she wondered how in the world the shower could compete with what had just happened—but it did.

Chapter 26

Mac and Aria were patient, and their diligence paid off. About two hours into their stakeout, Christopher appeared, exiting the manhole, and Mac was elated.

"Well, looky there," Mac interjected.

"Finally," Aria added as Christopher emerged from the manhole, turned, and walked toward the front of the Palace Hotel.

Mac was twitching with excitement as he readied Aria to follow him when the time came. CiCi and Dex were right. Christopher was here, and discovering this fact was a game-changer for Mac. While he thought there was a possibility his daughter saw Christopher Paloma, he was unsure. Christopher's emergence from the manhole confirmed CiCi's claims. And no matter how insanely crazy it seemed, it also proved that Christopher was being influenced by Tre. Now, Mac was a believer. No matter what, Mac and Aria had to follow this guy.

Christopher woke from his nap headache-free, but he was still feeling the painful effects of seeing CiCi with Dex. He wished Mitch would hurry up and get back, then he'd decide what to do about his unfaithful beloved. Right now, he would go to the front of the hotel, settle into a place out of the way, and watch for Mitch.

What Christopher really wanted was to go inside The Palace and look around. It had been a long time since he had been in Vegas, but being there now still felt like home. He wondered what the penthouse looked like now, and then that thinking circled his mind back around to CiCi and Dex. He was certain they were staying there since Aria inherited it when his mother died, which was another sore point that got his blood boiling.

Sitting there thinking of all he had lost was doing nothing but putting him in a foul mood, but finally, he spied what he had been waiting on. Mitch was walking up the Strip with some food.

"Feeling any better?" Mitch asked. "Man, I'm worried about you. You get those headaches now, and I'm going to be honest, Man, you act so different than you used to. It scares the shit out of me."

At that moment, Tre realized that Mitch knew him as Christopher Paloma, not Tre Halprin. Now that his full transformation had occurred, he understood Mitch's confusion. Being of one person's mind and another's body was a lot for even him to get used to, not to mention people with no background knowledge of the situation. Tre had come to terms with it, and although it didn't seem normal yet, his split existence was getting easier for him to accept. But he could see how people like Mitch, who only knew him as Christopher Paloma, would not understand, and he struggled with how much he should divulge. His story really was very unusual. Most people would say he was crazy if they heard what he'd been through. He decided he'd take one step at a time, and now was as good a time as any to make a huge leap.

"Yeah, being back in Vegas is weird for me. You may not believe me, but I used to own this hotel. My name is Tre Halprin, not Christopher Paloma," Tre revealed.

There—that's all Mitch needed to know right now. Hell, it was all he could effectively explain.

Mitch had a bewildered look on his face and finally let loose with, "Shit! You think you know someone."

Mac and Aria were patiently following Tre's every move, and now that he had a buddy, Mac was a little concerned.

"That's not good," Mac began, "That must be the guy who helped him bust out. That means this guy is loyal to the death. Now we have two crazies to worry about."

"Mac, let's just call the Feds and be done with him," Aria pleaded.

"Will we ever be 'done with him' that way?" Mac asked.

"So what do you want to do? End up in another showdown and kill him—again?" Aria asked, unable to mask her obvious sarcasm.

"Is that so horrible?" Mac asked, truly believing that this encounter with Tre Halprin was like all the other showdowns with Halprins—a matter of life or death, a battle between good and evil, and a necessary step for their lives to resume normally.

"I think it's reckless, especially with our daughter here and Dex," Aria admitted.

Mac thought about Aria's words. She had a point. He would never want to put CiCi in danger, and if Tre was already fixated on her, that was enough uncertainty to deal with. Even though he really wanted to go into a final face-to-face showdown with Tre, Mac pulled out his phone and called Chief Jackson.

The Chief thought it was a miracle that Paloma had been found, and Mac spent well over a half hour explaining their crazy theory about Christopher being affected by Tre Halprin's kidney now functioning in his body. Mac knew how ludicrous their story sounded, so he was very thorough with the details. The chief was confused at first, but then he started making connections to Mac's story, remembering some of Christopher's specific behaviors and mannerisms. Although Chief Jackson wasn't sure if their conclusion about Christopher Paloma was even medically or scientifically possible, Mac sounded like he knew what he was talking about. Besides, how would Paloma know about the bunker under The Palace Hotel if he wasn't actually Tre Halprin?

"My head is spinning, Mac. Do you know how crazy this sounds?"

"Yes, I'm well aware, " Mac answered simply.

"But," Chief Jackson began, "it's so crazy, it just might be true."

"Get the Feds out here. We'll try to keep an eye on him. And I know they know how to do their job, but they need to be undercover. Halprin knows Vegas like the back of his hand. If he sees the Feds come rolling in, he'll bolt and get lost in his underground maze of tunnels, and we'll be back to square one."

"Got it!"

"And you should probably keep my theory a secret. We'll let people draw their own conclusions," Mac added.

"Don't worry. I would never try to explain that fucked up shit to anyone," Chief Jackson replied. "Pardon my language."

Mac laughed.

"Alright, we'll wait for the Feds. Thanks, Chief."

The Chief hung up and leaned back in his chair, deep in thought. For years he knew there was something so very odd about Christopher Paloma, but this explanation was 'out there.' He sat for a few more minutes, wondering if something so unbelievably weird was possible.

"Fucked up!" he said, picking up his phone and dialing Agent Rice.

Chapter 27

CiCi was trying not to worry, but there had been no word from her parents, who left hours prior to verifying Christopher's presence in Vegas. She didn't dare text them for fear her message might have sound or light that drew unwanted attention. So she waited, hoping nothing was wrong and that one of them would contact her soon.

Aside from no contact from her parents, CiCi had another problem. She noticed Dex was being a little quiet, and she wondered what was wrong. They had such an amazing shower together, but now he just didn't seem himself. If the right moment presented itself, she was going to get to the bottom of his sudden sullen mood.

"Let's get some room service," she suggested, thinking she needed to get her mind off of her worries about her parents and about Dex.

"Sounds good," Dex agreed, pulling the menu out of the nightstand.

Before CiCi could call to order their food, she finally got a text from her mother. After reading it, CiCi smiled at its timing.

Go ahead and eat something. We're waiting on the Feds. It might be awhile.

CiCi felt a whole lot better getting the message that her parents called the Feds because she knew her dad all too well. She knew the infamous history her parents had with the Halprin brothers, and she feared her dad, especially, would have something to prove. CiCi worried that her mom and dad would try to handle Christopher the way they took care of the Halprins back in their prime. But now, she breathed a sigh of relief. Even though she was certain her dad would insist on being involved, at least her parents were not trying to take him down themselves.

She wasn't trying to get her priorities out of line, but she was a little salty that her spring break to Vegas was consumed with seclusion and danger instead of wild times on Fremont Street and phenomenal shows. Now, the Feds just needed to hurry up and arrest this guy.

She hadn't thought about it much until just this moment, but Dex had a pretty traumatic experience with Tre. Maybe the reality of knowing he was here had finally set in. Maybe dealing with the fear of past trauma had caught up with him and was part of his strange change in mood.

That settled it. CiCi was not waiting for their food to arrive to talk to Dex. She was jumping in right now.

"Hey," she said, walking up and grabbing his hands. "What's wrong? You're quiet. Are you worried about Tre? My dad has the Feds on it now. They'll get him, and everything will get back to normal."

Dex felt bad that his emotions were showing and that CiCi thought something was wrong. Nothing was wrong at all. In fact, everything was just perfect. His quiet demeanor was being dictated by some heavy-duty thinking about the future. In a few weeks, they would be graduating, and CiCi would start her job in Missouri, working on design plans for expanding locations around Lake Ozark. It was a wonderful opportunity, and they were both elated when Future Fortune Production and Construction offered CiCi a position. Future Fortune was CiCi's dream job, and she was shocked to receive her top pick. Dex, however, knew how amazing she was and that she would get an offer, but he hadn't given it much thought until now. All of a sudden, the reality of graduating and CiCi being in Missouri hit him like a freight train.

They had not really talked about their future since they got back together, and Dex knew that was his fault. Most of their fights back in the late summer and fall were about their future and his insecurities on the topic, so he knew CiCi would not approach the subject to keep the peace. But Dex felt like a different person now. He had been given a second chance at life, and more than anything, he wanted that life to include CiCi. Therefore, he felt it might be time to open the discussion on their future together.

"It's not that," he started. "I've been thinking about the future, and I know this has been a sore subject for us in the past, so I guess I'm just cautious, wondering how to say what's on my mind."

"Well, you just made the first step," CiCi said encouragingly.

"I guess so," Dex agreed. "I want to get engaged, and I want to move to Missouri with you."

They had never had more than a superficial mention of marriage, and CiCi wanted Dex to go with her to Missouri, but she had not mentioned it because she didn't want to limit his job search. She made up her mind that she would wait for Dex to broach the subject, and now that he had, she was pleasantly surprised. She had often thought about marrying Dex, and since their reunion a few months ago, she definitely knew he was the only one for her.

Nightmares & Premonitions

"YES, let's get engaged… and YES, I definitely want you to move to Missouri with me. Dexter Robertson, I love you so much!"

Dex was so relieved, and what CiCi thought might be an explosive conversation in the future had just played out perfectly. She had never been happier. She leaned in and kissed her one true love, who was now going to be her husband. She couldn't wait for her parents to get back and tell them. They were going to be so happy.

Just a few months ago, Aria and Mac were telling their daughter to cut ties with Dex because they were concerned about his controlling behavior. But now, he was the old Dex again, and they had every reason to believe their daughter and Dex belonged together and that they had done the hard work to repair their relationship and make it even stronger. CiCi just knew her mom and dad were going to be so happy and so surprised.

❖ ❖ ❖

"Dammit! Can't they just stay put?"

Tre and Mitch emerged from the manhole, and Mac was pissed.

"We know they'll be back here," Aria said, not understanding his anger.

Mac thought about it.

"This is why I need you, my Dear. I would have followed them and risked blowing my cover. As you said so brilliantly, we know they'll be back. We don't have to do anything but wait for the Feds, and we can do that from the comfort of our suite," he said, giving Aria a 'thank you' kiss.

Aria was relieved. Although she had insisted on going, now she was over it. She had to admit, she liked blood-racing danger better than sitting and watching a manhole for hours.

"Good! Let's go back, see the kids, and then get something to eat."

When Aria and Mac knocked on the penthouse door, CiCi ran to open it. She was glad her parents weren't using the private elevator that opened up right into the living space. She remembered that as being one of her 'ground rules' of her parents being on the trip with them.

When CiCi opened the door, the wide, excited smile on her face told Mac and Aria something was up. But Dex had asked her not to blurt out the good news. He had to do something first.

"What's up?" Aria asked, knowing that grin on CiCi's face all too well.

CiCi was afraid that she would scream from excitement if she opened her mouth, so she just kept smiling and opened the door wider to let her parents inside.

"What are you two up to?" Mac asked, a little afraid of the answer.

Dex got up from the couch and asked them to come sit down, and right away, Aria's 'mother's intuition' went into overdrive. She knew exactly what was about to happen. Mac, on the other hand, remained clueless but now figured it couldn't be anything too terrible by the looks on their faces.

Dex took a deep breath and went through his whole speech, ending with the crescendo.

"Mr. and Mrs. Brunner, I love CiCi with all my heart. I'll live every day doing everything I can to make her happy. I'm asking for your permission to marry your daughter."

Aria could barely control herself long enough for Dex to get through his whole speech. But finally, she jumped up with over-zealous confirmation that she approved 100 percent and hugged them both. Mac was beaming, and his smile stretched from ear to ear. He shook Dex's hand and then pulled him in for a hug, slapping him on the back as a 'welcome to the family' gesture. Then Mac hugged his daughter sweetly and kissed her on the cheek.

"You will make a beautiful bride, Sweetheart. You look so much like your Momma. I'm so happy for you both," he said, giving her another little peck on the forehead.

"So much planning to do," Aria said right away.

"Now wait, Mom. We are just getting engaged right now. We have to graduate, move to Osage Beach, and we both need to get settled in our careers before you can get all excited about a big wedding."

She and Dex had not discussed exactly when they would get married, but he definitely didn't want to wait that long, so he spoke up.

"We haven't really decided when we will get married. I think we need to discuss that before we make any rash decisions."

CiCi knew she had spoken too quickly and made a decision that affected both of them without Dex's input. So, she did her best to back up a few steps and try again.

"That's right. We're not sure of anything. We have to make those decisions together, and then you can help us plan Mom," CiCi said, noticing Dex smiling at her.

"Well, not to jump in here and cause problems, but we do know a fantastic jeweler here in Las Vegas," Mac added.

In all honesty, CiCi had always wanted to get her rings from the same place where her parents got theirs. The story of their wedding was so magical, and as a little girl, she loved having her parents tell her their love story. Even though she had heard the tale many times, CiCi was always in awe of their two different perspectives.

When her dad told the story, it was so different from her mom's version. But they both told an amazing tale that included the trips to the jewelry store, the proposal at the concert, and the details of making the commercial. She thought her parents were so lucky for the opportunity to advertise the store. Making the commercial was definitely a once-in-a-lifetime opportunity. She wanted nothing more than to get her engagement ring there, so this time, it was her turn to speak up.

"This might not be the trip when it happens because I know you may not be prepared," she said, addressing Dex. "But I do want to get my ring here. I just think their link to our family history is such a great way to start the rest of our lives together. I think it's kind of like a good luck charm, so to speak."

Dex was never happier. He really wanted to shop for CiCi's ring while they were in Vegas, but after her comment to her mother, he was worried that CiCi wouldn't feel the same.

"We'll go tomorrow," Dex confirmed with a smile.

"Really?" CiCi asked, a little uncertain. "Are you sure?"

"CiCi, I've never been more sure of anything. This idea of getting engaged has been on my mind for a while, and I have the money. Yes, we'll go tomorrow."

CiCi was uncontrollably happy, doing a little hop over to Dex and giving him a quick peck that she was certain would deserve an upgrade later when her parents were gone.

"I love you, Dexter Kane Robinson," CiCi said, giving him another kiss.

"And I love you, Adeline Celeste Brunner."

Feeling a bit uncomfortable, Aria and Mac excused themselves and headed out the door.

"To be young and in love," Aria said. "There's nothing better."

"Hum, I'm going to see what I can do to change your mind about that after dinner," Mac said, grinning and hoping Aria got his point.

"Well, I still consider myself young, Darling," Aria replied. "But I'm all for whatever you have in mind."

As they headed into their suite Mac had an ornery grin forming on his face, and he made one final comment in that conversation.

"We're ordering room service."

Chapter 28

Tre and Mitch had a lot of catching up to do as far as having fun goes. They had been on the run and hiding out for a couple of months, and they both thought it was time to cut loose. After getting their fill at the buffet across the street from The Palace, the two hit a casino bar and continued their night of fun.

After a few drinks, Mitch gingerly approached the topic of CiCi. Even though he was Tre's right-hand man, Mitch knew his boss had a temper, and more than once, he had seen it flair. In fact, Mitch frequently went hunting with Christopher and had watched him become enraged at the drop of a hat. One minute, he was fine, and the next, he was furious enough to kill.

Mitch remembered many years prior when Kelley Greene came on Christopher's property, also hunting, not realizing he was on private land. Christopher was so enraged he didn't even give the poor guy a chance to leave. After verbally attacking Greene, Christopher gave a warning shot up in the air, and when Greene turned to run, Christopher shot him—dead. Mitch also remembered how calm and normal Christopher sounded when he asked him to help bury the guy, as if cold-blooded murder was nothing.

It was these types of memories that kept Mitch a little guarded, so he approached his questions carefully.

"So, you said the girl is here. That's quite the coincidence, isn't it?"

Tre's mood shifted slightly, as it always did when someone mentioned CiCi. But nothing about his behavior alarmed Mitch.

"Yes, a coincidence, but also quite the opportunity," Tre said with a wicked smile Mitch had seen way too many times.

"What are you thinking?" Mitch asked, fearing that the answer was some devious scheme he wanted no part of.

"I told her I'd see her soon, and now I get to make good on that promise. It's distressing that she's with that little prick Dex, but he can be dealt with. And then it's just a matter of time before she falls in love with me again. She'll need a little reminding, a little coaxing, but Miss CiCi will come around. Mark my word," Tre elaborated, saying more than he probably should have.

Mitch was in no position to judge. He was along for the ride, and he learned a long time ago to agree with everything this guy wanted and not make waves. But Tre's next chilling words on the topic hit a nerve with Mitch, and he shuddered at the thought.

"Because if I don't get CiCi, no one will have her. She's mine, and I always take what's mine."

❖ ❖ ❖

Tre and Mitch were out all night, approaching The Palace Hotel hungover and weary. Maybe it was his lack of sleep or coming down off the alcohol, but Tre was in a pissy mood.

"I used to fucking own this hotel. I used to live in the penthouse up there," he said, pointing to the sky. "And now I'm hiding in the Goddamn bunker while Aria *Halprin* Brunner owns everything I used to have."

Mitch knew better than to comment. He just let Tre get it all out.

"I want to walk in that lobby, go up my private elevator, and walk in that penthouse. MY penthouse! I want to find that stupid little asshole Dex there and snap his fucking neck. I want to see CiCi, and when she lays eyes on me and sees that I have killed a man so we can be together, she'll love me again. That's what I want to do."

A whole bunch of red flags went up for Mitch, but this was not the time to talk unless he wanted all of that rage directed toward him.

And just as fast as the anger came on, it was gone, and Tre walked past the lobby doors toward the manhole to his bunker, and Mitch was relieved. Tre needed sleep and that's exactly how both he and Mitch spent the morning. But Tre would not get much rest. Instead, he tossed and turned, slipping in and out of a dream state, and his beloved CiCi was always there. Sometimes, she was kind and loving, and he held her in his arms. And other times, she was harsh and distant, and he saw that she was happy and in love with Dex.

Tre woke from his fitful nap, feeling as if he needed to talk with CiCi. He had to let her know Dex was no good for her, and he couldn't stand the thought of them together, making love, and creating a normal life. She was his and no one else's. As he had thought so many times since the incident, he wished he had killed Dex Robertson when he had the chance. Tre knew that he would have another chance, but he would have to create it.

Agitated and desperate, Tre felt there was only one thing to do. He was going to find CiCi and make her see things his way.

And in the process, her asshole boyfriend would be collateral damage.

As Mitch slept soundly, Tre grabbed his gun from the safe and made his way out of the manhole. He was headed to a side door of The Palace that he knew would be locked. He would just have to casually wait for someone to leave or go in. No one would question him following.

It didn't take long for a man to approach while Tre stood off to the side, smoking a cigarette. The man used his key card to open the door, and Tre took one last drag from his cigarette, flicked it into the air, and spoke.

"Hey, Man, hold that, please."

And just like that, Tre was inside The Palace Hotel after so many years. Tre noticed how different everything looked, but they were actually very tasteful changes, and he wondered if that was his sister's doing or Aria's. While the decor changed, he knew the layout of the building had to be the same. Tre knew right where to go to find the private elevator up to the penthouse, and even though he was certain the passcode had changed, he knew a secret. He knew how to bypass the code—or at least he used to know.

When the doors closed and Tre used his bypass code, much to his relief, the elevator began its slow and lengthy ascent. Tre knew the doors would open right into the foyer of the main living space. If CiCi and Dex were there, he would be immediately thrown into acting on his plan. But he had the element of surprise on his side. Wouldn't Dex's pathetic face be a sight to see when he realized he was about to die? This time, Tre was not showing mercy. Dex had to be eliminated.

"Bye-bye, Dex," Tre said to himself as the elevator passed the ninth floor.

Tre's euphoric state was short-lived as he now worried that he would catch his love in bed with the enemy. He knew he would never be able to handle such a disturbing scene. Although it would cause CiCi immeasurable trauma, he saw himself lifting his gun and shooting Dex right there in bed. It would be messy and gruesome but necessary.

"Necessary, yes, so very necessary," Tre mumbled as he passed the fifteenth floor.

Then Tre's mind went back to pleasant thoughts—precious, wonderful thoughts, actually. Now, he envisioned his love naked in bed, waiting for him to come to her. He remembered every curve and every smooth touch. He remembered all those glorious moments spent making love to his CiCi, and now he couldn't wait for the doors to open so he could see her perfect body trembling and yearning for him.

"I'm coming for you, CiCi," Tre said with passionate anticipation as he neared his goal— the penthouse on the twenty-fourth floor.

Chapter 29

Dex and CiCi left early to get some breakfast at a little diner across from the Flamingo before doing their ring shopping. They had all day together and planned to meet Mac and Aria at the Strat for drinks around four o'clock to hopefully show off her ring. Even though Tre was not apprehended yet, Mac felt they were safe to be out having some fun as long as they remained watchful. Mac was expecting the Feds any time, and he promised to let CiCi know as soon as any developments occurred. There was nothing left to do but to enjoy their day together and make their trip to the jewelry store magical.

In true Mac fashion and without CiCi and Dex knowing, Mac called ahead and made the jewelry store owner aware that his daughter and his future son-in-law were coming in to do some ring shopping. When CiCi and Dex arrived, the jewelry store was lively, and all the salespeople were busy helping other customers, giving CiCi and Dex some time to browse. However, when the owner spied CiCi, she just knew she was Mac and Aria's daughter and thought she had such a remarkable resemblance to her mother. Without hesitation, she hurried their way.

"You have to be Aria and Mac Brunner's daughter, CiCi," the woman said, approaching them. "I haven't seen you since you were a little girl."

CiCi smiled.

"Let me guess, you think I look like my mother," CiCi asked, shaking the lady's hand.

"Yes, yes you do, Dear. And who is this handsome young man?"

"Dexter Robertson," Dex said, offering his hand and a smile.

"So, your father tells me you are looking for an engagement ring."

CiCi just laughed to herself. Her good old dad. He just had to call ahead and get things started.

Dex and CiCi followed the woman, who pulled out two large trays of stunning diamond rings. CiCi was temporarily overwhelmed and a little shy about trying any on at first but soon began choosing some favorites and slipping them on her finger. CiCi thought all of the rings were beautiful in the tray, but once she put them on, they looked too bulky for her tiny hand.

"They're all so pretty, but do you have anything a little more delicate and simpler?" CiCi asked.

The woman knew right where to go and brought back a small tray of elegant solitaires, some haloed and some plain. Right away, CiCi spotted an emerald-cut solitaire haloed with tiny, sparkly diamonds. CiCi reached for it first and slipped it on her finger.

"That one is stunning, isn't it?" the woman commented.

The band was solid but thin, making it look perfectly delicate on CiCi's finger. CiCi's eyes lit up as she held her hand out away from her body, looking at the amazing ring. Dex could tell their shopping was over.

"It's beautiful," he said.

"I love it!" CiCi confirmed.

"We'll take it," Dex said, smiling and then giving CiCi a little kiss.

"It looks like it fits," the lady said. "Does it need any adjusting?"

"No, it's absolutely perfect," CiCi confirmed.

"Let me have it cleaned for you."

As the woman took the ring to the back for cleaning, CiCi gave Dex the biggest hug.

"Thank you so much!" CiCi said. "But it was expensive, Dex. Are you sure?"

"This might make you mad, and the only reason I agreed to it was because you deserve to have the perfect ring. Your dad told me to let you have anything in the store, and if it was out of my price range, he'd get it, and I could pay him back."

"That doesn't make me mad, and it also doesn't surprise me one bit," CiCi replied.

When the owner of the shop came back with the ring, it looked even more beautiful, and CiCi couldn't wait to put it on, but she thought she would ask Dex first.

"May I?" she said with her heart aching for a 'yes.'

"Of course," Dex said, giving her a sweet kiss.

"You two really remind me of your parents twenty-five years ago. So in love. So ready to take on the world," the owner said, finishing the sale.

"I'll take that as a compliment," CiCi responded.

The young lovers were on cloud nine leaving the jewelry store, and CiCi got to thinking about the woman's comments regarding her parents. They really were quite amazing, and she had always known them to be madly in love. She admired their respect and passion for one another and always hoped she would find love as genuine, and here she was with her best friend, her lover, her everything. CiCi never felt so grateful as she did right then.

❖ ❖ ❖

Tre grew tired of waiting in the penthouse. He was disappointed he missed out on seeing his CiCi, but he knew Mitch was awake and wondering where he was, so Tre exited the penthouse, slipped out the remote side door, and headed back to the manhole. Before he even got down the ladder, Mitch was ranting at him.

"Where the fuck have you been?" Mitch said angrily. "I have no way to get a hold of you and no money. He was not at all happy about being left in the bunker alone most of the day.

"Calm down," Tre said, annoyed with Mitch's bitching. "I was waiting on my CiCi, but she never showed."

Mitch hated the way Tre said, 'My CiCi.' He just sounded crazy and obsessed. Mitch was not at all impressed with Christopher's new personality. He always knew Christopher was eccentric and moody, but these days, he was just self-absorbed and distant, and Mitch was having serious second thoughts about staying with him. He thought many times that day when he was left alone with no way to go out and even get something to eat that his days as Christopher's—now Tre's—sidekick were numbered. And even though Mitch knew the possible hazards of his actions, he was wound up, and one damning comment after another spewed from his mouth.

"Well, I'm starving. I hope you're planning on going to get something to eat before you begin obsessing over *your CiCi* again," Mitch said with plenty of disdain and sarcasm.

Tre tried to let Mitch's disrespectful comment slide, but it pissed him off.

"Actually, we need to lay low a bit. CiCi and her prick boyfriend are out, and I don't want to risk a chance meeting that will ruin my plans."

Mitch was furious. He was not going to wait around.

"I'm not staying here. Give me some money so I can get something to eat."

Tre was not at all pleased with his partner's tone and began to feel a rage rising from deep in his core.

"I said we're laying low," Tre repeated in an authoritative voice.

"The bitch doesn't know me and won't recognize me," Mitch said before he realized what he had done.

Tre's whole face changed, and he could feel his fury rising faster now.

"Don't ever call my CiCi a name like that again," Tre said, grabbing Mitch's shirt at the chest and twisting it, pulling him up off the ground enough that his feet were only lightly touching the floor.

Mitch was terrified, and he wondered why he was so stupid. He had been so careful, tiptoeing around Tre's anger, and now this.

"Do you understand me?" Tre added coldly.

"Yes, Sir," Mitch said, fearing for his life.

Tre waited a few seconds and then smiled a diabolical smile and let go of Mitch's shirt, allowing him to breathe a sigh of relief. Tre knew right then and there Mitch's usefulness had run out, and he would continue to get in the way of his plans. It was decided. Tre went to the safe, put his silencer on his gun, and shot Mitch without hesitation.

Chapter 30

CiCi was obsessed with her ring and kept catching a look at it in the bright sunlight, watching its amazing sparkle. Dex, of course, was amused with her attempt to slyly catch a glimpse of the shiny, glistening prisms. He loved making her happy.

It was nearing time for their 4 o'clock meeting with her parents, so the couple headed toward the Strat, anxious to show Mac and Aria their perfect purchase. When they arrived, CiCi saw a man and a woman she didn't know sitting at her parents' table, and she figured they were the Federal agents her dad was waiting on. CiCi was momentarily disappointed that her ring reveal would have to wait but elated at the fact that Tre was about to go down.

Approaching the table, CiCi and Dex discovered the man and woman were exactly as they guessed—Federal agents. Mac and Aria were filling them in on Tre's hiding spot and the fact that he had a partner.

"That's probably his sidekick from, Deerfoot Mitch Henning," Agent Mankle offered.

Dex's mind went back to that awful night when he sat watching CiCi and Christopher have drinks and then Mitch tossing him out of the lodge bar. Dex tried not to ever let his mind go back to that dark place, but listening to the Feds talking about the case brought back painful memories.

CiCi could sense Dex's discomfort and placed her hand gently on his leg, trying to offer support, but as CiCi's parents and the Feds planned the raid, Dex felt the sudden need to get out of there. CiCi excused themselves and told her mother she would meet them back at the hotel. Aria gave her daughter a comforting look and mouthed, 'I'm sorry,' knowing their meeting had not turned out at all like they had planned. But CiCi got the big picture and knew she had many other opportunities to show off her new ring. Right now, apprehending Tre Halprin was top priority.

CiCi called for their Town Car, and she and Dex headed back to the Penthouse.

"I'm sorry, I ruined that, didn't I?' Dex asked.

"No, not at all. It just didn't go as I planned. I wasn't planning on the Feds being there."

"And I wasn't planning on getting so upset hearing them talk about Deerfoot," Dex admitted. "That was such a horrible time for me. I've tried to block it all, but lately, it all comes back and gets me all fucked up in the head."

CiCi snuggled close to Dex in the back of the Town Car and laid her head on his shoulder.

"We'll get through all of that together. When Tre is captured and behind bars, I'm sure our lives can get back to normal," CiCi shared.

"I agree. I'm just a little on edge with him out there somewhere, stalking us."

Dex suddenly felt horrible that he was being so negative at such a wonderful time in their lives, and not only that, he shouldn't be acting scared and disturbing CiCi. Rather, he should be strong for her.

"I'm sorry," he said. "This is silly of me. Your mom and dad are working with Federal agents right now to take this creep down. It's only a matter of hours before Tre or Christopher, or whoever he is, is out of our lives forever."

"You're right. Let's lay low in the penthouse until the Feds pick up Tre," CiCi agreed. "I'm sure we can find something to do for a few hours," CiCi added, giving Dex a little side-eye smile that helped change his mood considerably.

When CiCi and Dex arrived at the hotel, they were enthralled in conversation and didn't notice the man in a hat with a newspaper outside the hotel entrance. Tre had been patiently awaiting their arrival. After his disappointing trip to the penthouse with CiCi and Dex gone, he was making sure his next adventure was more productive.

Tre was upset with himself for not thinking about what he would do with Mitch's body before shooting him. He couldn't get it out of the manhole, and even if he could, what would he do with it. So, Mitch's body lay bloody and stiff in the middle of the bunker, making Tre's living space quite unlivable.

Tre had noticed that he had been excessively impulsive and impressionable lately. Looking back, he realized he didn't need to kill Mitch, but these days, when Tre got something in his head, it latched on and consumed him. And for the past few days, Tre was having compulsive thoughts about his future with CiCi.

He had convinced himself that she would love him if Dex was out of the way. And then he even started to believe that CiCi wanted him to remove Dex from their lives so they could be together. These delusional thoughts came frequently, and Tre was easily swayed by them.

Therefore, after thinking it over, Tre realized that his problem with Mitch's body in the bunker was not really a problem at all. Tre now believed that he didn't need the bunker anymore. He would be staying in the penthouse with CiCi as soon as Dex was out of the way. So before he left the bunker one last time, he cleaned his gun, grabbed his ammo, and gathered the rest of his cash. Then, he made his way to a secluded spot outside the hotel entrance to wait for CiCi to come home.

Tre knew CiCi would arrive with Dex, but he was unprepared for the closeness he saw between them as they exited the back of the Town Car and entered the hotel. He grimaced at Dex's arm around *his* CiCi and was more than a little miffed that she clearly entertained his affection. Seeing her just then with Dex and looking so chummy, Tre had a sinking feeling that his CiCi might be too far gone.

"He's all wrong for her, and she knows it. She told me so at the lodge, and here she is with him again. I just don't understand her lies and betrayal."

Tre was confused and hurt by CiCi's obvious feelings for Dex. At one time, Tre's plan was to surprise CiCi, and she would be so thrilled that he came for her and that he still loved her. But now her blatant affection for Dex had him rattled, and Tre began to feel his broken heart turning stone cold. While he would always have a special love for CiCi deep inside, Tre was a man who could not forgive. So when he saw CiCi with Dex, reality hit him hard and imploded all of the delusional dreams he had formed. Tre was now in revenge mode.

Tre took some time to collect his thoughts and decide his course of action, which had now changed. His obsessive love had completely dissipated, and he felt more anger towards CiCi than any other feeling. He was so distressed because he thought he had his plan all set until he saw her, and she disappointed him.

"I still have to take care of that prick, Dex, so that will be the first order of business," Tre said to himself. And then he fell into a deep, depressed mood. His anger for CiCi hit him hard once more, and he found himself wondering how she could be with an asshole like Dex. His disdain for her grew even more when he thought about how she had tricked him, seduced him, and now betrayed him. Had he only been a diversion until she made up with Dex? Did she use him to get Dex back? These troubling thoughts were eroding Tre's fond memories of CiCi, and he was beginning to see her as disloyal, and Tre despised disloyalty more than any other deception.

"I can't believe I've wasted so much time for such little reward," Tre thought.

He gathered his things and headed for the lobby door. This time, he was entering the hotel like he owned it again, not like a criminal sneaking into the side entrance. And this time he was going to live in the penthouse again where he belonged. But first, he had to deal with a couple of nagging problems.

Walking through the lobby, Tre had one more detail to work out: Should he make it quick and clean, or did these two deserve something slow and painful? That question was still on his mind as he entered the elevator. He had made this trip so many times in the past, and he was looking forward to a future that included this luxury. Amid other thoughts racing through his head, Tre finally made up his mind regarding his prior dilemma. He used his passcode once again, and the elevator hummed its way to the top floor. And as he slowly ascended, Tre felt revenge running deep in his veins. When he was almost to the top, Tre smiled and thought to himself—"I'm back!"

Chapter 31

Dex was feeling much better after returning to the safety of the penthouse. Now he was able to concentrate on CiCi's suggestion for passing some time while the Feds did their thing.

"So, what plans do you have for us?" Dex said, grabbing CiCi around the waist, and kissing her in that way he knew she loved.

"Well, *that* was a nice start," CiCi confirmed, kissing him again deeply and passionately.

"I think I'm beginning to understand your plans," Dex said with a smile while leading her out on the spacious terrace overlooking magnificent Sin City.

"I fulfilled my penthouse fantasy in the shower, but you, my dear, have not fulfilled yours."

CiCi's eyes lit up as she followed Dex out, and he settled in the chaise lounge. She immediately took her place, straddling on top. It was just starting to get dark, and the skyline was just enough romantic light. CiCi pulled her blouse over her head, revealing a sexy lace bralette that exposed just enough of her nipples to make Dex pull her to him and reward her with eager kisses on her neck.

When the familiar 'ping' of the elevator door sounded, they each scrambled out of the lounger, thinking Mac and Aria had arrived unannounced. Fumbling with her blouse, trying to get it back on, they heard a menacing and familiar voice.

"Yes, please put that back on, CiCi. I never pictured you to be a common whore, until now," Tre said gruffly.

Dex and CiCi were paralyzed with fear. They were completely cornered out on the terrace, and as Tre came closer, they noticed the pistol in his hand. Neither one knew what to say, so they stood there, helpless and afraid.

"Aren't you going to do anything to defend your woman?" Tre said, taunting Dex. "Some man you are. Really, CiCi, we decided you could do better. Remember that?"

When CiCi remained silent from fear, Tre's anger intensified, and he walked closer.

"I asked you a question. Do you remember that?" Tre said forcefully and with intense anger.

"Yes," CiCi forced, knowing not answering would only make their situation worse.

"Well then, you probably remember the nights we spent together, talking and making plans. Am I right?"

"Yes," she said again, backing away as Tre continued to move closer.

"And I have one more question. Do you remember how you couldn't get enough of me…fucking you…all night long?"

Tears began to roll down CiCi's face. She hated answering such a disgusting question, and she struggled with telling him what he wanted to hear or saying what was on her mind. Before she could answer, Dex piped up.

"Leave her alone!" he said with sheer hatred in his voice. Dex hated this man with all his being, and even with a gun in his hand, Dex couldn't let this monster assault CiCi this way.

Tre slowly turned his gaze to Dex, and the evil scowl on his face was terrifying, but Dex stood his ground. If he was going to die, he would do so, protecting CiCi from this horrible man.

❖ ❖ ❖

Mac and Aria led the Feds to Tre's manhole, and they carefully surveyed the area before descending. Right away, they saw Mitch Henning dead on the floor, and Agent Mankle went over to confirm the inevitable.

"He's been dead for several hours."

"Looking around, they could see Tre had accessed his safe and its contents were empty.

"Well, he's obviously out there somewhere, armed and equipped with whatever else was in this safe," Aria added.

"The good news is, he has an agenda that will keep him close to us," Mac replied. "Let's head back to The Palace. That's about the only other place he would need to be."

Suddenly, a wave of terror consumed Aria.

"Cici and Dex are back there alone!" she said, quickly making her way back to the ladder leading out of the bunker. Aria was manically running at a pace no one else could keep. Her mother's heart told her CiCi was in danger— grave danger.

❖ ❖ ❖

Tre didn't appreciate Dex's confrontation and thought about killing him right then, but realized he hit a nerve when he spoke of his brief but steamy time with Dex's precious CiCi. So Tre did what Tre does so well. He put fuel on the fire and then stood back and watched it burn.

"Oh, I'm sorry. Did I hurt your feelings when I mentioned the fact that I fucked your girlfriend?" Tre added.

"Stop, please," CiCi asked calmly, considering the circumstances.

"I was trying to be a gentleman, unlike you, who left her and her friends at the lodge. See, me fucking her brains out that first night was *your* fault."

"Please, please stop," CiCi was more frantic this time.

"She was afraid to go up to her room. She was afraid of *you* and wanted nothing to do with *you*—so much so that she went home with me—a stranger she barely knew."

"Shut up!" Dex yelled. He had enough.

"Oh, I see I'm still hitting nerves," Tre bragged. "Well, as I said, I was going to be a gentleman, but as you know, she's so fucking sexy, and she was so fucking horny. Well, you get it, right?"

Dex was like a wild animal, leaping on his prey. Fueled by hatred and adrenaline, he knocked Tre down, but not before Tre fired a bullet into Dex's gut.

CiCi screamed as Tre scrambled up off the terrace floor to grab her and stop her from running. Dex lay there, wide-eyed and in disbelief. He was shot and lost a lot of blood. He was certain he was going to die. He locked eyes with CiCi, telling her without words that he loved her and that he was sorry he didn't keep her safe. CiCi, now restrained by Tre, watched as Dex's eyes got heavier and heavier. She heaved and sobbed as she watched them close.

Aria, Mac, and the Feds were just entering The Palace when they heard the gunshot and a horrifying scream. Aria and Mac knew what was happening just above them and were desperate to get to the penthouse.

Holding CiCi from behind, subduing her, and muffling her screams, Tre felt her body surrender after Dex closed his eyes. She went limp, and she no longer cared what happened to her because Dex was gone.

Tre was disappointed in her reaction, and then he noticed something that enraged him beyond any level he knew before. When he saw CiCi's engagement ring, Tre unleashed an anger that even surprised him.

"You fucking Bitch! You were going to MARRY him?" Tre roared. And with cat-like reflexes, he switched positions and was now facing her and grabbing her around the throat with his free hand.

CiCi was powerless. She could feel Tre's tight grip compressing more and more, and she could feel her throat constricting her oxygen. Despite her efforts to break free, she could tell Tre was inching her closer and closer to the terrace rail. When she felt her back up against it, she began to think it might be better if Tre sent her over the edge. Dex was dead, and she knew she would never recover from losing him. But then CiCi thought of her parents, who would be devastated, and she didn't wish that misery on them—that would be too selfish. Therefore, she had no choice. CiCi began resisting again, but he was lifting her, and she could feel her feet rising off the floor. She struggled to kick and find the rail with her foot to get some resistance toward Tre's obvious agenda.

CiCi heard the 'ping' of the elevator, and she was overcome with both joy and dread. If her parents were coming in, they would be falling into her terror and Tre's revenge.

Mac instantly saw Tre holding his daughter by the throat, dangerously close to pushing her over the rail.

"Federal agents! Drop the weapon and put your hands up!" Agent Rice yelled.

Mac, too driven by personal emotions, never ceased his advance toward Tre, preventing Agent Rice and Agent Mankle from pursuing their target.

"Mac! Get back," Agent Mankle warned.

But Mac was too fixated on saving his daughter and continued his path.

"Stop right there," Tre said, coldly. "You know I give no fucks about shooting you right now."

Mac's steady advance told Tre he was going to have to make a decision, and it was only a matter of seconds before his decision was made.

When Tre's gun fired, Aria screamed and dropped to her knees. Now Mac lay slumped next to Dex with two fatal slugs in his chest. This whole scene was so unbelievable. But Tre still had CiCi, and Aria didn't have time to mourn, or she would lose everything to the man who had already taken so much from her.

Seeing her dad's dead body next to Dex made CiCi wild with panic. Tre tightened his grip on her throat, turned to her, and said his final sinister words.

"You ruined it. You ruined it."

Directly after, Agent Rice finally got a safe shot and pumped two bullets into Tre, causing him to let go of CiCi, who was teetering on the rail. As she fell, time seemed to slow, and despite Aria's efforts to catch her daughter before she fell, CiCi began her fatal descent with unbelievable fear in her eyes. Aria was helpless and could only watch her daughter's wide, pleading eyes in horror as she fell.

❖ ❖ ❖

Aria shot straight up in bed. Dripping wet with sweat, she frantically looked beside her and, to her relief, saw Mac sleeping peacefully. She ripped off the covers and ran into the nursery to find baby CiCi lying comfortably on her side with her thumb still in her mouth, fast asleep.

Aria dropped to her knees and wept tears of joy. Her husband and baby were safe. It took every ounce of willpower to fight off the urge to wake them both, grab them, kiss them, and hold them tightly in her arms. She was so relieved that her perfect little family was still intact.

Aria had been asleep for nearly twenty-four hours. The relaxation she felt after her passionate night of lovemaking and wine, paired with her total exhaustion, put her into a deep sleep that initiated a very vivid, extremely real nightmare. The trouble with these nightmares was that they eventually played out in real life, and if this was the case, Aria had just escaped her horrifying experience only to live her life waiting for it to manifest in the future. Aria thought there was no way this vision had any ambiguity. All parts were vivid and clear. It was like living in the future, and it scared the hell out of her.

Chapter 32

It took a long time for Aria to recover from her horrific nightmare. She had a lot of questions about people and events that happened because they were all so detailed and realistic.

How does my mind just know all these people and places from the future?

How can I have such a vivid dream that spans years in one day's time?

These questions and others often plagued Aria in the weeks right after the dream, but Mac told her that her terrifying visions and the events that played out were most likely intensified and altered by her stress level, exaggerating the ordeal. Deep down, he was just as freaked out as she was, but he had to keep her calm and help her believe what she witnessed was by no means actually coming true someday.

Not completely convinced of Mac's explanation, Aria consulted her doctor and asked about the medication she took that she once thought had no effect on her. To her surprise, the doctor confirmed that one of the side effects is intense, vivid dreams that seem eerily real. Aria also shared her ability with her doctor, and this fact made the doctor even more convinced that the medication had a unique and extreme effect on Aria.

Nightmares & Premonitions

Plus, the doctor explained that Aria's life had been filled with intense danger for quite some time, and now that the danger was over, her mind might be resisting. When Aria thought about it, her doctor was right. She now had no worries in her life. Tre Halprin was dead, and despite some crazy theory about his kidney affecting Christopher Paloma's behavior, Aria felt safe knowing the parameters of medical science were on her side. Therefore, as time went on, Aria let go of some of the most horrific parts of her dream, trying to convince herself that a medical professional had even concluded that her dream was drug-induced. When she was able to dismiss those unimaginable parts, Aria's mind calmed, and her life somewhat returned to normal.

❖ ❖ ❖

A couple of months after Aria's vivid and terrifying dream, Calysta decided to have a party at CiCi's Way to celebrate with friends and family. As she often did, Calysta threw this party for no particular reason except to have fun and enjoy life.

Mallory, Jason, and the boys were all coming, as well as Aria, Mac and baby CiCi. And, of course, the entire extended family would attend, including Mac's parents, Aaron and Maria, and Glen and Cheryl. All the guests enjoyed music and dancing and lots of food and drinks. Calysta had even rented a specialty coffee and hot chocolate truck and a cookie and dessert truck as extra special treats. Everyone agreed that no one threw a party better than Calysta.

Although Aria was having a wonderful time, she always felt a little uneasy at events where Christopher was present, and this made her feel horrible. But she had endured so much trauma at his hands in her horrible dream, and those events still seemed like reality to Aria. So when Christopher startled her in the kitchen while she was heating CiCi's bottle, Aria was frightened, and her anxiousness was impossible to hide.

"Oh, Christopher! I didn't know you were here," Aria said, trying to act natural.

Christopher was silent, making their meeting even more uncomfortable. Finally, Christopher cracked an innocent smile and apologized for startling her.

> "I'm so sorry," he began. "It seems I scare you even when I don't mean to."

Aria thought that was an odd comment. Did that mean he sometimes tried to scare her on purpose? Aria thought she might be reading too much into his words, but nonetheless, she wasn't sure she liked where this odd conversation was going.

"It's fine," she managed as Christopher stared directly at her with a queer little smirk on his face.

"You look tired, Mrs. Brunner. Are you sleeping well these days?" he questioned and then countered his comment with a common and logical reason for Aria's condition. "I mean... with a baby keeping you awake and all."

Aria now felt cornered and threatened. She reminded herself that he was just a fourteen-year-old boy trying to be polite.

"I'm fine. Thanks," she managed as she finished preparing the bottle and rushed out the door to go feed CiCi.

The rest of the night, Aria was fixated on Christopher, but as she watched him, nothing alarming happened. It seemed so strange to Aria that Christopher now behaved quite normally and befitting for his age when she had witnessed such odd behavior when they were alone. Without any additional incidents that night, Aria dismissed her strange encounter with him in the kitchen and went back to enjoying the party.

With the band playing in the background and an abundance of great conversation, everyone agreed this party was a welcome pause in the course of their busy lives. As it was getting dark, no one was particularly anxious to leave, so Calysta extended the celebration of friends and family beyond her original intent.

As the sun sank deep into the horizon, the crisp autumn air descended on the partygoers and made the night especially chilly. Calysta had fires in the outdoor fireplaces, but Aria worried that CiCi would get croupy if she were exposed to too much damp night air. Therefore, Aria decided to take her in, get her ready for bed, and lay her down in the crib Calysta set up in the room off the foyer. Once baby CiCi was fast asleep, Aria returned to the party, telling Calysta's housemaid to let her know if CiCi woke or needed tending.

After returning to the party, Aria joined Mac's conversation with Jason and Mallory. They were all having a wonderful time, and Mallory brought up the subject of maybe having another baby.

"I have to admit," Mallory began, "seeing your cute little CiCi has my Mommy instincts going wild. I think I might need another baby, Jason. She's just adorable."

"Thank you," Aria gushed. "But she can be a little pistol."

"Oh, who cares. She's such a cutie!" Jason added. "I love my boys, but I kinda always wanted a little girl, too."

"I think the boys wouldn't mind us having another," Mallory said.

"But Christopher is nearly fourteen. Maybe it's silly of us," Jason responded.

"My girls are my entire world," Mac said, kissing Aria on the forehead as she lay secure in his arms.

"Speaking of that," Aria interrupted. "I need to go check on the little darling. It's been a while."

"Oh, please let me," Mallory asked.

"Okay, if you don't mind."

"Oh, I'd love to!"

"And I'll come with you," Jason said enthusiastically.

Aria sat back down with her pumpkin spice coffee and nestled into Mac's arms.

"They seem excited about watching a baby sleep," Mac said, laughing a little.

"Hey, if they want to go check on her, so be it. That just means a little more time with you and this delicious coffee. Calysta spoils us, you know that, right?" Aria stated, taking another sip.

Mallory and Jason were thrilled to help with baby CiCi, and when they neared the doorway, they could hear her cooing and giggling, which warmed their hearts even more. But when they saw the reason CiCi was in such a good mood, they were even more overwhelmed with love and joy.

Christopher had made his way into the room and taken CiCi out of her bed where he was playing with her on the floor. Her giggles and little bursts of all-out laughter at Christopher's gentle play were so cute that Mallory and Jason just stood in the doorway and watched, debunking their fears that Christopher would be put off by having a baby brother or sister at his age.

"See how good he is with her?" Mallory said proudly.

"Yes, he's quite good," Jason confirmed.

And they just stood back and listened to their son pacify and entertain baby CiCi by playing a game where Christopher tickled her tummy, and CiCi would clap her hands and squeal for more.

"You're *my* CiCi," Christopher said, grabbing her belly over and over.

"*My* CiCi...*my* CiCi..." Christopher repeated playfully.

"I think she likes you, Christopher," Jason said as the two continued to play.

After thinking about it for a moment, Christopher responded.

"I don't understand it, but this little girl has captured my heart."

While Mallory and Jason thought that was a peculiar comment coming from their fourteen-year-old son, they also thought it was about the sweetest thing in the world, and they continued to watch the two play and laugh as a bond began to form. And little did anyone know, that bond would last a lifetime.

Part II:
The Future Plays Out

Chapter 33

It had been several years since Aria's troubling dream that left her husband, her only child, CiCi, and the love of CiCi's life dead. It was safe to say life as usual moved along, and even though Christopher Paloma once gave Aria a bad vibe, he had actually grown into a healthy, handsome, and accomplished young man. At twenty-seven years old, he owned his own business as a hunting a fishing guide in northern Wisconsin. Aria was a bit troubled by the odd coincidence of Christopher's location but had begun to realize that, once again, real life was playing out quite differently than her horrid nightmares.

Mallory, Jason, and the boys were a huge part of Aria and Mac's lives, and CiCi grew up knowing the Paloma brothers were not only some of her best protectors and friends—they were also like family. At age fourteen, CiCi felt as if Christopher, 27, Jeffery, 23, and Douglas, 20, were the big brothers she never had. But there was one more Paloma brother that Mallory and Jason were inspired to have after an intense bout of 'baby-fever' CiCi caused thirteen years prior. Despite their extreme desire to have a little girl, the Palomas welcomed Dexter Robert into the world and accepted their fate that the Palomas were a family of men.

CiCi was a year older than Dex, but they were in the same class at school. Apparently, Dexter was wicked smart and accelerated through his first year. Being so close with the Palomas and Calysta, CiCi spent an enormous amount of time with all the Paloma boys growing up, but her age made her the closest with Dexter. All through junior high and high school, CiCi and Dex were the best of friends, but there was never anything romantic between them. Dex dated Pixie Jones for most of his high school years, and CiCi more or less played the field with no serious contenders.

When it came time to head off to college, both CiCi and Dex headed to Millikin University in Decatur, Illinois. Pixie, however, was off to Stanford, which was the end of her relationship with Dex. He spent a short couple of days mourning his loss, and then Dex decided to enjoy his college experience, which included meeting lots of girls.

At the end of their freshman year, both Dex and CiCi went home to Peoria for the summer, where they both got jobs as lifeguards at the pool at CiCi's Way. While they remained close friends at Millikin, CiCi and Dex would go several days without seeing one another. Now that they were back home and especially because they were working together at the pool, Dex and CiCi were back to being best friends—or maybe a little more.

Both Dex and CiCi had fun that first year of college, partying, meeting new friends, and hooking up with a few people as well, but neither one could say they had anyone they were particularly interested in. CiCi always thought Dex had a nice body, but the first day he showed up to work and pulled off his t-shirt, CiCi was stunned by his smooth, tan torso and rock-hard abs. For the first time ever, Dex Paloma had given her goosebumps, and what a strange feeling it was.

Before leaving Millikin, Dex wondered if Pixie would be home for the summer, and even though he had not heard from her in months, he thought maybe she would be down for a little summer fun. But two weeks into the summer break, there was no sign of Pixie, so Dex decided he would have to look elsewhere for his summer activities.

"Part of me really wanted Pixie to come home," Dex admitted.

"Let me guess which part…your dick," CiCi answered with an ornery grin.

"Very funny…true, but very funny," Dex replied, a little embarrassed.

Just like CiCi was a bit shocked by Dex's ab reveal, Dex also noticed CiCi in a way he had never done so before. The uniform swimsuit was nothing revealing or sexy, but he had to admit, CiCi did that thing justice. His favorite part of the day was when CiCi finished swimming laps during their break, and no matter how hot it was outside, her tiny pinpoint nipples would poke through her suit, giving him a hard-on every time.

As the summer progressed, CiCi and Dex began flirting more and more, but now the summer was coming to a close. It was time for Dex and CiCi to make plans to return to Millikin, and for some reason, CiCi grew sullen.

"What's the matter with you?' Dex asked, noticing her blue mood.

"Nothing," she lied.

"Seriously, what's wrong?" Dex pressed.

"It's kinda stupid, but I'll miss you."

Dex had a little flutter right in the middle of his chest, and despite her despair, he thought her comment was the cutest thing ever.

"What do you mean? We're going to the same place."

"You know what I mean. I see you every day here, and when we get to school—not so much."

Dex was brimming with joy. For quite some time, he had been developing feelings for CiCi, but they had been friends for so long that changing the dynamic of their relationship seemed scary and risky. Now, he could tell CiCi was feeling some of the same things, and this reality made him extra brave.

Dexter bent down to where his face was dangerously close to CiCi's and flashed a gorgeous heartbreaker smile.

"Why do you want to be around me so much, CiCi?"

Dex was still grinning, and CiCi felt as if she was being set up, but finally said, 'What the hell ' and gave a truthful and sincere answer.

"Because I like you."

"You *like* me?" Dex questioned, still smiling.

CiCi could feel her soul being snatched by his fucking sexy smile and over-the-top confidence, but she didn't give him the satisfaction he sought and muttered a simple 'Yes' without elaborating.

With his face still inches from hers, Dex looked from her eyes to her lips, and CiCi prayed that he was going to kiss her. When Dex Paloma's lips first touched hers, CiCi went weak in the knees, and Dex literally grabbed her in a firm embrace.

The kiss was long and passionate, and neither one wanted it to ever end. But when they finally opened their eyes, they were different. They were now a couple. Neither one could explain how twenty-one years of nothing but friendship turned into a fiery, hot romance with one kiss, but neither one was complaining either.

CiCi knew Dex had been intimate with Pixie and probably a few girls from school, and she worried that her inexperience would bore him. She had hooked up with a couple of guys her first year at college, but CiCi was still a virgin. Until now, she was pretty proud of that accomplishment. Something inside her made it very clear that Dex would be her first. And while that thought made CiCi's mind wander down a pleasant path, she feared that he would be disappointed in her lack of experience. For this reason, CiCi began avoiding intimate situations, eventually putting a strain on their blossoming romance.

Dex, however, was completely smitten. All of CiCi's worries and insecurities were the furthest thoughts from his mind. He was happy just spending time with her. She had always been his best friend, but now that friendship was enhanced with true love, and he couldn't be happier. He did, however, long for more of a sexual relationship, but he also wanted CiCi to be ready for that step in their lives.

Back at Millikin, no one was really surprised that CiCi and Dex had upgraded their status. Most of their friends thought it would happen sooner. When the first semester of their sophomore year was nearing an end, Dex and CiCi, and four of their friends, began planning a snowmobiling trip up North where Dex's oldest brother Christopher lived. Christopher always bragged about his perfect life as a wilderness guide and his permanent placement at White Tail Lodge & Resort. Year-round, Christopher lived in a cabin at the resort where vacationers hired him to take them fishing, hunting, hiking, or snowmobiling.

When CiCi mentioned their plans to head up North and stay at Christopher's lodge for a few days before Christmas, Aria's heart dropped. It had been years since her terrifying nightmare, but the mere thought of her daughter going snowmobiling in Wisconsin over her winter break had Aria's senses on high alert.

Nightmares & Premonitions

"Why Wisconsin? Go somewhere warm with sand," Aria suggested.

CiCi didn't think her mom had a bad idea, but Dex and the others were dead set on the trip North, so finally, Aria had to have a heart-to-heart with her daughter. Aria never understood how her Grandma Tess knew of her abilities even before she had ever had a visionary dream. But the night of Aria's first dream while staying at her grandparents' house in Rockford, her Grandma Tess spoke as if she had been waiting for Aria's first vision.

When Aria had CiCi, she knew right away that she passed this peculiar ability to her child. It was unexplainable but obvious, and Aria felt as if this was how her grandmother knew as well. Aria had mixed feelings about passing on this insight, knowing firsthand that having these premonitions was a constant source of stress and worry. Then again, Aria couldn't deny that there had been several times the premonitions gave her the foresight necessary to approach perilous situations more prepared. Aria knew that this was her chance to not only tell CiCi about her unrealized abilities but also a way to possibly sway her daughter's mind regarding her winter break plans.

"CiCi," Aria began, "have you ever had a dream or nightmare that seemed unbelievably real?"

CiCi was confused at first because this question was so random, but the truth was that CiCi had such a nightmare recently. Even though the nightmare was horrifying, she had not mentioned it to her mother, thinking it was an isolated incident that had no real significance in her actual life. CiCi was at school with Dex when it happened, and once her initial terror was quelled, she put the unpleasant situation aside and went on with life. But there was something about her mother's demeanor that sent up a little red flag for CiCi, and she was not at all a fan of the dull flutter inside her stomach as she formulated her answer.

"Yes, how did you know that?"

Aria's heart sank just a little as she received the answer. For the next two hours, mother and daughter had their most crucial heart-to-heart ever as Aria explained the peculiar gift Grandma Tess continued to pass on from generation to generation. For CiCi, this explanation cleared up several odd situations that had occurred throughout her life but also instilled a dense fear of the future.

CiCi had heard the story of how her parents met, but now, knowing her mother's abilities, it all made perfect sense. It was time to reveal her dream to her mother. CiCi had not thought of it in quite a while, and now, knowing that she would live out this dream in some capacity terrified her.

"Let me tell you about a dream I had shortly after I returned to school in the fall," CiCi began.

Chapter 34

Their wedding was magical, and CiCi was on cloud nine, celebrating the promise of a wonderful future with her best friend and the love of her life. Like her parents, CiCi opted for a Las Vegas wedding, but the venue was not a simple wedding chapel. CiCi and Dex had the luxury of celebrating with family and friends in the grand ballroom at The Palace Hotel. The ceremony was over, and it was official. CiCi was Mrs. Dexter Robert Paloma. There was nothing else she wanted more on this earth. It was a dream come true.

Dexter was also elated that the woman of his dreams was now his wife. The day had a hectic schedule, but now he was dancing the first dance with his bride without a care in the world. His parents were so happy and so proud. They were, however, concerned about their oldest son, Christopher. He had been hospitalized just prior to the wedding with his recurring headaches and was not able to attend. Christopher had spent his life tortured by headaches and voices in his head. When he was *good*, Christopher was the nicest person in the world, but when he had these peculiar episodes, he seemed to be someone else entirely.

After the first dance, Christopher was supposed to deliver his Best Man speech, but this honor had been transferred to Dex's next oldest brother, Jeffery. As everyone settled in to hear the toast, a menacing disturbance began at the rear entrance of the ballroom. At first, it was just a loud door slamming, but then a terrifying vision of Christopher appeared from the darkness.

"Hello, Brother!" Christopher began.

It was obvious to all who knew of Christopher's ailment that he was not *Christopher*. He was being controlled by that dark entity no one understood. CiCi was terrified, and she moved even closer to Dex as Christopher continued his slow trek towards the head table.

Mac was on high alert. He didn't want to overreact too soon, but Aria could tell he was ready to spring into action any second. And Mallory and Jason Paloma were on the edges of their seats, knowing the unpredictability of their son in his current state.

As they all watched, Christopher maintained his deliberate journey into the center of the room. And when he spoke again, the entire room held their breath.

"CiCi, don't you look lovely," he began innocently enough.

But Christopher's cordial demeanor was short-lived, and in his next breath, he delivered a shockingly inappropriate comment.

"Mmmm," Christopher moaned. "Well, CiCi, you...you just look good enough to fuck."

With those words, Mac and Dex both sprang into action. Dex, addressing his brother first.

"Get out! You know you can't be here when you're like this," Dex yelled.

Christopher stopped his pursuit toward the table, seeing Mac on his feet and knowing that even though it was his daughter's wedding, there was a .45 in his shoulder holster beneath that tuxedo jacket. He couldn't, however, stop himself from making another crude comment.

"What?" he began innocently. "I was just stating the obvious. But then again, my CiCi always looks delicious."

With those words, Mac leaped in Christopher's direction and tackled him. Falling on the floor, Christopher didn't resist. He only laughed a sinister sneer that reverberated throughout the room. It wasn't long and Mac had him up on his feet, escorting him out, and Jason had called an ambulance.

At first, Christopher seemed to be calmly subdued as he waited in a private room for the ambulance with his father and Mac. Dex had taken CiCi up to the penthouse. Due to the disturbing interruption, the reception was cut short. CiCi was in shock and distraught. She had always loved all of the Paloma brothers, and at one time, she was awfully close with Christopher. She knew he had some problems, but he had never been so rude, and she didn't understand why he would ruin her wedding reception. CiCi was understandably distraught, so Dex helped her out of her gown and into bed to rest.

When he could tell CiCi was calm and resting, Dex decided to head down to the main floor and see what was going on with Christopher. Dex was extremely close with his oldest brother and used to his episodes, but this one was so much worse than any of the others. This one was a personal assault on CiCi, and Dex was livid.

Dex always knew Christopher had an unnatural attraction to CiCi, but it was usually limited to being protective. But this one was sexual and depraved, and Dex worried for his new wife's safety. Christopher was tall and muscular, and his alternative personality was capable of doing great harm—Dex had seen it firsthand.

When Dex finally found his father and Mac, he could tell something was wrong. He had gotten to know Mac pretty well, and that frantic pacing was a sure sign that he was worried or pissed or a combination of the two. Dex quickened his pace and addressed his father.

"What's wrong? Where's Christopher?"

Mac was still pacing, and he saw dread in his father's face. Before he could answer, Dex spoke again. This time more forcefully and frantically.

"I said, where's Christopher!"

Jason Paloma had no choice but to answer, but he knew what he had to say would be difficult for Dex to hear.

"He escaped from the EMTs."

"Escaped? So, you mean he's out there somewhere where he could hurt CiCi?"

Dexter was livid.

"Dex, you know Christopher thinks the world of CiCi. He wouldn't hurt her."

"But he's not Christopher at the moment. You heard him! You heard what he said about her!"

As if it was planned, all three men realized that if Christopher was on the loose and they were all together, that left CiCi alone and unprotected.

"Where's CiCi?" Mac asked with wide eyes.

Dex's heart sank, and before he could answer, he was on the run.

"Shit! She's resting up in the penthouse."

Mac and Jason were on his heels as they headed for the private elevator that opened up into the main living space.

When they reached the private elevator, they could tell right away it had been disabled, and all three instinctively headed for the main elevators.

"These elevators don't go all the way to the penthouse. We'll have to take the stairs after we get as far as we can go."

Mac's nervousness had disappeared, and he was on full auto pilot, racing out of the elevator doors and heading for the stairwell with Jason and Dex right behind him.

Arriving at the penthouse, Mac was disgusted when he learned that the door was locked from the inside, indicating a very disturbing fact—someone had gone in and locked it.

"Dex, do you have a pass key?"

"No, I always use the private elevator entrance."

Mac didn't waste time worrying about such a minor detail. He pulled out his .45 and shot the keypad, disarming its lock.

When they rushed inside, their worst fears came true. Christopher had CiCi by the neck from behind, leading her to the outdoor terrace. When the door burst open, CiCi screamed, and Christopher turned around, tightening his grip on her.

"Christopher! Stop it. What are you doing?" Dex yelled frantically.

He's not Christopher, remember?" Mac said boldly, staring straight into Tre's evil eyes.

A sinister smile formed on Tre's face. He was elated to finally be face to face with the man who delivered his fate. Tre couldn't help but notice Mac held the same .45 he stared down in St. Lucia in his final moments. Tre would recognize that gun anywhere.

"Well, well. Just as I thought," Tre began. "Daddy is here to save his little girl."

Mac had begun his determined pursuit across the room. He headed straight for Tre to free his daughter from the most evil man he had ever known. CiCi was struggling and wide-eyed as she looked helplessly at Dex. That was it. Dex also began making his way toward the man who had consumed his brother's body and mind and who had his new wife at his mercy.

"Let her go!" Dex screamed.

Before Mac or Dex could reach CiCi, Tre had her dangling on the edge of the rail, stopping them in their tracks.

"Don't come any closer, or I'll throw her over this rail and watch her pleading eyes all the way down!" Tre yelled.

Out of nowhere, a gunshot resounded, and time stood still. Tre loosened his grip on CiCi, and he began a slow slump toward the floor. Without Tre's supporting hand, CiCi teetered on the rail and suddenly became aware that she was slipping over the side. Dex watched helplessly as his new wife became dangerously close to falling twenty-four floors to her death.

Dex rushed to the edge of the rail, grabbing CiCi's arm with one hand and lunging desperately to grab her around the waist with the other. He wasn't quite sure how he managed such a feat, but she was safe. CiCi, the love of his life, his new wife, was safe in his arms, and his brother was dead at his feet.

❖ ❖ ❖

"And then I woke up," CiCi explained.

Aria sat there stunned at the detail her daughter had relayed. Worst of all, CiCi's dream made it clear to Aria that their dealings with Tre Halprin were most likely not over.

Chapter 35

CiCi absolutely loved Dex's brothers, and she had always had an especially close relationship with Christopher, but since her dream and her mother's explanation of their shared gift, CiCi's affection for Christopher had cooled considerably. Now that her mother had shared her vision that occurred in the Wisconsin woods, CiCi was also leery about the winter break trip. She wasn't ready to unload everything she had learned from her mother about their abilities to Dex, so it was difficult for her to explain why she was hesitant to go. Consequently, this situation created a huge roadblock in Dex and CiCi's relationship.

"CiCi, you're avoiding me and any situation we might have to be *together*. I don't understand why. I've never pressured you. That's not why I love you," Dex said, a little frustrated.

CiCi knew he had a point, but she just didn't know how she could explain everything she had just learned when she didn't understand it all herself. She thought she would tell him what she knew to be true.

"My parents aren't too keen about me going up there. I'm not even sure they would let me," CiCi said softly, looking down, knowing she was disappointing him.

"I don't understand that at all, CiCi. Our parents are best friends. They know me," he pleaded. And then he said something that nearly broke her heart.

"I'm sorry, but this all seems like an excuse to me. It's situations like this one that make me think that I must love you more than you'll ever love me. If you keep trying to find ways not to be alone with me, you obviously don't think I'm the one for you."

CiCi wanted to dispel his fears, and she wanted to tell him the truth, but she just couldn't find the words, so she stood there, speechless, as she watched Dex's eyes pleading for a response. When her words continued to fail her, Dex finally turned and walked off, and the heartbreak of two young lovers hung heavy in the air.

CiCi cried for two days before she had the nerve to reach out to Dex, but once she did, she wished she hadn't. When CiCi arrived at Dex's house off campus, she could tell there was a party, and Dex had not even invited her.

Nonetheless, CiCi walked up the steps and onto the porch, where the door was open, and she walked in. When she left her apartment for Dex's just a few minutes prior, she hoped to straighten out a mess she had made, but when she saw her friend Miley sitting on a very jovial Dex's lap, she realized her mess had developed into something larger, and CiCi was broken. CiCi stood there in disbelief, and when she locked eyes with Dex, he felt all the life drain out of his body. It looked bad, really bad, and Dex knew it. It had only been two days. They didn't even break up, and here he was, hitting on another girl.

When CiCi turned to leave, she felt numb inside, but she moved quite quickly from distraught to enraged and found her words when Dex jumped up, raced to her, and grabbed her arm to stop her from leaving.

"CiCi, stop!" Dex pleaded, grabbing her arm quite forcefully.

"NO!" she screamed as she flung her arm, freeing it from his grasp. Her eyes were fierce, and Dex let go.

The whole room was silent as CiCi turned and walked out, leaving Dex standing there, looking like an asshole.

When Miley approached him from behind to offer some *comfort*, he rudely dismissed her and headed out the door, looking for CiCi. He knew he didn't deserve her forgiveness, but he also knew he needed to talk to her. If this was the end of his relationship with the only woman he would ever want, he had to at least explain and apologize, even if his efforts were in vain.

CiCi was sporting a quick pace fueled by anger, heartbreak, and utter despair. Her mind was reeling. She had gone there to say she was sorry for making him feel so inadequate and to tell him he was the only man she'd ever love. She even thought she was ready to make love for the first time. But now, all her plans and efforts were destroyed by the sight of Miley on Dex's lap. Now she questioned if Dex loved her as much as he said he did if he could dismiss her so quickly.

CiCi made it back to her apartment before Dex caught up with her, and she was getting into her car as he ran to catch her. Dex desperately and uninhibitedly pulled out all the stops. He was certain he would never love anyone the way he loved her, and he had to make things right.

"CiCi," he said, touching her arm gently before she was able to retreat into the safety of her car.

"CiCi, I know you hate me right now, but I at least owe you an explanation and an apology. Can you please hear me out? Then, you can go wherever you want. Just, please, hear me out."

CiCi heard the desperation and sincerity in his voice, and she was suddenly curious what kind of explanation he could find for his actions, so she turned to him without words. The look on her face was one of strength, and Dex knew all too well that CiCi's independence and pride would not be in his favor. Nonetheless, he began his explanation, knowing it was very well dead in the water before he began.

"I'm sorry. I'm so sorry. I know I was wrong. But when I told you I must love you more, you couldn't say I was wrong. The fact that I love you will never change, but if you don't feel the same for me, you deserve to go find that person who makes you feel all the things I feel about you. I love you with all my heart, but if that feeling is not the same for you, it's not fair for either one of us to continue this."

CiCi was unprepared for such a heartfelt and selfless explanation. She had expected excuses and blame-throwing. Instead, he bore his soul, and it pained her heart because she knew this ordeal was not entirely his fault.

"Did you sleep with her?"

"No, I didn't even kiss her," Dex disclosed, moving a little closer, feeling the tension lifting slightly.

CiCi knew she should be satisfied with his answer but had to stretch her questioning further.

"If I hadn't shown up, would you have slept with her?"

Dex could have given her the easy answer that satisfied her curiosity with no other doubts, but he had to be honest.

"I don't know," he said, a little ashamed. "But I do know if that would have happened, I would have been very drunk, and it would be because I was missing you and heartbroken. I know that sounds cheesy and maybe calculated, but it's true. And you deserve the truth."

CiCi's heart was softening, and she respected his honesty. Besides, she had gone there to make sure he had no doubts about her affection. Dex Paloma was her one true love, and now it was time for her to deliver some honesty of her own.

"Let's go inside and talk."

Although it was uncomfortable at first, CiCi unloaded all of her insecurities about her inexperience, and even though she had shared this information to some extent before, this time, she made it clear that her fears were very real, not just excuses to keep from being intimate. And when Dex tried to assume some of the responsibility for her feelings, she stopped him.

"No, you've never been anything but patient and understanding. This problem is my own, and I know I need to work on it."

Dex moved to her, wrapped his arms around her waist, and pulled her close.

"You don't have to work on anything. I love you just the way you are," he said, kissing her sweetly.

CiCi's hard facade began to crumble, and she could feel a tear forming, which Dex tenderly wiped away.

"I have to tell you something I should have said before instead of standing there dumbly and letting you walk away the other day."

Dex was fairly certain this disclosure would aid their repairing process, but a tiny part of him felt a crippling fear that was quickly diffused when CiCi began explaining her mother's dream and the family trait that had been passed down to her. CiCi chose her words carefully and tried to make this situation as common as possible so Dex would not think she was full-on crazy.

After she got through her mother's ominous premonition regarding their Wisconsin vacation, Dex was visibly shaken by the vivid accuracy of what they had planned.

"And your mom had this dream when you were a baby?" he asked in amazement.

"Yes, a little freaky, huh? And it's not the kind of thing most people can digest. I was terrified that you would think I was crazy."

Even though Dex was on information overload, he was so very thankful that CiCi had a legitimate reason for her distancing. And as *crazy* as CiCi and Aria's unique ability seemed, he somehow understood it and instantly worried about how these premonitions would impact their lives.

Dex pulled her in for a comforting hug and kissed her on the forehead.

"I was so worried I'd lost you forever," he said, looking deeply into her eyes. "I love you, CiCi Brunner, and I know we'll have other disagreements in the future, but I'll never stop loving you and wanting you."

This time CiCi didn't stand there dumbly, not responding. Instead, she ran her hand through his hair and kissed him with her open mouth, confirming her feelings and leaving no doubts. When the kiss ended, the two young lovers stood wrapped in each other's arms, looking into each other's eyes. Mesmerized, Dex saw something incredible he had never seen before, and before he could speak, CiCi took his hand and led him upstairs.

Dex's heart was racing a mile a minute. He was certain he saw a passion in CiCi's eyes that meant she was ready for him to make love to her. When they reached CiCi's room, she closed the door and moved with sultry precision, leading him to the bed. Dex wanted to tell her she didn't have to prove anything to him, but he knew that the look in her eyes was one of desire. CiCi was proceeding of her own free will. Now that CiCi's intentions were clear, Dex decided to take the lead.

Kissing her lovingly but growing more passionate, Dex sat on the bed and gently pulled her to him. As she stood before him, a lump formed in Dex's throat as he thought about how close he came to losing her. When CiCi began unbuttoning her blouse, Dex pulled his t-shirt over his head. He stared in wonder as she unhooked the front clasp of her bra and slowly pulled it to the sides, allowing her full, gorgeous breasts to fall perfectly before his eyes.

Without hesitation, Dex cupped them in his hands and then began teasing her nipples until they were the rock-hard pinpoints he loved seeing so much at the pool last summer. CiCi moaned lightly, throwing her head back arching to meet Dex's hungry kisses. Finally, Dex stood and gave her mouth the same eager attention while he unbuttoned his jeans and let them fall. CiCi immediately slipped her hands into his briefs and pulled them down, giving him some relief from confinement. CiCi took him in her hand and slowly and sensually stroked him.

Dex was primed, but he wanted to give CiCi the attention she deserved, so he watched as she wiggled her jeans over her curvy hips and backside. He took the back of his hand and slowly slid it down the length of her bare torso. CiCi shivered with anticipation as he passed her navel and moved on to tease her over the top of her panties. Rubbing her more intentionally now, Dex watched as CiCi closed her eyes to enjoy every stroke.

Dex moved his fingers to the top of the elastic and slowly began pulling her panties down, and CiCi eagerly helped him. Still standing, Dex sat on the edge of the bed again and pulled her to him, kissing and licking her midsection, sending shock waves through CiCi's body. When he slipped his hand between her legs. She widened her stance, inviting him to continue his pursuit. Dex wasted no time, first circling his fingers near her opening and then sliding them inside to elicit a sigh of pure pleasure from deep inside CiCi's soul. When he took his thumb and rubbed up and down on her most sensitive spot, CiCi moaned with pleasure.

To make her more comfortable, Dex ceased his actions and gently helped her onto the bed. CiCi's eyes were fixated on his, and he saw that look again, begging for him to satisfy the fire burning deep inside her. Dex cupped her face with his hand and stroked her cheek with his thumb. She was his entire world.

When CiCi pulled her knees up and spread her legs, he knew he had read that look in her eyes correctly. He kissed her, and she eagerly reached for him with her open mouth and tongue. Dex rolled on top of her and gently eased into her, causing CiCi to involuntarily hold her breath only a couple of times until he was completely inside. When Dex gently began moving in and out, he could tell CiCi had untensed her body and was now moving with his steady rhythm. Her bottom lifted off the bed to meet his every inch, and Dex let himself go to experience the most wonderful orgasm he'd ever had.

When he slipped out, his fingers rubbed her with precision, making CiCi squirm and moan. Her chest heaved as she let go, and Dex slowly decreased the pace of his fingers to match the pace of her release. He watched her enjoy every second of the electric sensations pulsing through her body. He had just made love to the woman of his dreams, and when her big blue eyes opened, they landed on his. Simultaneously, the young lovers smiled, knowing that was just one of many pleasure-filled experiences they would encounter over the course of their lives.

Chapter 36

"CiCi, there's only one way you are heading up to Wisconsin for your winter break, and that's if your mother and I go, too. End of discussion," Mac said with the authority CiCi knew not to challenge.

"Okay, then."

CiCi had never been so relieved in her life. While part of her really wanted to spend that time with Dex and her friends, another part was freaking out about her mother's ominous premonition twenty-two years ago. So many of the details had already oddly matched up, so CiCi breathed a sigh of relief when her father took such a solid stance on the issue.

CiCi knew she would have Dex there to protect her, but for CiCi, there was just something about having her mom and dad close by that eased her mind. She had heard all the stories of their battles with the Halprins, and even though it didn't seem like it on a regular day, she knew her parents were pretty badass.

Dex was fine with the Brunners tagging along, but they sensed some of their friends weren't so thrilled. CiCi didn't care one bit. With her parents close by, she knew she could relax and have a good time. With this detail confirmed, she stopped worrying and began planning. Everything was going great, and the night before they were ready to leave, the group traveled from Decatur to CiCi's parent's house in Peoria, where final preparations were made.

It was the first day of their winter break, and CiCi was relieved that her classes were finished for the week. Even though there would be plenty of time for partying at the lodge, she was in the mood to celebrate and grabbed a bottle of wine from the cooler and poured a glass.

"Watch it, young lady," her mother teased. "You should always just have a half-glass to keep your wits about you."

"Please, Mother," CiCi said, rolling her eyes. "That's just silly. Who has just a half glass?"

"I used to because I didn't want to get out of control and, you know, do things I regretted."

CiCi looked at her mother, not sure if she was kidding or not.

"Well, I'm a full-glass kind of girl," CiCi responded as she splashed a bit more into her glass.

Aria just laughed and got a glass for herself, thinking CiCi was more and more like her father every day.

If CiCi's friends had any misgivings about her parents joining them, they dissipated over the course of the evening. The game room, open bar, and media room were big hits. But as all parents do eventually, Mac had to disrupt the fun and remind everyone of their pending early start with a nine-hour drive to the lodge. Not long after, everyone dispersed to their rooms for some much-needed sleep.

The drive to White Tail was uneventful, and upon their arrival, Christopher was excited and overjoyed by their visit. He was a bit taken aback by Mac and Aria's presence at first, and the actual reason they were there really couldn't be conveyed, so Dex and CiCi just ignored Christopher's inquiries, and he finally quit asking.

The first two days of the trip were fantastic, and the Brunners wondered why they were even worried. But when Christopher didn't show up on the third morning to take the guys ice fishing, Dex went to his cabin to find him. When Dex went inside, he witnessed an all-too-familiar sight. His brother was in the throes of a grippingly painful headache that was also painful to watch. From experience, Dex grabbed a cool cloth and some menthol ointment and went to Christopher's aid. Dex first rubbed the ointment on Christopher's forehead and then on the back of his neck. When he sensed his brother experiencing some relief, Dex placed the cool rag across his eyes.

Christopher's misery was hard to watch, but Dex stayed with him until the pain subsided enough that Christopher could talk.

"Thanks, brother. I hadn't had one of those for a while."

Dex went to put the ointment away and run the wash rag under some more cold water. When he returned to Christopher's side and handed him the fresh wash rag, Dex caught a glimpse of his brother's stare that sent a disturbing tingle up his spine. Dex couldn't explain it, but in just the brief amount of time he was gone from the room, Christopher's mood had completely changed. There was also an unexplainable coldness in the room, and Dex sensed a brooding anger emanating from his older brother. Dex had never experienced such an odd feeling from his brother. But it wasn't until Christopher spoke that Dex became concerned.

"You fucked her, didn't you?" Christopher asked with pure malice.

Dex was stunned at the total transformation of his brother's personality. He had witnessed his brother's mood swings before, but Christopher had never been rude or disrespectful toward CiCi, and Dex's mind went directly to the crass boldness she described in her dream. When Dex didn't answer, Christopher became more agitated.

"Answer me!"

"It's really none of your business, is it?" Dex replied, not knowing what else to say.

Christopher stared at his brother with pure hatred in his eyes. But his anger was short-lived as extreme exhaustion consumed him, and all Christopher could do was close his eyes and fall into a deep, healing sleep.

Dex decided not to relay this encounter to CiCi or the Brunners for fear they would overreact or that CiCi would be freaked out. But when he returned to the lodge to tell everyone Christopher was sick and couldn't take them out, CiCi, Mac, and Aria all got a bad vibe. And when Mac questioned him, Dex minimized the situation, saying it was just a bad cold Christopher needed to sleep off.

Even though Dex was justifying his brother's peculiar illness, he could not convince himself that all was well. Christopher's strange line of questioning was a source of constant worry for Dex and knowing his brother's history and now knowing of Aria and CiCi's dreams, Dex was uneasy, to say the least.

Without a guide to take the guys fishing, they decided to join the girls on their shopping trip into town. Aria had not said much the whole time, but this place and everything about the surroundings was eerily familiar. But when they pulled into the parking lot of the Moccasin Bar, a waft of dread consumed her, and her uncomfortable state was obvious to those who knew her best.

"Are you okay?" Mac asked, slipping his arm around her waist and pulling her to him.

"Yeah," she managed. "But this is the bar from my dream. Something bad is going to happen. I can feel it."

Mac instinctively touched his chest, confirming that his .45 was snugly in place.

After about an hour and a couple of drinks, Aria's somber mood lifted, and she was able to enjoy herself. She watched sweet little exchanges between CiCi and Dex and smiled, thinking how wonderful it was that her daughter had a perfect true love. Aria knew all too well the importance of that kind of powerful relationship, and she had always wanted nothing less for her daughter.

But Aria's peaceful contentment was interrupted when Christopher entered the bar. Aria instantly bristled, remembering the scene from her dream, but this time, Christopher seemed jovial and normal. He walked over to Dex and CiCi, ordered a beer, and stood and talked normally for quite some time.

"Mac, he seems okay, right?" she asked guardedly.

"Yeah, I was thinking the same thing."

So Aria let her wall down, thinking her dream had once again exacerbated the negative, putting her on edge for no reason. But when Christopher moved from the group with Dex and CiCi over to her and Mac, Aria was chilled to the bone by his intense, menacing stare. And just as fast as it appeared, it was gone, and he approached her and Mac cordially. Aria was a bundle of emotions but finally thought she must be overreacting. But when Christopher caught her eye again, she saw the same evil presence as before, and when he winked at her, there was no denying that Christopher's unnatural behavior was not her imagination.

"Mac, we have to go, and we have to get CiCi and Dex far away from here," she explained, standing and gathering her things.

Mac saw the fear in his wife's eyes and the determination in her movements. There was no way he was stopping that speeding train, so he quickly paid his bill and motioned for Dex and CiCi. Before they could cross the room, Christopher had his arm around Dex's shoulder, thanking him for the assistance in quelling his headache.

"Hey, thanks, Bro, I mean for today. It meant a lot."

Dex wondered if his brother remembered his crude question regarding CiCi, but it was clear from his friendly approach that he didn't.

"No problem, Man."

"Hey, I hitched a ride here from a friend. Can I ride back with you?"

Dex wasn't sure that was a good idea, but he supposed that if he sent CiCi with her parents, she would be safe. He really wasn't that worried that his brother would harm him, but he wasn't taking any chances with CiCi.

"Hey, Mr. Brunner, can CiCi ride back with you? I'm staying for a bit with Christopher."

CiCi was not at all happy about Dex's decision to stay, and all she could think about was her mother's dream.

"Dex, just come with us, please," she pleaded. "We can come get your car tomorrow."

Pulling her aside, Dex tried to explain that nothing was going to happen to him. But he definitely wanted her in the safe presence of her parents.

Mac felt a little uncomfortable leaving Dex there and then making him be alone in a car with Christopher, so he offered a solution that he hoped was well-received.

"Dex, we'll stay and follow you. We're in no hurry," Mac said casually.

There was something about Mac's voice that struck a nerve in Christopher, and his eyes took on that devilish darkness that Aria had dismissed too soon.

"We don't need a babysitter," Christopher growled, making CiCi jump and Dex wrap his arms around her.

CiCi's obvious fear and his brother's loving reaction to it seemed to enrage Christopher even more.

"And *you*," he barked, looking at CiCi. "You don't have to jump into his arms like a common whore at the sound of my voice."

CiCi was terrified, and Dex moved her as far away from Christopher as possible while Mac stepped in to give Christopher a piece of his mind.

"I don't know who the fuck you think you are all of a sudden, but that's my daughter, and you'll never refer to her in such a degrading way—ever again."

Mac's delivery was slow and powerful, with just the right amount of force, and Christopher's demeanor softened slightly.

"Fine!" Christopher responded. "Don't worry about me. I'll find my own way back." And with that, Christopher headed to the back of the bar, detaching from everyone and everything.

Aria and CiCi breathed a sigh of relief and couldn't get out of there fast enough. Mac made the executive decision that Dex and CiCi were riding with them, and they could retrieve Dex's car later. All the way back to the lodge, Aria's eyes kept darting to the side mirror, even though she knew Christopher didn't have a vehicle to pursue them. The silence in the car was overwhelmingly awkward, and finally, Dex felt compelled to relay the details of his encounter with Christopher earlier that day.

"I didn't say anything earlier because I didn't want to cause unnecessary panic, but I had a run-in with Christopher earlier today, and his attitude toward CiCi was similar," Dex admitted.

"Similar? What do you mean, similar?" Mac inquired.

"Degrading and…" Dex was afraid to say it, but he managed. "Sexual."

The pit of CiCi's stomach felt hot and hollow. She also had an admission that she knew would send her parents and Dex reeling.

"I really hoped all of this was over and that he'd just leave me alone," CiCi replied.

Momentarily, the silence was deafening, and then Mac spoke. "What do you mean?"

"Christopher has always privately commented on things like my outfit or my makeup. I used to think it was him being overprotective, you know, like a big brother, but since knowing about Mom's dream and then having my own dream, well, his behavior seems like something different."

Dex was mortified.

"He's said things like that to you before?"

"Not that crude, but, yes, he's said things many times," CiCi admitted.

"That son-of-a-bitch!" Dex responded. He was furious. "I don't understand him at all. He needs more help. He's spiraling out of control again. I have half a mind to just call an ambulance and make him go to the hospital."

Aria had been silent, but now she finally spoke.

"*Christopher* would agree to go to the hospital, but *Tre* will fight you tooth and nail."

Dex looked bewildered.

"Tre?" he asked, wrinkling his eyebrow to accentuate his confusion.

Aria looked at Mac. His silence seemed to be permission to unload their theory regarding Christopher's split personality.

"Before you were even born, Christopher received a kidney transplant from a very evil man. It's always been your grandmother's theory—and ours, too—that Christopher is tortured by this man whose personality randomly makes an appearance. We think we're his trigger since Mac killed the man who ended up donating the kidney. His sick obsession with CiCi began when she was just a baby."

Dex and CiCi were stunned and took a moment to process that quite unbelievable information.

"I knew about the kidney but not about where it came from," Dex admitted.

"I don't understand why he's fixated on me," CiCi questioned.

"Because you're ours," Aria said, using her hand to point back and forth between her and Mac. "We love you with all our being, and I believe Tre wants to destroy that. He wants to hurt us as a punishment for all we did to him."

Realizing her words and her story sounded crazy, Aria explained some more.

"I know it sounds unbelievable, but your dad and I have had a lot more experience with Christopher—Tre—than either of you, and, well, he's just evil, and poor Christopher suffers."

"Why hasn't anyone told me this before?" Dex said, unable to conceal his agitation.

"In some respects, your parents are in denial," Mac piped up. "This is a difficult theory to get behind," he added.

"Believe us," Aria began, "we've spent a lot of time wondering if Christpher's situation is medically or scientifically possible, but it's really the only explanation for his odd personality disorder."

Hearing this outrageous theory helped CiCi put a lot of her encounters with Christopher—or Tre—into perspective. She now noticed that Christopher's personality generally changed suddenly and secretly and then returned to normal quite quickly. But this time, he had shown his malice boldly in front of Dex and her parents, and she wondered why.

"In my experience, Christopher's odd change in character has always been covert. I wonder why he's so bold this time," CiCi voiced.

Mac thought for a second and then voiced a possible answer.

"It's because we're with you. As I said before, your mom and I are Tre's trigger. He hates us so much; he can't stand to lie dormant when we're around."

"This is crazy," Dex interjected. "Christopher grew up around you guys. You're like family."

"But we've always had this effect on him if we spend enough time around him," Mac replied. "He usually has to remove himself from the situation because he gets one of his debilitating headaches. I think that's Tre breaking through and manipulating his mind. Christopher probably moved up here to get away from us so Tre would stop haunting his thoughts."

"Did he know we were coming with you," Aria asked.

"No," Dex answered.

"So, Christopher was caught off guard, and Tre was in heaven with all three of us present," Mac suspected.

"This is difficult to believe," Dex responded. "But it does seem to explain a lot."

The remainder of the ride home was in silence as Dex and CiCi struggled to accept such an outrageous explanation for Christopher's strange personality shifts. But CiCi knew one thing, her dad was right. He and her mom had far more experience with Tre Halprin; therefore, their theory was most likely true. Now knowing why Christopher appeared in her terrifying dreams, she worried and wondered which dream would play out in real life—hers or her mother's.

Chapter 37

Back at the lodge, CiCi and Dex sat at a bar table with Aria and Mac, trying to make connections between their dreams and reality and trying to get a battle plan for dealing with Tre Halprin once again.

"Both CiCi's dream and mine come to a tragic end in Las Vegas," Aria said. "Both of us dreaming that this fiasco ends in the same place makes me feel pretty confident our worries up here at the lodge are minimal."

"Never underestimate Tre Halprin, Aria. That's when he'll get the upper hand," Mac said, almost scolding her naive assumption.

"I feel as if I should let my mom and dad know Christopher is bad again," Dex interjected. "I feel like we need to get him to a hospital."

"Agreed," Mac said, "before he hurts himself or someone else."

Before they could finish their first drink, Dex had a text from his friend Matt who stayed at the Moccasin Bar.

> Your brother is going to get the police called on him if he doesn't cool it. What the fuck is up with him?

The look on Dex's face told the group that his text was bad news. CiCi put her hand on his leg—a meager attempt at providing some comfort, but it was all she could think of doing. She watched as Dex called his friend. He had no patience for texting under these conditions. When Matt picked up, it sounded like utter chaos in the background.

"What's going on?" Dex said, eager to get this issue resolved once and for all.

"Christopher is freaking the fuck out. He's screaming and holding his head. There's something really wrong. The owner just called the police and an ambulance."

Dex had Matt on speaker, and it sounded like an all-out brawl in the background.

"I'll be right there," Dex said, clicking off his phone.

"I gotta go," Dex said, downing his beer and grabbing his coat.

"Now, hold on," Mac said. "Your car is still at the bar. I'll drive you. You gals just stay here where it's safe and have a few drinks. We'll be back before you know it."

CiCi and Aria didn't have to be told twice to stay put. Neither one wanted to be anywhere near Christopher. The only bad part about staying behind was that they had no idea what was going on.

"You text me and let me know what's happening, Mac!" Aria yelled as Mac gave her the 'thumbs up' rushing out the door.

❖ ❖ ❖

By the time Mac and Dex got back in town to The Moccasin Bar, Christopher had pulled himself together. When the police arrived, as well as the ambulance, there was really no reason to arrest him or take him to the hospital. In fact, the bar manager was willing to overlook all of the chaos if Christopher left.

"Fine, I'll get my car and take him back to the lodge," Dex said, hoping to just get out of there as fast as possible.

"Now, wait a minute," Mac intervened. "Let's all stay together. We'll come get your car later."

Dex was not really afraid to be alone with his brother, but the look Mac shot him indicated that staying together was a much safer plan.

"Okay then, let's just get out of here," Dex said, motioning for Christopher to follow.

When Dex started to get in the front seat of Mac's Tahoe, Mac motioned for him to get in the back. There was no way Mac was having his back to Christopher all the way home. Even though Christopher seemed completely fine at the time, Mac knew he could erupt into Tre at any moment. In fact, Mac worried that there was no way they could make it all the way back to the lodge without Tre making an appearance.

Therefore, Mac was on high alert all the way back, but it seemed that Christopher had worn himself out ranting and raving at the bar, and he was sleeping like a baby. When they pulled onto the lodge grounds, Dex guided Mac to Christopher's cabin, where he stopped, and Dex proceeded to wake his sleeping brother.

"Hey…hey! We're back. Let's get you inside and to bed."

Christopher was groggy but receptive, and Dex and Mac helped him inside.

When Christopher first saw Mac, he was confused. He thought he had been with Dex alone on the way back.

"Oh, hey, Mr. Brunner. Thanks. I…I must have had too much to drink. I haven't been myself lately. I'm having headaches again, and when that happens, I black out. I hope I didn't do anything stupid."

Both Mac and Dex were taken aback. This person was 100 percent Christopher. Mac had anticipated an all-out war in the car on the way home, and all he got was a contrite Christopher who appeared to have no recollection of his tirade at the Moccasin Bar.

"Christopher, what do you remember from the past four hours?" Mac asked.

Christopher thought for a minute.

"The last thing I remember is walking into the Moccasin Bar to meet you guys. I got a beer and talked to you for a few minutes."

"That's all you remember?"

"Yes. Why? I've done something bad again, haven't I?" Christopher said, closing his eyes in utter despair.

"We're going to get you some help," Mac promised. "But for now, we're going to get out of here and let you get some sleep."

As Mac and Dex walked out, they were both flabbergasted that Christopher could not recall any of his violent antics at the bar.

"This just goes to show that Christopher is innocent, and his alter personality is the one causing all the problems. Unfortunately, his alter personality is a diabolical killer."

The next couple of hours were actually quite pleasant for mother and daughter, who rarely had the chance to catch up these days. But when the clock indicated Mac and Dex had been gone for nearly two hours and had no update, Aria wondered if no text meant trouble or if it was just Mac, who rarely texted anyway.

Aria was quick to scold Mac for keeping them in the dark. Mac could tell right away Aria was beyond tipsy, and he quickly paid the bar tab and escorted her upstairs. There would be plenty of time to tell her everything when she was sober.

That left CiCi and Dex at the bar, ready to engage in some much-needed alone time. CiCi was buzzed, but as a seasoned college co-ed, she handled her alcohol much better than her mother, who tried to match her drink for drink.

"So…" CiCi began.

Anticipating her line of questioning, Dex stopped CiCi short.

"Ya know, I don't want to waste one more second worrying about my brother on this trip, especially when my gorgeous and sexy girlfriend is by my side, and we're finally alone."

CiCi felt a hot rush of pure passion move through her as Dex spoke. She was also tired of being afraid and tired of being consumed with the details of her dream.

"Well then, whatever would we do?" CiCi said quite flirtatiously. And when Dex looked at her face full-on, and saw her biting her bottom lip, he found it difficult to prevent his growing excitement, and he didn't want to anyway. And when CiCi put her hand on his thigh and moved it close to, but not touching, his crotch, Dex wanted to get out of there as soon as possible. When he hailed the waiter to make sure the tab was taken care of, CiCi stopped him and whispered in his ear.

"Not yet. Let's stay here. This could be fun."

And when she ended her plea with a breathless "I promise" in his ear, Dex adjusted himself in the booth seat, making more room for CiCi to address his aching crotch.

CiCi teased him lightly at first on the outside of his jeans, and when she saw the desperate look in his eyes, she applied more pressure and maintained a slow, steady pace up and down his long shaft bulging inside his pants. She was quite enjoying watching his face tense and his eyes close as he experienced the pleasure. Finally, he spoke. He was at his brink.

"CiCi, I really need to get you upstairs, like NOW," he whispered, fearing his pleasurable state had already drawn attention. But CiCi had other plans.

"No, now…you can't be selfish. I've so enjoyed watching you squirm, but I think it's time you do the same for me."

Dex blinked once and then he knew the assignment. He felt CiCi spread her legs under the table, and although she was wearing jeans, his firm pressure grabbing her excitedly between the legs made CiCi jump slightly, and then, as he got into a rhythm, CiCi settled in to enjoy. When Dex saw her slowly throw her head back and lick her lips, he was certain this was the hottest thing he'd ever done.

Feeling bold now, Dex unbuttoned her jeans and unzipped them just enough to get his hand inside. When he moved his fingers past her smooth mound and into her wetness, he was certain the entire bar heard her carnal moan. But his fear did not deter his mission. Dex landed his fingers on CiCi's swollen spot and moved them in tiny circles, which made her twist and moan.

Dex could feel her pushing her feet off the floor, making room for him to move on down, but before he could comply, CiCi voiced exactly what she wanted.

"Finger me, Dex."

Without hesitation, Dex continued his path and started to put his fingers in slowly when CiCi pushed her hips forward, indicating that she wanted a more forceful push. Dex read her signal perfectly and plunged his fingers deep inside her, wiggling them and thrusting them in and out until CiCi was writhing on the verge of exploding.

"Do you want me to finish you, CiCi," Dex whispered in her ear.

"Yes, yes, please," she panted breathlessly.

Dex placed his thumb on that spot and rubbed up and down in the same rhythm his fingers were thrusting in and out. Within seconds, CiCi was in the throes of a wildly intense orgasm. Her body flinched and twitched for seconds afterward, and Dex kissed her neck as she began to come down.

When CiCi opened her eyes, and they met Dex's, they both smiled a naughty little smile and collected themselves before going upstairs to finish what they had started.

Chapter 38

The next morning at breakfast, Dex and CiCi enjoyed some carefree time with their friends, which they felt bad about ignoring the day before.

"So, do you think your brother will be up for taking us out ice fishing today?" Matt asked.

"Or, we could get on the snowmobiles and hit the trails," Lance countered.

"I don't know," Dex answered honestly. "He's been feeling pretty bad."

About that time, Christopher came strolling in the lodge restaurant, looking happy and healthy.

"What's on the agenda for today, folks?"

Dex was amazed at Christopher's good mood.

"Well, ice fishing?" Dex responded.

"Ice fishing it is!" Christopher replied. "I'll go get all the gear. You finish breakfast and meet me down at the dock in a half hour." And with that, Christopher slapped his brother on the back and headed out of the restaurant.

Dex and CiCi looked at each other with the same puzzled stare, and secretly, they wondered how long Christopher's good mood would last.

"Well, we've already explored the town. What are we going to do while the guys are fishing?" Mia asked with a concerned frown.

"Let's explore some of the shops and bars on the other side of the lake," CiCi replied. "I bet my parents would drive us so we can drink and have fun."

"Sounds good to me," Mia replied. We only have one more day here. Let's party!!!"

Mac and Aria were happy to escort their daughter and her friends for the day, but Mac kept thinking about his conversation with Christopher the night before. He knew Tre would eventually rear his ugly head, and Mac hoped to get Christopher some help before that happened.

When the fishing excursion was over, Christopher invited the guys to follow him on the snowmobiles for some drinks. Dex could tell Mac and the girls were not back yet, so he consented. Christopher had been completely normal all day, and Dex was actually building his hopes that all of this nonsense with his alternate personality was quelled for the time being.

"Follow me, guys. The best bars are the most hidden," Christopher said with a huge grin as he put his helmet on.

About half hour into the trek, they were getting pretty far from the lodge, and Dex was getting a little worried. When he spied a small shed in the distance, he knew this had to be Christopher's destination since there wasn't another building anywhere in sight. Suddenly, Dex had a bad feeling about the whole ordeal.

When Christopher did, in fact, stop at the remote shed, the guys were all a little pissed.

"What the fuck, Man? We drive a half hour for a fucking shed? I thought we were hitting some hot bars," Matt said.

Christopher silently headed to the door and let himself in, gesturing for his companions to enter.

Dex started to pull out his phone and text CiCi, and Christopher couldn't help but notice.

"Who are you texting, Brother?" Christopher began. "Don't tell me it's your little piece of pussy you have to check in with."

Those words hit Dex like a freight train. When he looked up, Christopher's eyes were dark and threatening, and Dex had a sinking feeling of dread.

"Or maybe it's her asshole dad and bitch of a mother who couldn't let their precious CiCi out of their sight for a few days."

Matt and Hal were confused and didn't understand how Christopher could go from the nicest guy ever to a total dick so easily.

Dex had no response to Christopher's attack, and he continued his original plan of texting CiCi, which enraged Christopher even more. Dex was a stout, muscular guy, but his older brother had several inches of height on him, so overtaking him was out of the question. And in Christopher's current state of agitation, Dex was a bit afraid of what he might do. So when Christopher told him to stop texting and turn over his phone, Dex did so. In the next breath, Christopher told Matt and Hal to relinquish their phones as well.

"What the fuck!" Hal blurted.

But when Christopher brandished a huge hunting knife, the guys were silent and did as they were told.

Fearing the worst, Dex put in a desperate plea.

"This is between you and me, Christopher. Why don't you just let them go?"

Christopher thought for a moment, and then he had a change of heart.

"You know, you're right, little brother. You are *so* right," Christopher agreed.

Matt and Hal were frozen with fear, so when Christopher handed them their phones and let them leave, they wasted no time.

Although they didn't say so, Dex was confident they would send Mac to rescue him. It would just take a little time for them to get back and then for Mac to get all the way out to him. Dex worried about what he would endure in the meantime.

Once Matt and Hal were long gone. Christopher addressed his brother again.

"You know why I let them go, right?"

Dex was silent, fearful that he would say the wrong thing.

"They are going to lead Mac and Aria right to me. And this is MY territory. Once they're dealt with, no one will find them way out here."

Dex was now a little less hopeful that Mac would come to save him. But before he had more time to worry about that, Christopher began his full-on assault.

"I can't believe you're fucking *my* CiCi," Christopher said with a malicious tone that made Dex shiver to the core.

Dex knew that anything he said was wrong and would just be fuel to Christopher's fire, so he remained silent.

"Tell me—I mean, since you know all about it—how is she?"

Christopher's tone was rude and probing, and his dark eyes stared directly into Dex's when he asked that disturbing question. Dex was sickened by the thought of this man, who could not possibly be his brother, lusting over CiCi, and he didn't know how much longer he could stay quiet.

"She was supposed to be mine. You know that, right?"

Dex saw pure evil in his brother's eyes and knew that Christopher was gone, and the man Mac and Aria knew was now in control.

"We're going to get you some help, Christopher," was all Dex could think to say.

The man before him stared menacingly into Dex's eyes and then released a sinister, guttural growl.

"You can't help him. He's *mine.*"

Dex felt a gripping chill overpower him, and more than ever, the gravity of his situation became real.

The man moved slowly and deliberately toward Dex, and when he reached his goal, he just stood there glaring at Dex with pure hatred in his eyes. Dex wanted to look away but maintained his eye-lock bravely until this monster of a man hauled off and slugged him in the jaw as hard as he could.

"That's for fucking my CiCi!"

There were several minutes of awkward silence, and Dex was trying to determine precisely when his friends would make it back to the lodge and retrieve Mac. But after only a short time, this man, who used to be his brother, was moving toward him again, grabbing him by the arm and dragging him to a steel pole in the middle of the shed. When the man chained him to the pole, Dex recalled Aria's dream and thought how unbelievably eerie this whole ordeal was.

"So, are you just going to leave me here?" Dex asked. "I'm your brother, for Christ's sake."

"You're not my fucking brother!"

Dex found it so terribly difficult to realize the man before him, who looked just like Christopher, was not the brother he knew. And with that sobering thought, his hopes fell, and Dex wondered if he would get out of this predicament alive.

Nightmares & Premonitions

When the guys finally made it back to the lodge, Mac, Aria, and the girls were just getting back from across the lake, and it was only a matter of seconds before Mac was geared up and following Matt and Hal back out to the remote shed. Aria desperately wanted to go, but she felt it best to stay with CiCi and the other girls, trying to calm their fears. In the meantime, Tre Halprin's mind and will inside Christopher Paloma's body continued his vicious assault on the defenseless Dex.

"You do know that every time I hit you, I get so much pleasure," Tre bragged. "You have no idea how much I hate you."

Dex was now swollen, bloodied, and broken. He had endured numerous malicious blows for well over an hour and worried that Matt and Hal might have gotten lost. But when they heard the roar of approaching snowmobiles, Dex's hopes lifted, and pure excitement consumed Tre's dark face. Dex knew this man had some diabolical plan for Mac and hoped with all his heart that Mac was cautious.

When Mac barreled into the shed, Christopher had the large hunting knife to Dex's throat.

"Well, hello, Mac! Finally!" Tre said boastfully.

"Drop the knife, Tre. You and I both know I can pop you in an instant."

"But will you? Will you kill your little innocent friend, Christopher?"

Mac thought for a moment. That would certainly not be optimum.

"That's what I thought," Tre gloated.

"So, here's how we're gonna play this, Tre dictated. "First, you're gonna give me that gun or something worse than *this*," Tre stated as he took his hunting knife and sliced through Dex's cheek, "will happen to Loverboy here."

Dex screamed at first but then tried desperately to mask his pain, not wanting to give Tre the satisfaction of seeing his agony. Matt and Hal, who had guided Mac back to the shed, were frozen with fear as they watched this unbelievable display of horror.

Mac had two options: he could surrender his gun or pop Tre right then and there. Mac was conflicted because he had witnessed the real Christopher's innocence and ignorance of his situation with Tre, and deep down he wanted to get him some help. Killing Tre would also be killing an innocent man, and Mac was not ready to take that leap. Still holding Dex in a precarious position, Tre told Mac to toss his gun to the side, and even though Mac cringed at the thought, he did as Tre asked.

Dex's hopes sank when the gun fell to the ground out of reach. He certainly hoped Mac had a plan. But Mac's only thought was that at some point he would have to overtake Tre, and now he would have to do so using pure strength and try to keep from getting sliced by Tre's massive blade.

Outside, the faint roar of a snowmobile became audible, and a sly smile consumed Tre's face.

"Just as I hoped. Someone else has come looking for you."

Mac's mind was reeling, wondering how he could use Aria's presence to their advantage. But when she opened the door suddenly, he hadn't had enough time to wrap his head around a plan. With an unconscious reaction, Mac slightly turned his body away from Tre and toward the door, inviting Tre to release his grip on Dex and quickly wrap his arm around Mac's neck. Putting the knife dangerously close to Mac's face.

Mac was now rendered helpless and could kick himself for making such a stupid move. Although released, Dex was still bound to the steel pole and was no help whatsoever. Now, their escape and Tre's demise were all on Aria.

When Aria came barreling through the door with her Glock in her hand, her sights went immediately to Tre.

"Well, well… the gang's all here!" Tre bellowed, followed by a mocking laugh.

"Let go of him!" Aria demanded. She had the voice of a woman who had enough of the chaos and turmoil Tre Halprin had created in her life. She had the voice of a woman with zero fucks regarding the fallout that might ensue as she saved her husband and Dex from the most sinister man she ever knew.

It was at this point that Tre wished he had Mac's gun that lay on the floor, but he stupidly had Mac toss it to the side rather than place it in his hand. When Tre's eyes darted in that direction, searching for its exact location, Aria delivered a harsh reality.

"There's no way you can get to that, so let him go!"

"Or what?" Tre mocked. "Your husband couldn't do it, and you won't either."

Tre was fairly certain Aria would not shoot him. Again, he had the ultimate protection— he held Christopher Paloma's life for ransom. When Aria didn't answer, Tre repeated his question with more anger and force behind his words.

"I asked you, OR WHAT?"

Aria had thought about this moment many times, and deep down, she knew the only way their nightmare with this man would be over was when he was dead. They had thought that once before, but they had no idea Tre would still haunt their lives from inside an innocent man's body. And if Tre was capable of such an unbelievable feat, the only way they would ever be rid of the danger he posed was when he was dead and gone for good. It had been that way with Tre's brother. Aria remembered the feeling of complete freedom after pulling the trigger in The Grotto that day and killing Deuce Halprin.

It was that thought that made Aria pull the trigger again. Their nightmare was finally over.

❖ ❖ ❖

The trip back to Peoria was a somber one, but no one could deny the liberating sense of peace that came with Tre's death. It was beyond unfortunate that Christopher Paloma lost his life in the process, but no one disputed Aria's decision, not even Christopher's parents.

Even though the end of this saga did not exactly match either of the ominous dreams that paralleled the action, Aria always knew that real life played out differently. And on the same note, if her decision did, in fact, change the course of fate, she knew it was for the better. They were all finally free from the sinister side of her family. That left Mac and Aria to live their lives peacefully with CiCi and Dex, and the rest of their friends and family. And thanks to their daughter CiCi's namesake, they would manage a multi-billion-dollar estate.

❖ ❖ ❖

The only detail left to convey in the Brunners' lives is a simple one…

And they lived happily ever after.

A SPECIAL BONUS FROM

The Wanted

The Desired

The Craved

A DARK NOVELLA

Chapter 1

Gianna Stevens had to admit, being back on campus felt good—really good. Her semester studying abroad was a once-in-a-lifetime opportunity that unexpectedly came her way last spring. And frankly, at the time, she was ready to escape some harsh realities at Briarwood University.

Trying to focus on a new year and a new beginning, however, was more difficult than Gia imagined. And as hard as she tried to move on, dark thoughts were doing their damnedest to take control. Shaking off the unpleasantry, Gia tried to focus on the electric vibe of campus, and quite suddenly she was back to being full of hopeful anticipation about finishing her senior year at Briarwood.

An art major, Gia spent the first semester of her senior year touring the museums of Europe and learning from some of the best artists in the world. It was no secret among her peers that Gia possessed a phenomenal talent, and like most artists, she longed to make a living from her work. But she was also a realist, and even though she thought her true bliss would be for people to pay an insane amount for a Gianna Stevens original, Gia knew she needed a backup plan. Since getting rich quickly from her art was just a fantasy at this point, Gia would settle for sharing her gift in a different way. That's why she also took education classes and looked forward to becoming a high school art teacher after graduation.

Walking the scenic pathway to class, Gia was invigorated by the sights and sounds of campus life. Until now, she didn't realize how much she missed this place over the past semester. Her parents, however, were apprehensive about her return to Briarwood.

Her last semester on campus was filled with anxiety and fear for Gia's parents. One of Gia's classmates, Celine Tibbs, went missing, and once the case went cold after a few months, it was like she never existed. Debra Stevens and her husband Mark were mortified that a human being, someone's daughter, could be dismissed so quickly and coldly, and they shuttered to think what they would do if something so horrific ever happened to Gia.

Gia and Celine were in many of the same classes before Celine disappeared. They weren't close friends, but they saw each other every day and were even working on a project in Professor Graham's class when Celine went missing. Gia's parents thought their daughter should be more upset, but Debra was convinced Gia was masking her feelings and being strong so she could better cope with losing a friend.

The truth was Gia and Celine were rivals, and their 'friendship' was based on their common talents and mutual respect, not on the fact that they actually liked one another. Both girls were talented artists who competed in many ways throughout their college years. Deep down, Gia couldn't help but think that with her biggest competition eliminated, she would be more of a shining star. Gia sometimes felt bad for having such disturbing thoughts and wondered how she could be such a bitch sometimes.

Gia noticed, though, that her parents were right. It was like Celine never existed. Gia had been back on campus for three days, and still not a single mention of the tragedy from last spring. Like her parents, Gia briefly wondered if people would be this cold if she were the one missing. Maybe all the other students were like her—not talking about Celine's mysterious disappearance but aware of it and the related dangers that might still be lurking.

Gia returned to campus with all the hope in the world that her final semester of college would be fun and normal. And she remembered having the same hope about being abroad for an entire first semester and being away from Briarwood. But Gia was beginning to discover that it didn't matter where she was, she couldn't completely escape that dark place she visited during the time of Celine's disappearance. And even though she was eager to return to Briarwood at one time, being back there resurrected all those complicated feelings. The last thing in the world she wanted was to return to that soulless place that consumed her when she last called Briarwood home.

❖ ❖ ❖

About a week before finals last spring, and only a few weeks after Celine went missing, Professor Graham gave Gia an extension on the project she was working on with Celine. And right after he mentioned giving Gia extra time, Professor Graham left campus. The semester wasn't over, but he was heading home to Chapel Hill, North Carolina. It seemed Celine's disappearance and the scandal that prefaced it were too much for Professor Troy Graham to handle.

It was no secret that Celine and Professor Graham's relationship crossed a line and went beyond one of a student and professor. The campus was abuzz with rumors connecting Professor Graham to Celine's disappearance. Gia knew it was impossible for an outstanding, talented, gorgeous man like her professor to be responsible for horrific acts like kidnapping and murder. But after being cleared by the police last spring, Professor Graham's hasty departure from campus made him look guilty as sin.

Gia thought the circulating rumors were unfair and hated that Professor Graham had to justify such unfounded allegations. While his hasty departure was devastating for Gia initially, she honestly couldn't blame him for bolting early. At one time, Gia worried that she'd never see Professor Graham again. But even though she was not on campus during the fall semester, news traveled her way that the handsome art professor was back teaching at Briarwood, and he looked as sexy as ever.

This was the day Gia had been waiting on for months. It was finally the day she laid eyes on her strong, devilishly handsome professor for the first time in nearly a year. She hoped he had not already dismissed and replaced Celine with another student lover. Gia's reasoning had little to do with mourning her friend and much to do with wanting Professor Graham in her bed, not someone else's.

While the word around campus was that the sultry and mysterious professor was single, Gia knew another indiscretion with a student would undoubtedly be hush-hush. She hoped that when she arrived in his class this semester, he was, in fact, unattached and that she could capture his attention and devotion. At one time Gia believed she was over these unnatural thoughts, but just the anticipation of being back in his class made all of her lustful fantasies reappear.

This year I will be the wanted— the desired— the one he craves.

Walking into Professor Graham's classroom, Gia was disappointed that she didn't arrive before her classmates. She had hustled tail to get there, but now she would have to wait until after class to speak privately with her favorite teacher, and Gia knew from experience that she probably wouldn't be the only one vying for his time and attention.

At least the class content was engaging and made the time go faster. Gia had waited years to be in the Honors Watercolor Painting course. Typically, this class was reserved for the best of the best. Gia had been dreaming of such an honor ever since her senior year of high school when visiting the class during a campus visit. Professor Graham was not at Briarwood then, but Professor Lyons did an excellent job telling her all about the art courses after his class ended, and Gia remembered his blunt advice specifically.

"Honors Watercolor only has six spots a semester, and if you're lucky enough to get one, by all means, don't fuck it up."

So here she was, checking a long-time goal from her list. And the cherry on top was seeing the beautiful man teaching the coveted course four times a week. Looking around, Gia saw the students she expected to be there. Last spring before he left, Gia remembered Professor Graham reminding them of the competitive nature of Honors Watercolor.

"I would love to move you all to Honors Watercolor, but as you know, that class is reserved for the top six senior students. We've always thought competition is a good motivator. Work hard and do your best this semester, and you'll have no regrets."

After that speech, Gia remembered feeling nervous and scared that maybe, just maybe, she wouldn't be one of the chosen ones, killing her dream. Looking back on it now, Gia couldn't help but wonder who wouldn't be there if Celine was still around. Gia hated to admit it, but she was confident her rival would have made the cut. But this was a new year, and she was sitting in the most honored position in the art department as one of the six most talented and promising artists who would graduate from Briarwood in a few short months. Gia wouldn't waste time worrying if she was number seven and got an upgrade when Celine disappeared. That was the past, and this was a new year.

Maybe it was the seriousness of the course and the responsibility of instructing the best of the best, but Professor Graham was all business, not wasting a single minute of his two-hour lab course. Gia immersed herself in the atmosphere and before she knew it, the class was over. With time sneaking up on her, Gia still had to clean up her station when most students had left. Kimi, Gia's housemate, said she would wait for her, but Gia declined and said she would just meet her back at home later. So, just as she planned, Gia found herself completely alone with her gorgeous professor, which further aroused past feelings Gia had hoped to keep suppressed.

As Gia cleaned her brushes, her glances darted his way, half hoping he wouldn't catch her watchful eye and half hoping he would. Gia already knew her excuse to talk with him. With his abrupt departure last spring and her absence during the fall semester, Gia still didn't have a grade recorded for her extended project. Unfortunately, her segue into a conversation with Professor Dreamy had to be tied to the tragic past. Gia didn't want anything to do with stirring up old memories for the professor. Therefore, asking about her grade from last spring was both bitter and sweet. But much to her surprise, Gia didn't get to initiate the conversation because Professor Graham beat her to it.

"It's good to see you, Gia," he said, more as a courtesy than stating facts. "How was your semester abroad?"

Catching her off guard, Gia's heart was about to burst out of her chest, and she had to take a second to compose herself.

"It was fabulous," she replied. "But I'm glad to be back."

And before she could ask about her pending grade, Professor Graham addressed her question.

"By the way, I'll have your project grade from last semester recorded by the end of the week. Sorry it's taken me so long," he said, maintaining a matter-of-fact tone while nervously gathering his things.

Gia could tell he was trying to broach the subject casually, but his haste and a slight tremble of his hands told her that this topic was still tricky and stressful for him. Even though Celine was gone, Gia still felt she was competing with Celine for Professor Graham's attention, and she wasn't the least bit happy about it. Nonetheless, she managed a cordial reply.

"Sure, that's no problem at all."

And before she could continue the conversation, Professor Graham cut her off. He was uncomfortable being alone with Gia, and he felt a deep need to hurry, get his things, and get out of there.

"Okay then, check your online portal in a few days, and it should show up. See you tomorrow." And he was gone, leaving Gia both dreamy-eyed and salty. She understood that her professor was uncomfortable with lingering elements of the past, but he didn't even give her a chance to respond or change the subject. In fact, his behavior was borderline rude.

Boy, that was a fast exit! She wasn't at all impressed with her much-anticipated conversation with her beloved professor, and this disappointment had her feeling that her inner bitch was about to appear.

"He never hurried out that fast when Celine stayed after class. Oh well, we have time, Gia. We have time."

Chapter 2

It was Friday afternoon, and Troy Graham knew that Rosa would be waiting for him at his condo by the time he got out of his last class. Her 'welcome home' the last time she visited had Troy's head spinning, and he could barely make it to the end of his Honors Watercolor course thinking about Rosa's naked, voluptuous curves lying in bed waiting on him.

Troy met Rosa while on vacation in Cabo last July. And what began as a chance meeting escalated into a spicy love affair over the course of a week. Troy was trying to forget some questionable decisions from the months prior and shake the judgment and suspicion that accompanied them.

Admittedly, he fell hard and fast for the shy, cute, and talented Celine Tibbs, who transferred into his class at midterm. When Professor Carter became ill and couldn't finish the semester, he arranged for Celine to enter Professor Graham's section of the course to continue pursuing her study abroad semester in the fall. Without finishing all her courses, going to Europe during the first semester of her senior year would have been impossible.

From the first day Celine walked into his classroom, Professor Graham was smitten, and his feelings were difficult to suppress. Gia, as well as everyone else, noticed the professor's attentiveness to his new student. Now, all of the attention Gia had been getting was directed to the shy, talented newcomer, and Gia was pissed.

As Professor Graham's attraction grew and became a full-blown affair, his behavior was a hot topic on campus. When the board of directors came down on him for his poor judgment and lack of professionalism, Troy tried to figure out how to have his cake and eat it, too. So, when he didn't read between the lines of his first warning, the board returned with more precise consequences. Professor Graham needed to make a choice—his job or Celine Tibbs.

Being quite fond of Celine but in no position to lose his job, Professor Graham decided to end things. He waited for her that night at the little diner on Highway 64, but when Celine was a half hour late, he began to get worried and texted her but received no reply.

Troy remembered thinking that maybe she saw the writing on the wall, and she just decided to spare herself the agony of the disappointing news. When Celine wasn't answering his texts, he progressed to phone calls that went straight to her voicemail. Troy also discovered Celine wasn't at her apartment and didn't show up for any of her classes the next day. Now, *this* was a problem.

Troy discovered later that Celine's roommates had been trying to contact her all night and reported her missing when she wasn't home the next morning. Wanting information but feeling more exposed than ever asking for it, Troy was going crazy not knowing Celine's whereabouts. Of course, once the detectives discovered Troy and Celine's affair, they had lots of questions for him. But his alibi at the diner was rock solid and much to everyone's surprise, Professor Troy Graham was eliminated as a suspect.

Even though the police cleared him, public opinion surged in the opposite direction, and Troy couldn't take the rumors and suspicions. His solution was to leave school early, return home for the summer, and then decide if he would return to Briarwood in the fall. After getting himself together, Troy figured a nice vacation would be just what he needed to relieve stress and get his mind in the right place. And then he met Rosa.

Rosa was also mending a broken heart and treating herself to a lavish vacation where she wanted nothing more than to sit by the pool with a drink in her hand and read a book all day, every day. When the handsome professor had no choice but to take the last lounge chair right next to hers, Rosa did a double take. Initially, she was not looking for romance on this trip. But now, she had to admit, the man next to her was putting some pretty dirty thoughts in her head, making the steamy love scenes in her romance novel pale in comparison.

It's a good thing I have sunglasses on. The places I'm staring are shameful, she thought, sporting a naughty grin.

Professor Graham was not innocent in this encounter. He remembered thinking how lucky he was that the last chair was beside a smokin' hot Latina. Troy was also not actively seeking a relationship or even a brief romance on this trip; it just happened.

"Do the bartenders come around and take orders, or do I need to go up to the bar?" he asked, innocently.

"They come every now and then, but if you're really thirsty, you'd be better off just going up yourself," Rosa replied.

"Do you mind saving my place here?" Troy wanted a drink, but there was no way he was going to lose this prime spot. "What are you drinking?" he asked, noticing hers was nearly gone. "I'll bring it back."

"Aperol spritz," Rosa replied. "Thanks!"

Rosa watched the muscles in Troy's legs pop in and out as he made his way up to the bar. As he stood there and waited, she noticed his broad shoulders and flat abs.

This guy is out of my league. Oh well, I'm not interested right now anyway.

But there was something about this guy. He was good-looking, for sure, but even in their brief exchange, she could feel his confidence. And confidence was sexy.

That's it! Be confident!

But this was a tall order for Rosa, who had just been dumped for a tiny twig of a woman. But Rosa was too hard on herself. She had the kind of curves that drove men crazy. And Rosa had another bewitching feature that she was about to unleash.

Rosa had long, silky black tresses that were now bunched up in a clip, but usually, they flowed past her waist. Her thick mane was layered into long pieces that flipped up here and there, giving her a uniquely retro look. Rosa knew if she wanted a chance with this guy, she would have to pull out all the stops, specifically setting her locks free.

When Troy returned with Rosa's drink, he introduced himself, and they engaged in small talk. He admired her flawless, sun-kissed skin that was hard to ignore in her cut-out one-piece. But when Rosa unclipped her hair and shook it out, using her fingers to fluff it up, Troy knew he wanted to get to know this woman beyond just talking in pool chairs. He was mesmerized by how her smooth, shiny mane fell on her bare shoulders and down her back and how the sun glistened and made its coal-black hue emit a slightly bluish color. Troy watched in awe as Rosa effortlessly ran her fingers through the silky strands. Rosa's plan worked, and that day was the beginning of Professor Troy Graham's best vacation ever.

That was five months ago, and even though Troy and Rosa still had a long-distance relationship, it seemed to be working. She lived in Hot Springs but had the time and the means to travel, so she frequently made St. Charles a stop. Even though the semester had just begun, and they had just seen each other over the holidays, this week happened to be one of those times. When Rosa mentioned spending a few days with him, Troy was thrilled. For obvious reasons, Troy Graham was not missing a single opportunity to be with Rosa.

When Professor Graham returned to St. Charles and resumed his job at the university, he changed his address, trying to make a fresh start. Too many students knew where he lived before, and he needed more privacy after all that had transpired. He now lived in a condominium community on Lake Ferris, several miles from campus. He was pretty sure his new address, as well as his relationship status, was still unknown regarding his students. Professor Graham was being extra careful with his private information these days. The last thing in the world he wanted was another scandal.

Now home with the work week behind him, a burst of electric excitement shot through Troy's body when he saw Rosa's Audi in his driveway. Opening the front door, he heard music playing and smelled a spicy candle burning. When he didn't see Rosa in the living room or kitchen, he was sure she was in his bed, and the mere thought was making him hard. But when Troy rounded the doorframe into his bedroom--- still no Rosa.

A huge smile formed when he realized Rosa was probably waiting for him in the jacuzzi. He peeked his head around the door to find the jacuzzi filled, candles burning, and music playing, but Rosa was not in the tub. Instead, she was in her bitsy lace underwear and a crop top with one leg up on the vanity shaving. She turned her head and greeted Troy with the kind of smile that starts a fire.

"You're early," she said, puckering her lips in the air, waiting for a kiss.

"I guess I was anxious to get home," he replied, kissing her passionately and giving her a soft pat on the behind that finished as an arousing rub. The professor had a steamy way of making his intentions clear.

"That was nice," Rosa said, watching his eyes as they bore into hers. "I'll be done here in a minute. I bought some wine. Why don't you get us some? By then, I should be finished," Rosa said, raising her eyebrow in that flirty way that Troy thought was so sexy.

"I'll be right back."

When Troy returned with the wine, Rosa was by the bed, clipping up her hair.

"Leave it down," he said.

Rosa removed the clip, tipping her head back and shaking her long locks. That silky, jet-black mane of hair was his weakness. He stood there and watched as she continued to amaze him. Rosa could feel his eyes on her when she slowly pulled her top over her head, revealing her large, tanned breasts. Troy loved how they looked so round as her arms were over her head and how they fell slightly after her arms returned to her sides. Rosa could feel her lover's eyes on her skin as she tempted him with the simple things that always made the biggest impression. The vision of Rosa's nearly naked body made Troy put down the wine glasses and go to her.

Standing there in only her lace panties, Rosa was stunning. Troy wanted to rush her and make hot, passionate love to her. Instead, he slowly approached, slipped his hand under her silky hair at the nape of her neck, and firmly pushed his fingers along her scalp. Rosa knew what was next, and she was trembling with desire. Gently at first, but then with a little more force, he grabbed Rosa's hair and pulled her head back. She closed her eyes and released a submissive sigh.

Rosa's mouth opened slightly, and Troy took full advantage by kissing her long, slow, and deep. When the kiss ended, Troy unbuckled his belt and removed his pants before unbuttoning the cuffs of his dress shirt and pulling it over his head. He grabbed Rosa around the waist and pulled her to him, stopping when his lips nearly touched her neck. She could feel his warm breath caressing her, and she was wild with anticipation, craving his lips and tongue, dying for them to explore every inch of her body. Finally, he gently placed his lips on her neck, giving her goose bumps, making it harder and harder for her to maintain her composure. She could feel he was ready for her, and she wanted him to lay her down and make love to her with long, slow waves of pleasure.

But Troy was in no hurry. He moved to the bed where he sat and positioned her standing in front of him. He put his hands on her hips and pulled her close enough to kiss and lightly lick her smooth midsection. When Troy gently hooked his fingers around the top of Rosa's panties and slowly pulled them down, Rosa released another one of her gentle sighs. Troy lightly caressed her hips, up and down, and kissed her midriff, allowing his tongue to dip lower occasionally, turning Rosa's sighs into moans.

When Troy slid his hand between her legs and slowly moved it up her thigh, Rosa was ready to beg.

"You really do know how to tease a girl, Professor," she managed breathlessly.

Troy was not deterred from his mission. When he reached his goal, Rosa's knees got weak, and Troy was ready to satisfy her aching needs. When he finally laid her down, Troy smiled as he moved inside her, and she arched her back to meet his push. She was beautiful. She was perfect. Troy Graham was falling in love, and it was such a delicious surprise.

Chapter 3

Gia Stevens was both exhilarated in the presence of Troy Graham and also disappointed. It had been nearly a year since she laid eyes on her favorite professor. His strong and sexy mannerisms were all still there, but he was not interested in her the way Gia had hoped.

Gia also hoped that her crush was not too obvious but noticeable enough that Professor Graham would take her hints. She often found herself staring at his muscular forearms as he painted, and her heart pounded an extra beat when she got a glimpse of the intellectual, pensive stare he gave when contemplating a piece of art. Professor Graham was young and handsome and sexy in a way that she could only imagine at this point. But Gia was going to change all that. She was going to be his. She just knew it.

Gia spent many nights dreaming about being Professor Graham's lover. She never had the chance to actually kiss him, but in her mind, she knew exactly how it felt. His lips were not too big, and they were well-defined. Gia often found herself staring at them in class. Therefore, in the privacy of her own room, she could visualize them perfectly. In her dreams, they were soft, but his kisses were firm. Professor Graham was an excellent kisser, or at least Gia made him out to be in her frequent fantasies.

Gia never understood how Professor Graham fell so hard and fast for Celine Tibbs. She was pretty, for sure, and she was a talented artist. But Professor Graham had dozens of students each semester. Why Celine Tibbs? Gia wondered why she continued to contemplate such nonsense. These things didn't matter anymore. Celine was out of the picture; that was a fact. With that hurdle cleared, Gia was determined to take her place in the delectable professor's bed.

Gia remembered a time before Celine when her professor was far more personable and relaxed with his students. Gia loved how he flirted in class and always used to find reasons to engage in a physical closeness that made Gia aroused. But all that special attention was suddenly over, and Gia noticed the way he now fawned over Celine.

Recalling the details from last spring, all of the heartbreak and rejection came flooding back, and Gia would not stand being dismissed again. She had been so sure Professor Graham would turn his affection her way with Celine gone, but so far, that had not happened.

He's just playing a little hard to get. Understandably, he's guarded, but if I don't make a move, someone else will.

Gia was convinced her professor was attracted to young, beautiful students, and this time, once she had charmed him, he would stay where he belonged. She would not lose her spot to the competition ever again. If Professor Graham was going to have another affair, it would be with her.

This conquest might take more effort than I thought. It's time to get serious!

But Gia's efforts were in vain. Everyone except Professor Graham seemed to notice she was wearing her sweaters tighter and her skirts shorter. And when her actions became more desperate, her roommate Kimi called her out.

"Gia, I don't want to be mean, but he's obviously not interested. I hate to see you throwing yourself at him. People are talking."

Gia was shocked by her friend's words at first but eventually dismissed Kimi's plea. No one understood that the professor was meant to be with her. She just needed to get his mind back to that time before Celine when their attraction was bold, uninhibited, and obvious.

Once a spark ignites, it never really goes away. It's just a matter of time before he realizes he belongs with me.

But Kimi's comment made Gia think it may be time for a different approach.

I think it's time to find out where the sexy professor lives and catch him away from the watchful eyes on campus.

After giving the situation some thought, Gia was sure that her professor was leery of another scandalous romance and catching him in a different element would have him more relaxed and ready to show his true feelings.

I know he felt something for me before Celine took him away. I know I can get him back to those feelings. I just need the right chance.

When she arrived back on campus, Gia was certain she had gotten past all those toxic emotions from last spring. She was even hopeful that her final semester at Briarwood would be productive, fun, and normal. But unsubstantiated beliefs that she once had a relationship with Professor Graham allowed Gia to drift back to an unstable time. At this point, Gia was too far gone, and she didn't even realize it. This delusional state kept her mind in a fantasy, and Gia was about to cross a line.

❖ ❖ ❖

Gia knew the dreamy professor often hustled out of class as soon as possible on Fridays, and he had to be going somewhere. Gia bet he had a favorite bar off campus and jump-started his weekend with a few drinks. That was precisely the atmosphere she needed to loosen up her guarded teacher. This Friday, Gia was getting her shit together as soon as possible after class and following Professor Graham. At the very least, she would find out where he lived, which would be decent progress toward her goal.

As usual, Gia caught Professor Graham checking his phone during the final half hour of class, and it didn't dawn on her that maybe he had plans and was meeting someone. Gia's misguided explanation for her professor's actions was that he was in a hurry to get to his favorite watering hole, and this week, he would be so excited to see her there.

Lately, Gia's mind overflowed with similar delusional thoughts that she could not control. She allowed herself to believe that Professor Graham was inhibited by last spring's unfortunate events and fearful of showing his true feelings for her this year. She just knew that being unable to reveal his passion was killing him as much as it was killing her. But she could not have been further from the truth.

Believing she was creating a wonderful surprise for her professor, Gia followed him across town, away from campus. She was intrigued by the possibilities of his destination, and when he pulled into the lot in front of The Hideout, a knowing smile spread across her face.

"I knew it!" Gia said excitedly.

She had heard about The Hideout and should have figured it would be her teacher's favorite bar. Gia giggled a little at the name and grew excited to see how a real bar for professionals differed from campus bars. She was anxious to sit beside her love at a cozy table, hold hands, and catch up on each other's lives. Hanging back a safe distance, Gia watched her dreamy teacher exit his car.

He's so damn sexy.

Gia watched him run his fingers through his hair and noticed how fucking amazing he looked in his tailored dress pants that were snug in all the right places. To Gia, he was the perfect man, and she would not stop her pursuit until he was hers and she experienced the full benefits of belonging to Professor Troy Graham.

"I'll give it a minute," Gia said, checking her look in the visor mirror and applying a little color up her lips. "I'll let him get a drink and get settled. He's going to be so surprised!"

When Gia entered the bar, she discovered her instincts were dead on. There was a different kind of energy there than the campus bars she was used to, and it made her feel grown.

So, this is how life will be with the professor.

Gia's mind was racing, and she could not stop thoughts of cozy dates at places like The Hideout. And lately, her mind even took her to thoughts of a proposal, a wedding, and an entire life with the professor. Gia's return to Briarwood had not only resurrected all her old feelings, but it had also taken her further down a dark path she had hoped to avoid.

When her mind cleared and her focus returned, it wasn't difficult to spot her love at the bar drinking a beer, which surprised her. Gia had pegged the intellectual professor as a mixed-drink guy for some reason.

I guess there's a lot I need to learn about my lover.

Once again, Gia got swept away in her fantasies and got chills thinking about looking into those dark gray eyes and having a real conversation. Before she knew it, Gia's mind was engulfed in a vivid and delusional scenario, and her heart allowed her to drift into the bliss. She envisioned herself sitting across from the gorgeous professor with sexual tension hanging heavy in the air. She looked into his eyes and saw pure desire. And then her most outrageous delusion swept her away.

Tonight, might be the night!

And as Gia thought about this beautiful moment of lying naked next to her professor, a tingling sensation rushed through her body. And when she allowed all the intimate details of their lovemaking to play in her head, Gia felt her body surrendering. Once the perfect moment was over, Gia's mind came back to the present.

So, here's the plan. We drink. We talk. We laugh, and I see that delicious look in his eyes. The look that's undressing me as I speak to him. Finally, he takes me home and makes love to me exactly as I envisioned it.

This plan now consumed her, and Gia wondered if he was spontaneous and free or if the intellectual professor was more traditional in the bedroom. She didn't care one bit, but in her dreams, the Professor was naughty. And now, she was about to discover all of his deep, dark secrets and desires. The Professor would make love to her, but first, she needed to join him for a drink. Gia took a deep breath and prepared herself for the grand meeting. This was it. This was her moment.

Maybe I need to recheck my look, Gia thought. Feeling a bit nervous, Gia headed to the ladies' room for a little pep talk.

"This way, he'll be a beer in, and all that seriousness will be defenseless," she said, looking into the mirror as she fluffed her hair. And then Gia giggled a naughty little giggle as she turned and headed for the door.

When Gia exited the power room, she saw that her beloved teacher was still where she left him. It was time. This was what she had waited a year to experience. Right here, right now, would be the moment that made it all worthwhile. Gia confidently took her first few steps toward the bar, more than ready to make a past spark reignite. A few steps in, Gia couldn't help but notice a beautiful, professional woman with striking, long dark hair enter and walk to the bar as if she knew the path well.

The woman was dressed in a flattering, snug magenta dress and black pumps, and Gia was certainly not the only one in the bar noticing the unassuming but alluring way she walked with purpose.

Although temporarily stalled by the woman's entrance, Gia resumed her journey until she noticed that she and the woman had similar paths. Gia paused again and watched as the woman walked directly to her professor. Gia was stunned. When the woman put her arms around Professor Graham's neck, hugged him from behind, and kissed his cheek, Gia saw red. And when her professor, her man, her love, turned to the woman with a huge smile and returned her kiss with one on the lips, Gia didn't understand such betrayal. She watched as he stood and pulled out the woman's barstool, helped her get seated, and slipped his arm around her back and then down to her waist, pulling her closer to him.

Gia wanted to cry the same way she cried when she watched Professor Graham give all of his attention to Celine last year. Once again, Gia was crushed. She had convinced herself that with Celine out of the picture, she was the one he wanted. And now, this.

Gia rushed out of the bar, growing more upset with each step. When she reached her car, she hurried inside, put her face in her hands, and sobbed. When the tears were all dried, Gia remained in her car for a long time, sorting through the mire of emotions consuming her mind.

"It was all for nothing," Gia said out loud. "He was supposed to be with me. It was all planned. Celine was gone, and my going to Europe for a semester was supposed to give him time to escape the rumors and accusations. Then, when I returned, we were going to be together. It was planned."

Gia's broken heart grew stone-cold as she worked through her unrealized dreams of a steamy affair with her beloved professor. He had been so perfect for her, but now he had betrayed her again, and this time, Gia was not so sure she could remain hopeful.

"I tolerated you straying once, Professor," she said under her breath. "You can't keep fucking up and expecting my forgiveness."

Gia sat in the lot long enough to arrive at a conclusion.

"Poor Celine. I'm so sorry. Obviously, *you* were not the problem."

Chapter 4

Class with the two-timing professor was painful on Monday. It was all Gia could do to keep from confronting him. And as she once used to admire his chiseled jawline and delectable body, now she detested the sight of him. When he came around to ponder over her painting, Gia could feel her skin nearly rippling to a boil. What once would have been sweet ecstasy was now spoiled.

Gia pondered her options all weekend and decided that surely the professor wouldn't retreat to The Hideout on Monday after class, and maybe if she followed him, she could discover where he lived and then make final plans accordingly. Once again, Gia made sure she was ready to go directly after class ended. Being Monday, however, Professor Graham was not in such a big hurry, and Gia wondered if he was ever leaving campus. Finally, long after Gia was usually back to her house, the professor made a move to his car, and Gia pulled out of the lot behind him.

Troy thought maybe he was crazy when he spied Gia Stevens in the Commons Building when he went to retrieve his campus mail. That situation would not have been too unusual, except he had just seen her in the Union Food Court as he stopped to grab a bite to eat.

This has to be the most peculiar coincidence, he thought. *I hardly ever see students after I leave class, and now I've seen Gia twice.*

Getting into his car, Troy thought he must be seeing things. Gia Stevens was also getting into her car, a red Mustang.

I know I'm imagining this. But is Gia Stevens following me?

Professor Graham pulled onto Dunkin Street only to see Gia's red Mustang a few cars behind.

"Well, really, that's not unusual," he said out loud. "She only had two directions she could go."

As he approached the first stoplight, Troy decided to test his potential tail. Without indicating his turn with a signal, he turned right. Looking in his rearview mirror, he saw the red Mustang also turn in his direction.

"This is getting fucking ridiculous!"

It was safe to say, the professor was getting nervous. What he thought might be an odd coincidence was now a reality, and Troy searched his mind for reasons why Gia would be so bold. Landing on an honest answer, the professor knew he could only blame himself.

Before the unfortunate events with Celine Tibbs, Professor Graham was more than a little reckless with his affections. Looking back now, he saw the error of his ways. Being a young, good-looking professor, constantly surrounded by enticing female students, Troy Graham gave in to temptation more than once. True, he had an eye for Gia and even gave her some special attention on several occasions. Still, he never crossed a line, and he never gave her a definite indication that he was interested in getting together outside of class.

Still locked in his thoughts, Troy admitted that when Celine entered the class at midterm, the dynamic with Gia changed.

He was now enamored with his newest student and could not entertain the thought of any others, and he could tell Gia was disappointed.

Additionally, this semester, it was quite apparent that Gia begged for his attention with her new wardrobe and style. He'd be a liar if he said she was not tempting, but Professor Graham learned a lesson with Celine Tibbs. He was never going down that road again. Besides, he was in a real relationship now with a woman his age. He was happy, and his days of having wandering eyes were over. With the red Mustang still pursuing him, Professor Graham wondered if Gia Stevens had an unhealthy attachment to him. If so, he needed to stop it right away.

Seeing Gia's car in his mirror, the professor pulled into the BP station, parked by the door, and went inside. When he saw Gia stop on the fringe of the lot, his suspicions turned to full-blown fact.

"Hey," he said, addressing the attendant. "Is there a back door here?"

Wondering what was up, the attendant was hesitant but finally pointed in the proper direction.

"Thanks!"

Troy slipped out the back door and found a roundabout path to Gia's location. Sneaking up to her window from behind, he knocked on it to get her attention. Gia was startled and frightened at her exposure. When the professor motioned for her to roll her window down, she complied but had no idea how she would explain herself. Before the window was all the way down, the professor was firing off questions.

"What the hell? Why are you following me?"

Gia had no choice but to tell him the truth.

"You disappointed me, Professor. I did so much for us, and you tossed it away."

"What do you mean *us*, Gia? There is no *us*."

"Well, not now that you've been unfaithful. I saw you with her. Who is she?"

Troy was now really freaked out. Apparently, this was not the first time his student tailed him. Suddenly, he was fearful for Rosa. Thank goodness she was not there and was not planning to come for a few weeks. This ordeal had to be settled by then.

"Gia, I am your professor, and you are my student. We are not involved in any way other than that relationship," Troy said slowly and deliberately.

Gia looked directly into his eyes with a cold, hateful stare.

"Professor, *that* situation is entirely *your* fault."

And with those words, Gia rolled up her window and sped off, leaving Troy shaken to the core.

Troy went directly to the police station and relayed his most recent encounter with Gia Stevens. The detective listening to the story seemed disinterested until it dawned on him that this was the professor at the center of last spring's scandal.

"I'm telling you, this girl is crazy," Troy relayed.

Thinking this was possibly more than just the professor getting caught with his dick in the wrong place again, the detective proceeded with some questions.

"Excuse me for asking, Professor, but have you been intimate with this woman?"

"NO! Maybe last school year I flirted a bit. But that was before the tragic circumstances with Celine. I'm in a relationship this year and have never given any of my students, including Gia, any indication that I'm interested in pursuing a relationship outside of class."

Detective Edwards was a seasoned law enforcement officer and an excellent judge of character. He believed the near-desperate professor.

"Okay, so you said today's incident was not isolated?"

"That's right. She referred to my girlfriend, who she would never be able to know anything about unless she had been following me before today. I don't talk about my private life in class; as far as I know, not even my colleagues know about Rosa."

The urgency and desperation in the professor's voice were enough for the detective to do some investigating.

"Alright, Professor. I'll look into it."

"I have a class with her tomorrow, Detective. I hate to be pushy, but when can I expect you to *look into it*?"

Troy's voice and request were nearly desperate, and his point was valid. Detective Edwards liked Troy Graham and could sympathize with his situation.

"I can do it today. I'll run down her address and visit her. I'll call you and give you an update later tonight."

Satisfied with that answer, Troy shook the detective's hand and exited the police station but was suddenly fearful that Gia was watching his every move. He would love to go home or to The Hideout and settle his nerves with a few beers, but evidently, Gia knew he frequented that place.

She also knows about Rosa.

As far as he knew, The Hideout was the only public place they had ever been in town. That had to be where she saw them together.

I'll hit The Gin Mill instead, he thought. *It's just far enough on the outskirts of town that none of the students go there.*

Obsessively looking in his rearview mirror all the way across town, Troy parked in the lot, and stood by his car for several minutes, waiting to see if any cars pulled in behind him. Professor Graham was officially paranoid. When his fears were quelled, he went inside and positioned himself at the bar with a direct view of the door.

❖ ❖ ❖

Detective Edwards knocked on Gia's door at about 7:30 pm. Gia answered to find a strange man, and her knees went weak when she discovered who he was and his purpose. Despite her efforts, the detective saw through Gia's innocent demeanor. Before he left, he warned her sternly.

"The only contact you can have with Professor Graham is in the classroom. If you follow him again, your situation will be far more grave than just a warning like this one."

Gia was so pissed that she had been that reckless, and she was smart enough to see the big picture. Her careless pursuit of her professor could easily stir up the past. People like Detective Edwards might start asking questions, and Gia certainly didn't want that.

I let myself get too far gone again.

Gia was distressed. Whether it was Professor Graham's confrontation or Detective Edward's warning, her mind was somewhat back to reality. She was consumed with her professor but not so far gone that she was willing to throw caution to the wind. Gia knew she had to lay low for a while, and that's exactly what she planned to do.

You thought you could get rid of me by calling the cops. Well, you don't know me that well then, Professor.

Gia's current mental state was caught between loving the professor and loathing him for his infidelity. And while she still believed they were meant to be together, Gia knew better than to push forward.

I'll be as fucking normal as anyone else in that class Monday and give him the space he thinks he needs. But mark my words— the first opening I see to draw out his real feelings, I'm taking it!

Chapter 5

Kimi and Gia's other friends had pretty well given up on trying to include her in their social activities. Kimi, especially, was hurt and disappointed that her best friend had been so distant since the semester started. They had been apart for the entire fall semester, and Kimi was so thrilled when Gia returned to campus.

When Gia first got home from Europe at the beginning of winter break, they had a ball going out and catching up, and Kimi was hopeful that Gia would not get consumed with Professor Graham again. It was Gia's unreasonable fantasies about the hunky professor that pulled Gia away from everyone and everything last spring.

Kimi and Gia each had their own rooms in a little house on Carroll Street. They had been so excited to secure the rental last year because the house was close to the art building and also on Party Row. When Gia suddenly discovered she would be abroad for the fall semester, Kimi was bummed at first, but Gia leased her room to another friend for the fall semester while she was gone, making the rent manageable for Kimi. It wasn't that Kimi didn't like Rachel living there, she was just excited for Gia to return.

Sadly, it wasn't very long after the spring semester began when Kimi noticed Gia slipping into an old pattern. She was becoming less and less interested in being with friends and more intrigued with staying home in her room. And now that Gia was acting weird again, Kimi wished Rachel had never moved out and that Gia had never moved in.

Back when they signed the lease, they looked forward to hosting parties, and now whenever Kimi broached the subject, Gia thought of a reason why they shouldn't.

"I don't get you, Gia. This is what we wanted. You've already missed out on college life here in the first semester. Why don't you ever want to do anything anymore?" Kimi asked with genuine distress.

"It's childish. There's more to life than getting wasted and hooking up with some immature college boy," Gia argued.

Kimi knew exactly where that comment came from. Last year, she had wiped some tears when Professor Graham broke her heart, and Kimi had watched how Gia acted around the professor this year. Gia's heart was still fixated on Professor Graham, but this time, her infatuation was upgraded to obsession, and Kimi just didn't know how to help.

When the detective came to speak with Gia, Kimi was desperately trying to listen from the next room, and she wasn't surprised at all to discover that Gia was caught stalking Professor Graham. Kimi had tried to help and be Gia's friend, but Gia always pushed her away. Now, the police were getting involved with Gia's weird obsession, and even though they had once been best friends, Kimi wanted nothing to do with her.

❖ ❖ ❖

The remainder of the semester came and went, and despite Gia's uncontrollable feelings for Professor Graham, she gave him no reason to think she was still obsessed with him in any way. Inside her head, however, a storm was raging. It was all Gia could do to finish the semester. And all she could think about was finding the perfect moment to let Professor Graham know that she forgave him for his infidelity so they could finally be together.

When the curvy, gorgeous, dark-haired woman from The Hideout accompanied Professor Graham to graduation, Gia felt her blood boil from the depths of her soul. On a day that should have been a celebration, Gia was scornful and bitter. Getting through the ceremony was brutal. Professor Graham was sitting with the faculty and not with his dark-haired love, but Gia had a direct view of the woman who lay in his bed at night. Full of emotions, Gia was caught between being sickened by her classic beauty and being awestruck.

Rosa wore a cream-colored jumpsuit that cinched her waist and hugged her curves. The color paired well with her golden-brown skin and jet-black tresses. Gia thought she had never seen such strikingly beautiful hair, and for a brief moment, she couldn't blame Professor Graham for falling in love with her.

But her rage flared once again when Gia accidentally caught sight of a sweet exchange of affectionate glances between the Professor and his lover. Unable to excuse herself from the ceremony, Gia tried to look away to curtail her anger, but she was drawn to the enchanting woman and couldn't help but think she and Celine Tibbs were so different.

He obviously doesn't know what he wants. This is why he needs me, Gia rationalized. But after seeing how happy and in love her professor looked, the reality seemed to override her more delusional thoughts, and Gia was angry.

Gia thought about the after-party for the art students she had once looked forward to. As an undergrad, she spent three years planning graduation parties for the seniors in her department, and now that it was her turn to be honored, there was nothing to celebrate. Her world was in shambles. Besides, she was sure Professor Graham would be there with his dark-haired love, and the thought of watching them merrily chit-chat with the other students made her stomach churn.

When the ceremony was over, Gia had one goal. She wanted to find her parents and leave.

"We're leaving," Gia demanded.

"Gia, Honey, we want to go to your senior party and meet your professors and friends. We're not going home. That's just silly," her mother stated.

Gia was sure that her comment was not a request. To clarify her demand, a dark presence overcame Gia's demeanor, and she spoke with malice and authority.

"We're *not* going to that stupid party. I don't give a fuck about my professors, and I don't have any friends."

Gia's parents were horrified by their daughter's response. They had noticed her becoming more and more sullen and introverted in their phone conversations throughout the course of the semester. Now being with her in person, they experienced the full wrath of their daughter's unhappiness.

"Gia! Control your language!" her mother snapped. "And, of course, you have friends."

"We're not going. I'm getting in my car and heading home right now."

"What about your things at the house?" her dad questioned.

"I can come get them later. I'm getting out of here."

Gia's parents didn't understand the reason for their daughter's immediate distress, but they complied and began the three-hour drive back to Taylorville, Illinois.

Gia's thoughts settled a bit while driving home in her car, but her mind went to some disturbing facts. She now had a diploma, but she didn't have a job. Instead of attending to the usual senior tasks like sending out resumes and going on interviews, Gia's final months of her college experience were consumed with thoughts of Professor Graham. And even though she could not have any contact with him, the police could not control her manic brain that fluctuated between a wild, passionate love for her professor and a scornful hatred that only a betrayed woman knows. At this particular moment, Gia was on the scornful end of that spectrum.

"Just another reason to hate that prick," Gia said. "I did so much for him, and he ruined me."

This thought, and others similar, continued to simmer deep inside, making it difficult for Gia to focus, even though she was home and far away from the source of her stress. Her parents were concerned with her apathy at first. Then their concern turned to displeasure as Gia continued floundering, uninterested in looking for a job, seeing friends, or even coming out of her room most days.

A few weeks after school ended, Gia got a message saying she needed to go get her things out of her campus house because the summer session had started, and new students had moved in. If she didn't get her things soon, her old landlord would donate them to charity. It was time for Gia to return to campus and clean out her room at the house, but the thought made her cringe.

Visiting the house and gathering her things was not as bad as Gia imagined. With her car packed and still a lot of time left in the day, she contemplated heading to the Union or the Commons. Although she initially dreaded her return, she softened a bit after being there for a few hours and decided that a walk around campus might do her some good. Visiting her old favorite places without recognizing a soul, Gia strolled to the art building.

"You know you're playing with fire here, Gia," she said to herself. But she wasn't even sure the Professor was there. "He might not be teaching any summer classes." But when she glanced at the bulletin board outside the department chair's office, she saw the summer schedule and a familiar name gave her chills.

So, the licentious professor is teaching Ceramics II on Wednesday night.

Although Gia was somewhat relieved that she had not run into Professor Graham, now she thought that surprising him after class might be a lot of fun.

"Well, what do you know? Today is Wednesday!" And then a rush of reality swept through her.

Stop it, Gia! You are just going to stir up shit and cause trouble for yourself, she thought, trying to counteract the delusional dreams from consuming her thoughts.

But the image of the sexy professor, caught off guard and alone with her in the classroom, gave her a thrill. It had been a while since she had those burning feelings, but for some reason, at that moment, they returned. And now Gia found herself at a crossroad.

Part of her wanted nothing more than to make Professor Graham pay for what he did to her. And the other part was toying with the idea that the right moment and the perfect circumstance could make him realize he loved her. As in every situation before this one, Gia's irrational side dominated her mind. Once again, she was swept up in the fantasy of being Professor Troy Graham's lover.

Gia sauntered out of the art building with a new purpose, determined to talk with Professor Graham after his class. She knew she wasn't supposed to, but her heart told her to give their love one more chance despite his betrayal. But Gia's new, positive outlook was short-lived. She was about to witness the unthinkable.

Sitting in the Commons, she spied her professor and his beautiful companion. Instantly, her back stiffened, and a knot gripped her insides. She saw that they hadn't lost any of their wide-eyed passion, and the sight of them made her stomach churn and her head pound. They sat beside one another, with their backs to her, holding hands, talking, and smiling. All of the rage Gia had tried to suppress came rushing back like a flood. And when the professor took his hand and lovingly stroked the woman's long, alluring ponytail, Gia got a sickening feeling in her stomach. Gia was now consumed with hatred, and she burned with envy.

That hair...he should be stroking my hair. I did so much for him...for us, and once again the cheating professor betrayed me.

Consumed with her malicious thoughts, Gia began slowly and deliberately walking toward Professor Graham and his companion as if a magnetic force drew her to them. Knowing her limits, Gia stopped at a safe distance and painfully endured their loving gestures, smiles, and laughter. She continued to watch her professor's obsession with that coal-black mane and her hatred for it was intense. Gia remained fixated and undisturbed by her surroundings until she heard two girls comment on the lovers' affectionate display.

"Aren't they the cutest?"

"Yes, I always see them now that she's moved here. He told us in class that her name is Rosa, and she finally quit her job and moved here to be with him."

Gia's hyper-focus on the happy couple was now interrupted by this unsettling news.

First, why is the professor divulging personal information to his class? He never told my classes his personal business.

And then the magnitude of the girls' comments hit her. If Professor Graham was making his personal life with this woman common knowledge, their relationship must be serious. Now, Gia's feelings of despair and betrayal were too much for her broken heart. She didn't know how much more she could take. But seeing the two love birds in the Commons once again gave Gia new determination. She would visit her professor after his class that evening. Only now, her visit was to confront him about his infidelity.

Chapter 6

Gia's hostile attitude towards her professor did not dissipate this time. She remembered a time last year when she was so certain her relationship with Professor Graham was about to change and she would become more than just his student. However, when that didn't happen, Gia was quick to blame Celine. It's unclear how Gia's mind went to such a dark place after her rejection, but her actions followed her thoughts, and everything about the situation went far beyond normal jealousy. The only solution Gia could think of was to get rid of Celine, and after figuring that out, she waited for an opportunity.

Looking back, Gia felt she had pulled off the perfect crime. She knew she could do it, but she didn't expect every detail to be so fucking perfect. At first, all she wanted to do was get rid of Celine so Professor Graham would return his attention her way. But getting rid of Celine had other benefits that made killing her such a sweet reward.

❖ ❖ ❖

Two weeks before Celine's disappearance, the best of the juniors were all vying for the coveted semester abroad spot. Every year, only one junior got to say they were the best of the best and study in Europe for the first semester of their senior year. This award was the most honored achievement in the department and certainly one of the most respected in the whole university.

Gia was certain she was in the running but also knew her grades and accomplishments were quite similar to Celine's. When Professor Graham and Professor Burke announced that they had narrowed the field of prospects to Celine and Gia, Gia was excited but worried. She wondered how Professor Graham could be fair with his vote since he was sleeping with Celine. When the department head stated that an outside panel would evaluate their portfolios, Gia felt her chances improve. Even though her portfolio was rock solid, Gia knew Celine was very talented, and she wondered how her work would compare to Celine's.

When Gia took care of Celine once and for all, not only did she think she was securing her place in Professor Graham's bed, she knew she was ensuring the semester abroad. Looking back now, Gia admitted Europe was amazing, but she was irritated that her plans didn't turn out the way she imagined with Professor Graham. Even though Gia didn't get all she wanted from her gory crime, she wasn't sorry she killed Celine. After all, life had been much easier without her rival constantly pushing her to her limit. For that reason alone, she had no regrets.

Although Gia had been thinking of ways to get rid of Celine for some time, the opportunity came so unexpectedly, and Gia wondered how she could ignore its perfect timing. Even though Gia's hatred for her rival classmate was fiery, she felt she could mask it well when necessary. Therefore, when Professor Graham paired her with Celine for their final project, Gia was repulsed but had to play the part of being okay with spending copious amounts of time with her archenemy. Gia wondered how she would tolerate Celine's constant comments, suggestions, and incessant need for the final say.

But as the two became more involved in the project details, Gia began to see the wisdom in Professor Graham's method. As much as she hated to admit it, Gia could learn something from her rival, and Professor Graham was quite clever in pairing his two best students. Apparently, he knew each would bring something unique to the project.

Gia, however, was not fond of Celine's constant worry and discussion regarding their competition for the semester abroad. And Gia even felt as if Celine was being excessively humble, by making annoying comments.

"I just know you'll get it, Gia."

To Gia, these comments seemed to be a diversion from Celine's obvious advantage— fucking Professor Graham. Every time Celine complimented, Gia was suspicious that she was fishing for reciprocated praise. The night Gia killed Celine began with one of these situations, and Gia had reached her limit.

"Oh, now there is an outside panel judging us," Celine began. "You've got me beat—hands down!"

This time, Gia could not resist blurting out her snide reply.

"Oh, I'm so sorry that the fact you're fucking Professor Graham won't help you win now?"

Celine was flabbergasted and could not respond before being hit with another verbal assault.

"You heard me. I'm tired of you getting everything you want because you spread your legs. Aren't you ashamed of yourself?" Gia asked and then followed with, "Whore."

Celine figured her *secret* was probably not so secret anymore, but to be confronted so blatantly was a shock. All she could do was say something shocking in response.

"What's wrong, Gia? Are you disappointed that it's not *you* he's meeting at the diner tonight? And not *you* he's taking home, making love to, and then lying next to all night long?"

A part of Gia wanted to kill her right there, but she maintained some composure. But that comment was the beginning of the end for Celine Tibbs because Gia began formulating her plan, and it went off without a hitch.

Needless to say, their working session ended abruptly, but now that Gia knew where Celine was headed, she could make sure she was never in the perfect professor's bed again. Knowing Celine would make a beeline for her lover, Gia had to get moving and stay one step ahead of her doomed rival. Taking a few back streets as fast as she could, Gia made her way onto the highway, and she was reasonably certain Celine did not get ahead of her. The diner was out of town about three miles, and the area between the last semblance of city and Celine's destination was remote.

Gia pulled off to the side of the road, turned her lights off, and watched anxiously for headlights in her rearview mirror. When she saw the faint specks of light heading her way, Gia got butterflies.

As the two headlights grew larger, Gia composed herself. This was serious shit, and once she committed to the act, there was no going back. She knew Celine drove a white Chevy Malibu, so as soon as she confirmed it was her nemesis, Gia pulled out behind her. Sure enough, the car that sped by was Celine on her way to meet their professor. The thought sickened Gia, making what she planned to do a little easier to justify.

"Once I get rid of Celine," Gia said blissfully, "I will be the one he wants—the one he desires—the one he craves. Professor Graham will be so surprised."

When Celine pulled into the diner's remote parking lot, Gia followed, knowing her enemy was oblivious to her plan. But when Celine saw Gia, a lump formed in her throat. That lump grew when Celine saw the menacing look on her enemy's face.

"Are you following me?" Celine asked in a worried but perturbed tone. "You know Troy is just inside that door over there, right?" Celine argued.

The way Celine called their professor *Troy* disgusted Gia, and she approached her victim quickly and without mercy. Before Celine knew what was happening, Gia lunged at her with a tire iron, cracking it squarely across her skull and face, making a wet *thud* sound before dropping her to the ground.

That was easy, Gia thought. "Now comes the hard part," she said, struggling to get Celine's limp, lifeless body into her car. Once Gia was able to flop her victim into the front seat, she entered the vehicle on the driver's side, relieved that Celine's car was a push start and that it started up right away with no keys.

I can't go too far, but far enough that no one will find her for a while, Gia thought.

Noticing a lane or maybe a river road behind the diner, Gia decided that was as good a plan as any. About a half mile down the thickly wooded lane, Gia decided she needed to dump this vehicle and the burden inside, so when she saw the lake glistening beyond the trees, Gia knew her next move.

Getting as close to the bank as possible, Gia prepared to move quickly. She put the car in neutral, letting it progress toward the lake. Once rolling, Gia jumped out before the laws of motion did their thing. As planned, the car and Celine rolled into the murky depths of Lake Ferris. Gia was surprised at how quickly the vehicle bubbled to the bottom. Wasting no time, she hightailed it to her car, still waiting in the secluded diner lot.

Back at the parking lot, Gia noticed nothing unusual except a small trace of blood in the dirt where Celine's head met the ground. Gia got a couple of pieces of paper from her glove box and used one to scrape the bloodied dirt onto the other. She carefully carried the papers to her car, got in, drove off, and tossed the evidence out the window a mile or so down the road. Laughing out loud, Gia was both amazed at her boldness and relieved that the main barrier between her and the sexy professor was eliminated.

❖ ❖ ❖

That was nearly a year ago, and to her benefit, it seemed everyone lost interest in finding Celine Tibbs way sooner than they should have. At one time, Gia second-guessed herself, wondering if her disposal of the body was crafty enough. While she was in Europe, Gia longed for any and all information she could retrieve concerning the missing art student from Briarwood.

When no news was to be had, Gia began to relax, and by the time she returned from her semester abroad, her murderous act was the furthest thing from her mind. In fact, she was ready to reap the reward of her actions—having Professor Graham's attention and affection all to herself.

After all that, she was still not Professor Graham's lover, which was heart-wrenching. Gia discovered that after all she had done to secure her spot in the dreamy professor's heart and after all she risked so they could be together, the unfaithful professor had strayed again. Gia cried over losing Professor Graham's affection a year ago, but today she had a newfound strength. She had a plan, and she would not waste time feeling sorry for herself.

Chapter 7

Troy Graham didn't draw attention to the fact that he saw Gia Stevens out of the corner of his eye while visiting with Rosa over his supper break. He didn't want a confrontation and didn't want to expose Rosa to Gia's wild imagination and unstable mind. Therefore, he pretended he didn't see her but secretly wondered what in the world Gia would be doing there.

As soon as Rosa left, Troy quickly surveyed the area, but there was no trace of Gia, so he immediately called Detective Edwards.

"Hey, this is Troy Graham. I thought this bullshit was over, but I just saw Gia Stevens staring at Rosa and me in the Commons. First of all, I have no idea why she would still be hanging around, and second, she was creepy looking, staring at us. I'm not going to lie. I'm a little worried, Detective."

"She drives a red Mustang, right?" the Detective tried to confirm.

"Yes, Sir," Troy replied.

"Alright, I'll drive around. She shouldn't be too hard to find."

"Well, I have class tonight at five in the ceramics lab. It's in the basement of the art building. It's pretty secluded, and I'm a little freaked out."

"I'll look for her around campus but stake out around your building during your class," Detective Edwards assured. "Keep your phone handy. I'll call if I happen to see her."

Professor Graham was satisfied with that answer and proceeded to the art building to prepare for class.

❖ ❖ ❖

Walking down the hallway to the ceramics lab, Gia could hear Professor Graham's strong, sexy voice. She missed that and the way sitting in his classroom made her feel electrified and brimming with passion. She had been robbed of that experience the last month of school when she forced herself to suppress her true feelings. The visit from Detective Edwards was a bit too real, and Gia knew that putting some time and space between her and the professor was the best course of action at that moment.

But hearing his deep, powerful voice was like music to her ears, and as she walked, she became aware of the tire iron's cool metal handle in her hand and wished things didn't have to be like this. She probably should have gotten rid of the evidence by now, but she was sure that by keeping it, the weapon would be of some use to her. Tonight, she gripped it tightly, knowing it was the tangible object she needed to prove her love.

Detective Edwards spotted Gia's red Mustang in the parking lot across from the art building at about 7:45 p.m. He had forgotten to ask Professor Graham when his class ended, but looking at his watch, he suspected it was 8 o'clock.

Detective Edwards exited his car and headed toward the building, expecting to encounter Gia Stevens and haul her to jail for violating their agreement. He knew he wouldn't be able to hold her there very long, but hopefully, the whole ordeal would scare the shit out of her, and she'd give up this unnatural fascination with the professor.

When Gia heard class wrapping up, the butterflies in her stomach returned. She dipped into a janitor's closet momentarily and struggled to collect her thoughts. She was suddenly aware that her purpose was unclear. At one time she was resolved to teach the professor a lesson, but her mind and her heart were playing tricks on her.

What would be so bad about giving him another chance?

Trying to control her breathing, which was getting more labored, Gia peered out of the cracked door and into the hallway. She was certain the last student had exited, so she had to move fast. She knew the professor would be in a rush to leave, having been there all day.

As Gia was about to enter the lab, she heard voices coming from inside, but she could tell Professor Graham was not talking with a student. She had heard this voice before, but she wasn't sure where. Carefully peeking in the door, Gia saw Professor Graham talking with the detective who had visited her.

"I saw her car parked across the street, so I came in. I haven't seen her, but she's here. I'll find her and take her in. She knows she's not supposed to be near you."

The two men chatted some more, and as Gia listened, she now wondered what she should do. Then suddenly, she was moving down the hallway, up the stairs, and out to her car.

"I'll just move my car to the faculty lot on the other side of the building. The smarty-pants detective won't see it there, and he'll think I'm gone," Gia thought, smiling at her cleverness.

When Detective Edwards walked out of the art building, he was relieved to find Gia's car gone.

Good! She wised up, he thought, taking his phone out and texting Professor Graham.

> Hey, Professor, Gia's car is gone. I think you're safe, so, I'm heading home.

The Professor's phone pinged when Gia Stevens quietly entered his classroom. Professor Graham had his back to the door, reading the Detective's text, unaware of her stealthy entrance. Once again, Gia was conscious of the tire iron in her grip, and she no longer pondered her motive. She wanted nothing more than to prove her loyalty by exposing the one unselfish act she performed in her beloved professor's best interest. She killed Celine Tibbs to get her out of the picture. Once Celine was dead, Professor Graham was supposed to be with her, and even though that didn't happen, Gia now wanted him to know the depth of her love and sacrifice. The tire iron was her proof.

"Hello, Professor," she said in her most alluring voice.

Startled and alarmed by Gia's boldness, Professor Graham turned quickly and stumbled on his words when he tried to speak.

"Gia," he managed. "What are you doing here?" His eyes instantly darted to her hand, which had a death grip on the deadly weapon. Becoming more fearful, Professor Graham instinctively looked at the phone in his hand.

"I'll take that," Gia said.

Noticing Gia's hand on the steel weapon again, the Professor complied.

"Interesting question," Gia began. "I'm not quite sure. I guess my purpose is entirely up to you."

Professor Graham saw a wildness that he had never seen in Gia's eyes. It was almost as if she was a different person completely.

The rigidity in her voice gave her an angry, unstable sound, and the darkness behind her eyes told him to tread lightly.

"What do you mean?" he replied, backing away a bit, and trying his best to remain calm.

When Gia didn't answer, Troy became even more nervous, and his eyes once again went to the weapon she carried at her side. The sight of it along with Gia's unnerving presence made him compelled to give her a reminder. "You know you can't be here."

Gia smiled and then finally replied, "Ah, no one will know. You don't deserve it, but I'm giving *us* one more chance, Professor. I would never forgive myself if I didn't. I have already sacrificed so much for us. It would be silly to give up now."

Considering Gia's mental state, the cornered professor knew he must choose his words carefully.

"Well," he began nervously, "let's talk then." His eyes were glued to the tire iron, and Gia was once again reminded of its presence.

"Oh, don't be alarmed. I brought this as proof of my loyalty. Even though you have betrayed me twice, I brought this to show you the lengths I will go to be with you."

Professor Graham now had a sinking feeling and dreaded Gia's extended explanation.

"See this?" she said, lifting the weapon and pointing out the visible dried blood. "This is Celine's blood. I killed her for us," Gia admitted proudly. And as she smiled and looked into his eyes, Troy Graham's heart dropped. At one time, he longed to know what happened to Celine, but now, at the moment of his gruesome discovery, he was repulsed by Gia's confession. Still, he knew he had to play along, or he'd never leave there alive.

"Okay," he managed. "Thank you," he said. His voice cracked nervously, and he was still backing away.

"Professor, you don't sound very convincing. And why are you still backing away from me?" Gia asked. Her displeasure was obvious in the way she cocked her head and raised her eyebrows as she asked her question. It was like she was daring him to be truthful even though her fragile state couldn't have handled the agony.

Many thoughts went through Troy Graham's head in this tense moment. For one, in a normal situation, he knew he could subdue Gia, but this was not normal; Gia was not normal. The way she walked, the way she spoke, and the way she constantly adjusted her grip on the tire iron told the professor that Gia Stevens was fueled by adrenaline and all the emotions of a scorned woman, making her a force beyond her normal capacities. His eyes went to the weapon in her hand once more, and he only briefly had time to let his thoughts go to Celine—poor Celine.

"Put the tire iron down, and I'll feel better. Then we can talk, okay?"

"I don't want to talk, Professor," Gia began. "I want something more," Gia said seductively, moving even closer.

The professor was sickened by the sound of her voice. He wondered how she got so delusional and regretted that he had ever given her reason to think he was attracted to her. In this crucial moment, Professor Graham recalled a time before Celine when he was quite flirty with several young women in his classes. He knew his behavior was inappropriate but couldn't help himself. Thinking back on those times created a churning, hollow place in his gut.

"I want you to kiss me… a real kiss…a kiss that shows you crave me with all your being. If that kiss satisfies my curiosity about your feelings, we're good. But if I feel the kiss is ingenuine or forced… well, we have a problem."

The thought of kissing Gia repulsed Troy, but kissing her would preoccupy her, and he could get the weapon out of her hand. Without the weapon, Troy knew he would be safe. Therefore, Troy reluctantly agreed.

"Sure, I'd like to kiss you, Gia," he managed. As the words exited his mouth, that sick feeling in his stomach gave him doubts that he could actually pull off this farce. But his rational mind told him, it was his only chance.

It's a matter of survival.

Apprehensively, Troy inched closer. He was well aware that with one swift move on her part, he was a goner. And with that thought, his mind once again went to Celine. His heart ached, wondering if that was how it was with her. The vision of it was haunting and heartbreaking, making what he was about to do nearly impossible. Still, it might be the only way he could get the weapon from her, so Troy did his best to shove thoughts of Celine's last moments aside.

As he leaned in for the kiss, he saw Gia positioned and ready, and for a brief second, he thought he could wrangle the tire iron from her without filling her repulsive request. When he saw Gia raise the weapon slightly, right before their lips touched, he knew better than to test her, and his plan to overtake her was impossible.

Apparently, Gia's idea of a kiss was much more aggressive and passionate, and when she opened her mouth and presented her tongue, the professor tensed and pulled back ever so slightly. Just as he suspected, the professor was emotionally incapable of kissing this vile woman, and now he had to prepare for her response.

"You failed the *kiss test*, Professor," Gia managed, gritting her teeth to keep her voice from trembling with anger. She stepped back from him quickly and repositioned the firm steel weapon in her hand. "Why was it so hard for you to kiss me?" Gia asked with anger and hatred in her voice. She stood staring at him and then shaking her head.

"Why can't I be the one?" Gia asked, softly. The anger had been replaced with sadness in her voice, and the professor wasn't sure if she was retreating or if this moment was just the calm before the storm.

Before Professor Graham could respond, Gia turned and walked out of the room. Troy thought about going after her, but honestly, he was just so damn relieved he was safe, he just let her go.

Gia walked numbly to her car and sat emotionless for several minutes. When she reached into her pocket for her keys, she realized she still had the professor's phone. She quickly pulled it out and held it to her heart. The mere sight of it spurred new life. Almost instantly, Gia dismissed her funk and got moving. It wasn't long, and she was on Highway 64, the one that led to the diner where Professor Graham once waited for Celine, but she never showed.

The sun had set, and it was nearly dark. Gia pulled off on the side of the road, pulled out the professor's phone, and initiated her satisfying solution. It wasn't difficult to pull up his text thread with Rosa, and once she did, Gia began crafting her fake message from the professor to his lover.

> Troy: Hey, let's have a date night! Meet me at that little diner out on Highway 64. It's a cute little place. You'll love it!

After she hit *send*, Gia placed the phone at her side and let her mind wander. She didn't realize when Rose texted back, but when she saw the tiny pin-point orbs appear out of the dark night behind her, Gia's attention peaked. She sat patiently on the side of the road and watched them grow, first with an icy stare and then a sinister grin when the white Audi zoomed past her. She had a white-knuckle grip on the weapon which lay beside her on the seat. When Gia pulled onto the highway, she was exhilarated at the thought of confronting the woman standing in her way of being with her one true love.

"If I can't be the one he wants, the one he desires, and the one he craves, then no one can have him. Once the dark-haired beauty is out of the picture, I'll take care of the professor, too," Gia said, confidently as she turned into the diner's eerily familiar lot and parked.

Gia had all her wits about her as she watched Rosa check her look in the visor mirror and then step out of her car. This was a woman with confidence. This was a woman who had everything Gia desired, especially the gorgeous professor. Gia was mesmerized when the professor's lover reached up and unclipped her long, gorgeous mane, letting it fall onto her shoulders and down her back. Even Gia could not deny Rosa's hair was magnificent. She watched as Rosa effortlessly ran her fingers through it and then tightened it all up enough to make a long ponytail that perked up a bit at the base and then hung in bewitching waves down her back.

Once again Gia's innocent victim was caught by surprise. And once again the deadly tire iron did its job with one vicious blow. Gia noticed that the thud of steel on Rosa's skull was remarkably similar to the sound last spring when her first rival met her match. And just like her first kill, Gia placed Rosa's body into the Audi and made the familiar trek down the lake road to deposit yet another victim into the cold, murky depths of Lake Ferris. Rosa's death might have been punishment enough, but this time she had a special surprise for the professor—something that would ruin his world. The thought of Professor Graham's pitiful face as he realized his lover was gone gave her chills—the good kind.

It was pitch dark—darker than Gia had ever seen the night and walking back up the lake road to the diner, she thought about the final stages of her plan. It was late and the diner was empty, but calm as can be, Gia went inside and ordered a soda before pulling Rosa's phone out and texting a message to Professor Troy Graham.

> Rosa: Meet me at the little diner out on Highway 64.
> I can't wait to see you! You're going to love what
> I've done with my hair.

Gia hit *send*, took a drink of her soda, and looked in her bag. She felt a wicked smile form on her face and her chest was bursting with pride.

"Gia, you've really done it this time!" She always amazed herself at the lengths she would go for a little self-satisfaction. "I guess I'll have to settle for the consolation prize," she murmured. "If I can't be the one he wants, the one he desires, and the one he craves, I'll be the one who ruins his world—again."

Gia sat and looked out the diner window where she saw two tiny headlights growing in the darkness. She had wasted the best years of her college experience obsessed with a man who wouldn't—who *couldn't* kiss her. She grew sullen as she thought about her humiliating rejection, and her eyes grew dark with thoughts of revenge.

"Poor Professor Graham. He thinks he's meeting his lover."

With that thought, Gia's anger began to dissipate, and a gentle smile formed on her face. From the very first moment she saw Rosa, Gia was fixated on the gorgeous sophistication of her hair. She knew that it must also have a bewitching effect on the professor, and this thought made her do the most sinister act.

Gia timidly opened her bag to gaze at the trophy inside. Shiny and alluring, a long, black ponytail lay at the bottom, and Gia hoped it was the perfect gift for the professor. Gia had accepted that she was not the one Professor Graham loved and settled for being the one who destroyed the ones he wanted, desired, and craved.-

"He's going to be so surprised!"

The End

Author Bio

Marcy Bialeschki is an award-winning, #1 bestselling author, speaker, and entrepreneur. A retired English and speech teacher and a school counselor, Marcy is an avid writer, published in numerous online magazines, including *Harness*, *Mentor's Collective*, and *Women Thrive*. She also created *Aria's Closet*, an adult coloring book that provides insight into the world of Aria Donaldson, the unforgettable protagonist of The Vengeance Series. With the release of *Deception & Consequences*-- the first book in the series-- Marcy won the Titan Literary Award and the Publisher's Choice Award. She became a #1 bestselling romance-suspense author just fifteen days post-publication. Aside from writing, Marcy is the founder of Tastefully Sexy by Marcy B, an online business that coincides with her world of fiction. Marcy is also an aspiring mind coach and public speaker and was selected to speak at the Women's Thrive Summit in March of 2025.

Milton Keynes UK
Ingram Content Group UK Ltd.
UKHW031353011224
451755UK00004B/341